'   rin.

"Mamor . . . Roy . . .
Can You Fight?"

Diver had used his stun-gun with measured
force; already those that he felled had bounced
up again, and as he altered the setting two of
the largest brutes leaped upon him. Vel Ragan,
behind a tress now, fired his weapon, and I saw
Red-Belt, the leader, clutch a wounded arm,
pierced by a dart.

"Devils!" panted Red-Belt. "Nest of devils!"

I felt Old Gwin come closer, placing the whimpering Tomar in my arms. "Keep back, for the
fire of Eenath has consumed your souls! We
know you all, and you are all accursed! You
will go down into fire . . . !"

THE
LUCK OF
BRIN'S FIVE

Cherry Wilder

PUBLISHED BY POCKET BOOKS NEW YORK

I would like to acknowledge the help given by Ken Ozanne, astronomer and Science Fiction Wizard of Faulconbridge, New South Wales.   C.W.

POCKET BOOKS, a Simon & Schuster division of
GULF & WESTERN CORPORATION
1230 Avenue of the Americas, New York, N.Y. 10020

Published by arrangement with Athenuem Publishers
Library of Congress Catalog Card Number: 77-1590

ISBN: 0-671-83032-5

First Pocket Books printing October, 1979

10 9 8 7 6 5 4 3 2 1

Trademarks registered in the United States and other countries.

Printed in the U.S.A.

CAST OF CHARACTERS

BRIN
MAMOR
HARPER ROY
OLD GWIN *A Family of mountain weavers. All bear the family name Brinroyan (of Brin's Five).*
ODD-EYE (Eddorn) BRINROYAN *The first Luck of Brin's Five.*
SCOTT GALE *Lieutenant-Navigator of a Biosurvey team from the planet Earth. Adopted as the Luck of Brin's Five. He is given the nickname* DIVER *and is also known as* ESCOTT GARL BRINROYAN, *a version of his name which is easier for Moruians to pronounce.*
DORN BRINROYAN *Eldest child of Brin's Five, who tells the story.*
NARNEEN *Second child of Brin's Five.*
TOMAR *Youngest child of Brin's Five.*
HUNTER GEER *Neighbor of Brin's Five on Hingstull Mountain.*
WHITEWING *An albino. The Luck of Hunter Geer's Five.*
BEETH ULGAN (Beeth the Weathermaker) *A Diviner in Cullin, the local township. Friend and adviser of Brin's Five.*
GORDO BEETHAN *Her apprentice. A Witness or telepath.*
RILPO RILPROYAN GALTROY
TEWL RILPROYAN GALTROY *A married pair. Grandees of Clan Galtroy.*

TSAMMET *Their servant. An omor: one of a caste of female workers noted for strength.*

MOONEEN *A twirler or religious fanatic rescued by Diver and Harper Roy.*

PETSALEE, Host of Spirits *Leader of the band of twirlers.*

ITHO

LANAR

MEEDO *Three ancients who sailed a bird-boat on the river Troon and carried passengers.*

TIATH AVRAN PENTROY *The Great Elder, elected leader of the Council of Five Elders, chosen from the five clans of Grandees. A powerful but unscrupulous governor and landowner, dedicated to preserving clan power. His nickname is Tiath Gargan, which means "Ropemaker," "Lawmaker" or "Strangler."*

NANTGEEB *A powerful Diviner and scientist, out of favor with the Great Elder for the use of fire-metal-magic. Also known as the Maker of Engines.*

VARB'S FIVE *A family of shepherds living at Whiterock Fold.*

AT THE BIRD CLAN

THE LAUNCHER *The leading Bird Clan official.*

ABLO *A townee from Otolor who serves as Diver's mechanic and remains with Brin's Five. Later he is called Ablo Binigan or Ablo the Fixer, the one who picks up dropped stitches.*

JEBBAL FALDROYAN LUNTROY *A pilot at the Bird Clan.*

VALDIN

THANAR *Her children.*

MATTROYAN *A merchant of Itsik.*

ULLO MATTROYAN *His child; a pilot at the Bird Clan.*

MURÑO PERAN PENTROY *A young grandee, known as Blacklock. He is a popular hero on Torin for his athletic feats. A pilot at the Bird Clan and a pupil of Nantgeeb.*

SPINNER *Blacklock's first officer, who takes care of him.*

FER UTOVANGAN *Blacklock's copilot, whose name, which can mean Second Pilot or Former Bird Farmer, hints at his former identity. Antho, a birdfarmer from the outskirts of Fintoul, is a famous designer of flying machines whose adventures have passed into legend.*

DEEL GIRROYAN *A town-grandee of Otolor, pilot at the Bird Clan.*

VEL RAGAN (Vel the Scribe) *A scribe from Tsagul, the Fire-Town.*

ONNAR *A Witness, in his service.*

VARADON

MEETAL

ARTHO

TRANJE

TROY

ALLOO

BANO *Vassals in the service of Tiath Pentroy. Members of a Gulgavor or seven-fold band, who have sworn to capture Diver or die in the attempt.*

TILJE PAROYAN DOHTROY

ARN LORGAN (the Bridgemaker) *Friends of Vel Ragan, from Tsagul, where they were in the service of:*

TSORL-U-TSORL *Former Deputy of Tsagul, who has disappeared on an errand for Tiath Pentroy.*

AT RINTOUL

GUÑO GUNROYAN WENTROY *The Wentroy Elder on the Council of Five. Known as Guño Deg—Old Crosspatch.*

LEETH LEETHROYAN GALTROY *The Galtroy Elder on the Council.*

ORN ORNROYAN DOHTROY *The Dohtroy Elder on the Council, known as Orn Margan— the Peacemaker.*

MARL NOONROYAN LUNTROY *The Luntroy Elder on the Council. Known as Marl Udorn, Blind Marl—the Luck of Noon's Five.*

AV AVRAN PENTROY *Old Av, Tiath's elder sibling, the head of his Family.*

URNAT AVRAN PENTROY *A dwarf. The Luck of Av's Five.*

THE
LUCK OF
BRIN'S FIVE

Prologue

A low mountain range straddled the northern coast of the continent; it was massive and striking, rising in places straight out of the grassy plain. The highest peaks lay to the north, snow-capped in summer because they were close to the polar circle. A hot summer sun burned down on the craggy lower slopes; there were stands of a straight-limbed tree with a red-brown trunk and small leaves of a particular bronze green. Campsites clustered among these trees; some were old and permanent as small villages, with a stone wall or a stockade. In summer many of the camps were empty: the campers had wandered off on their travels, to the fairground and the riverside. In other places there was a murmur of voices, the rhythmical clacking of looms; no open fires were lit, no smoke curled above the treetops.

There were cool places to be found even in high summer; caverns full of the sound of rushing water; noisy brooks and torrents. Hunting trails ran along the tops of the ridges and dipped into the valleys that led down to the hot grass of the plain. There were natural plantations of a plant that looked like flax; its flat leaves rattled and shook, never still, in the prevailing north wind.

A man, travelling through this rough, pleasant, hill country could drink at the streams, eat berries if he dared, breathe the mountain air. Yet the creatures that scram-

11

bled up the trees as he passed, the little bouncing deerlike animals that took off into the scrub, the slow, dipping flight of the birds would remind him, finally, that he was not on Earth.

The continent and the world itself were called by the same name: Torin. When Esto, the Great Sun, set in the west, its strong golden light gave way to darkness, then to a silvery light, six times as strong as the reflected light of Earth's moon . . . the light of Esder . . . the Far Sun. It was possible to read, to hunt, to maneuver a flying machine by the light of Esder.

Down below on the plain, during Esder light, other flickering lights clustered at fords and river crossings. In an old shallow crater a sheet of water threw back the far sun's light oddly; the water steamed and gave off its own phosphorescent glow. Beyond the northern bank of this lake twin peaks rose up, two of the highest in the range, and below them, on a stone terrace, stood a long oval building.

It was a mild summer night in the year 274 of the New Age, two hundred and seventy-four Torin years since the last Torlogan or Great Builder handed power to the grandees. The only sounds here in the mountains were natural ones: bird calls, a stone dislodged that rolled down into a pool. When four Torin hours of darkness had passed and ten of Esder light, a new sound grew sharply in the clear air. The flying machine came buzzing in from the southwest and landed neatly on the terrace. It was strong and shapely, made of woven, stiffened fabric over a frame of bent wood. The wingspan was large; there was a propeller mounted on the nose and four smaller ones on the wing itself. On the hindmost panel, to the left, there was a row of painted characters; in the corresponding position to the right there were block letters: TOMARVAN II.

A man climbed down out of the machine and reached up to help down his companion, a young Moruian, an inhabitant of Torin. They talked softly, as if the silence of the mountains made them lower their voices, but the man's voice, his laughter, rang out sometimes. They came down from the terrace and began walking briskly towards the lake, just visible through the trees. The light of Esder picked out quite clearly their sameness and their difference. The man, Scott Gale, was well-built, broad-shouldered, muscular, a head taller than his young companion. He wore a synthetic blue zipper suit, a regulation garment hardly weathered by four hard years of an alien climate.

Dorn, the Moruian, was seventeen years old; he was wiry, thin, long-limbed. He walked with a lithe, swinging motion; the carriage of his head, his hips, his thin, long-fingered hands, were all distinctive. By contrast Scott Gale was over-controlled, muscle-bound. Dorn had thick mid-brown hair, perfectly straight and cut off, carelessly, above the collar of his fine woollen tunic. His face was broad at the forehead, and tapering, with a straight nose, a long upper lip and a firm jaw. It might have been a human face, in certain attitudes, except for the eyes, which were widely spaced, very large, and set, up-curving, into his temples.

Scott Gale was, in comparison, round faced and round headed, yet in cloak and hood he had often passed for a Moruian. His hair and beard were black; he had often, during his first days on Torin, cursed the Irish ancestors who gave him blue eyes. This strange pair walked on, talking in Moruian, until they came to the lake shore. Esto, the Great Sun, came over the shoulder of a mountain and turned the warm waters of the lake to gold.

"There!" said Dorn, "and not even a stone for memorial!" Scott Gale laughed. "Memorial to the loss of a good air ship," he said.

"Ah, but it is strange!" exclaimed Dorn. "Don't you feel it? To remember the past so clearly . . . We stand where the party from the hunting lodge was standing . . ."

He looked back to the oval building on the terrace. "They carried torches and lances, that night, and a Galtroy banner . . . star and spindle." He knelt at the water's edge, wrinkling his forehead, and skipped a stone across the steamy water.

"I've heard the story, from the Family," said Gale, "until it's like a story from my own childhood. I don't know what I remember or what was told to me." He pointed to a narrow beach on the far side of the lake.

"Was it about there that you pulled me ashore?"

"Yes," said Dorn.

They walked on, around the head of the lake, with Dorn running ahead and clambering over fallen logs. When Gale caught up again, Dorn was staring ahead at a particular rock above the little beach. Over the rock arched an old, gnarled tree, a mountain black-thorn, which had been struck by lightning and scarred along one side of its bent trunk. The rock was scratched and indented with written characters; the tree itself was strung with loose clumps of thread, of varying thickness, knotted in certain patterns.

"Well, someone has not forgotten," said Scott Gale. "What do the skeins say?"

They walked to the tree, and Dorn climbed the rock and felt at the largest message skein. He read off the woven symbols: "Praise to our Mother, the North Wind, and to Eddorn who found great fortune for his Family." Then he reached for another skein.

"Send us a luck to equal the Luck of Brin's Five."

Scott Gale shook his head and smiled sadly. "I wish them better luck than that," he said. He came to the rock and stood with Dorn looking down, between the rock and the tree, at a narrow grave, carefully covered with round stones.

They went down and sat on the strip of white sand by the water's edge.

"It should all be told," said Dorn. "It is part of this world's history."

"The way human beings came to Torin?"

"Our part of it," said Dorn, "the part that I remember . . . that first winter and the spring that came after it, when you first joined our Family and travelled with us."

"Then you must write it," said Scott Gale. "No one else could do it so well. You will be Dorn Utragan pretty soon . . . Utragan, the scribe in two languages. The first on Torin."

"It has been a long time," said Dorn. "I am hardly the same person."

"You are not an ancient yet . . ." Scott Gale grinned.

Dorn blinked and laughed; he was about to throw a stone into the lake but instead he pointed, with a hand to his lips for silence. A bird, about the size of a large kingfisher, came gliding out of the trees and swung down low over the surface of the water; its wings flashed a dark, iridescent blue.

"What is that called, then?" Dorn asked in a whisper.

"Great Wind!" said Scott Gale, "it must be a Diver!" They laughed so loudly together at a shared joke that the bird flew off, startled.

I

I will tell how we found our luck, the great Luck of Brin's Five, and how, being found, it led us on to good fortune beyond all dream-spinning.

I am Dorn, eldest child of our Family. When the Luck came, I was twelve years old and we lived high on the slopes of Hingstull Mountain, near the Warm Lake. It was a hard winter: our fingers were stiff with cold as we worked at the looms; the snow bore down on the fabric of our house. A blizzard had ripped families of spinners from our home trees and rolled them down the mountainside like dead birds.

Food was scarce; two families had quit the glebe and now only two were left. Hunter Geer, who boasted many thick pelts, and, as we said, a thick head and a thick hide, was bound in under a rock wall across the glebe, watching us perish with cold by the east gate.

We could not go down the mountain because our Luck was dying. At first we sang; Old Gwin boiled herbs after scratching them from the snow; dearest Brin embraced us all; but it was no use. Mamor and Harper Roy talked all night apart, but they could not find a solution. Our Family, Brin's Five, and a perfect five it had been, five adults with no outclips, was doomed. Odd-Eye lay in his bag, spinning yarns still in a dream voice, with the marks of death on his face.

I remember Narneen weeping at night in the sleeping bag, because the spring would not come if our Luck died. It seemed perfectly possible to me. No good thing would ever happen again: the suns would not rise, the spring would not come, our webs would break and our youngest child, still hidden, would never be seen. In the city, as I have since observed, people live in a different way and have no Family, no Luck to bind them, and they survive very well, but as mountain people we followed the old threads.

We did not give up easily. Every day we fought against our doom by searching for a new Luck. Sometimes Brin went out as far as the lake, alone or with Mamor. Harper Roy went out in the night, and we heard him singing against the storm and harping for our deliverance. When the wind died down, they sent Narneen and me to the lake shore, with instructions to walk in circles, to pray, to call, to bring back news of any stranger passing.

It is strange to stand in winter by the Warm Lake. Clouds of steam rise up off the surface into the frosty air, and where the cold mist from the pass meets the steam they form spiral patterns. I remember once standing hand-in-hand with Narneen, letting the water play over our frozen feet. We looked up and saw two figures watching us from a crag, Hunter Geer and Whitewing. One fierce and ruddy, with hair the color of dried blood hanging over a wolf-skin tunic. The other even more frightening, immensely tall and thin and white as the snow, for Whitewing had no color. Whitewing was the Luck of Hunter Geer's Five . . . white-haired, bloodless, from the first showing.

From where we stood by the lake, we could not see those pink eyes flashing ill-will upon us. I bent down and seized a warm pebble, then molded snow around it. I flung it at Whitewing, high on the crag, crying out as it fell short, "We will find our Luck again!"

Whitewing laughed aloud, a high, jagged laugh that rang and echoed from the farthest shore.

Two days later we ate the last of the preserved game birds; there was nothing left but blackloaf and dried sun-

ner. A blizzard was blowing, and Mamor could not hunt.
Odd-Eye did not speak, and we felt sure our Luck was
dying; but suddenly, towards noon on the second day, his
mind became clear. Odd-Eye spoke to each of us in turn
and prayed for the hidden child. I felt desolate and strange
when my turn came to sit beside him. Odd-Eye had a long
hatchet face; one of his eyes was green, the other brown.
He was short and misshapen, but in all the time I could
remember, he had been so agile I could not think of him
as old. He was a good Luck, for he had made it his calling;
he was "a Luck out of the bag."

Every Luck has suffered some misfortune: there are
dwarfs and cripples, the blind, the deaf, the mad and the
half-mad. I have never seen a hunchback who was not the
Luck of some Family or some grandee. It is equally correct to adopt as a lucky person someone who has lost a leg
or been scarred in a fire or maimed in some other fashion,
though some say a "born Luck" is best.

Odd-Eye said to me, when my turn came, "Cheer up,
Dorn. I have dreams for you that are as fine as Blacklock's
mantle."

I could not help smiling. We had often talked in summer, at the loom or in the woods, of Blacklock, the swag-
gering hero from Rintoul. I had half-persuaded Odd-Eye
to take me downriver, across the plains, to see the great
city of Rintoul and watch Blacklock perform his feats.
The fame of Blacklock had certainly reached our mountain. Hunter Geer, who had visited Rintoul, claimed to
have shaken Blacklock by the hand, but Hunter Geer is
a liar.

"Now Dorn, you must take me!" said Odd-Eye in a
quavering voice. "Take me out to the lakeside, to our rock
under the burned tree, and I will have a last try. I must
find my dear family a replacement."

They looked sideways at me, to make sure I was not
afraid, then Harper Roy bound Odd-Eye upon our sled
wrapped in the thickest rugs we had and covered with our
only wolf pelt. I was wrapped up just about as tightly, and
when the wind dropped, I started on my way.

Before I left, Old Gwin came up with a basket of hot

stones and three roasted graynuts that she had been saving. The stones went at Odd-Eye's feet to warm him, and I had a warm pocketful of graynuts. I have had to laugh, since those days, when I have heard scholars in Rintoul swear that the "primitive Moruia" use no fire. Indeed we were chary of fire . . . our home was made of flaxen cloth pulled over a tree! I never saw a blaze or a flame in our glebe, but we certainly used fire in winter, and we warmed our food. A point in the scholars' favor is this: we never spoke of fire or called a flame, a flame. We were superstitious. Old Gwin made us say instead "the kind one."

It was a weaver's mile to the lakeside; but after the first rise outside the western gate, it was downhill all the way. The sled was light because Odd-Eye was nothing but skin and bone. I trudged through the snow numb with anxiety as much as cold. This journey was like stepping off the edge of the world; I felt that the worst was about to happen, that I was hard up against the cruelty of life and could do nothing to change it.

I had a hard time hoisting the sled to our comfortable place under the burned tree. Then I checked to see if Odd-Eye was alive; his odd eyes blinked at me. I went down and warmed my hands and feet at the lake, then I came back to sit on the rock and eat my graynuts. There was no snow falling, and the winds were still. We saw Esto, the Great Sun, go down, a smear of orange in the distant west; it was the time of "runar," the little darkness before the rising of the Far Sun. Trails of phosphorescence sprang up on the lake's surface and overhead the stars blazed. I was dozing when Odd-Eye gave a thin cry.

"Glider!"

"What is it?" I was frightened, sure that he was dying, that his mind was wandering again.

"A glider!" He was straining against the thongs that bound him to the sled. His voice was so weak that I had to put my ear close to his lips.

"Look, Dorn . . . coming down over the lake . . ."

I stared and saw what he meant, but it was no glider. It was more like a falling star, then blazing closer, like a fireball or meteor. I thought, in fact I hoped, that it would

fall short, a long way from us, behind the peaks on the far
bank of the lake. But Odd-Eye was whispering in my ear,
and the fireball came closer, "A glider! A balloon! It will
strike in the lake and your Luck is there, I know it! A great
Luck is there!"

The light from the fireball grew from white to orange
to pinkish red; I was terrified now, for I could see that it
would *not* fall short. I was sure it would crush us, right
there under the burned tree. It came on and on, and I
could not look away until it fell hissing and burning into
the lake near the far bank. Then I saw two other things:
a hunting party on that bank, near the dark peaks—city-
dwellers with banners and lances—and in the upper air
floating towards our side, two little white tents on strings
wafting down among the tendrils of steam.

I left Odd-Eye without a word and ran back along the
track. Halfway to the rise I cannoned into Brin and Harper Roy, coming to relieve me at my post, and blurted out
my story.

"We saw the fireball!" said Brin. "What's this about a
tent in the air?"

"The Luck!" I gasped, "don't you see? It will land in the
lake!"

"Odd-Eye called it a glider?" asked Harper Roy.

"Some *vessel*," I said. "Some air ship. Oh please come
. . . the Luck is in the lake by now . . ."

They were coming along with me as I babbled, and we
came in sight of the lake. The white tents floated in a
tangle about fifty feet from the shore.

"Something came down . . ." said Harper Roy.

There were shouts and torchlights springing up on the
far bank. The hunting party was trying the steamy water,
to probe the place where the fireball struck. Suddenly
there was a movement near us; I saw the tents and their
cordage wrap against a heavy body, circling slowly in the
wide whirlpool eddies of the warm lake.

"Quickly!" said Brin, "reef in the cords . . . there is
someone bound to them!"

We waded into the warm water until I was swimming
and dragged at the cords and fought with billowing heaps

of warm, wet fabric, soft as silk. There was a grotesque figure floating in the water: ballooning legs, stiff arms, square head with one dark, glistening eye, big as a whole face. Then it came to rest on the shore, and we all saw what it was . . . a kind of body-shaped bag of fine metallic cloth. The dark eye was a piece of glass. Someone lived inside the bag, and we knew it must be our Luck.

"Blood . . ." said Harper Roy, ". . . on the sleeve . . ." From within the helmet there came a feeble gasping cry, for all the world like that of a hidden child.

Brin struggled with the square helmet while Harper Roy got to work with his knife on the strangling mess of cords. He reefed in the two white tents. I could see that Roy did not mean all that wealth of white silk to go to waste. Brin gave a soft cry; the helmet was off. There in the night, with no light but a radiance off the snow, we could just make out a face. A young face, with pale soft features and short hair; black hair, black as night. The eyes were open now, and a deep voice implored and questioned; we did not understand one word. We all replied at once in the most soothing tones we knew: You are safe. You are our dear Luck, come in answer to our prayers. We will help you. You have come to Brin's Five. We are your Family, and we will love you.

There was a confused shouting and splashing from the far bank.

"Do you read that crest?" asked Harper Roy.

"Star and spindle," said Brin, peering through the mist at the torchlit banners. "Some grandee. But they will not have our Luck."

The Luck lay still now, eyes closed; I could not look away from that pale face. Then suddenly Harper Roy was beside me with our sled and coverings, gently rolling the Luck upon it, still in the body bag. I started up. "Odd-Eye!"

But Brin pulled me down again into the shadow. "Odd-Eye has no need of these things any more."

Then I was filled with remorse and sadness and almost hated the new Luck because I had left Odd-Eye alone to die, by the burned tree.

The hunting party had not seen us, but they were beginning to move around the head of the lake towards our beach. We took everything including the bales of white silk; the Harper dragged a branch over the places where we had been. We went quickly up the track, bent double, dragging the sled, and a light snow fell behind us, covering our traces as we bore the Luck safely home.

II

We were afraid of pursuit that same night, but it did not come. We sat in the dark, retelling the miracle to Old Gwin and Mamor and Narneen. Then Brin made a bold decision and lit two candlecones from Gwin's secret store.

"We must not lose the Luck now it is come!" said Harper Roy, in answer to Old Gwin's protest. "Pray to the Kind One or whatever you like, but we must tend these wounds."

"A glider?" rumbled Mamor. "Burn us but it must be some rich grandee that will never stay with mountain folk!"

"An *air ship!*" I insisted, "not a glider!"

"You sure it ain't some Hairywing, some goblin come through the void from Derrin?" teased Mamor again.

Narneen whimpered.

"Hush!" said Brin. "It is a person . . . a Moruian. Perhaps it is an Islander."

Old Gwin who had been wrestling with the shining body bag found the way to work the fastening and began to peel it off.

"You see, Mamor?" I said. In the confined space we slid off the body bag and had it folded away quickly.

"Not bad . . ." said Old Gwin. "Fetch clean snow in a basket. There's a cut . . . oh poor dear . . . the Luck has a burn. The Luck's poor dearest hand is burned."

23

"If it were perfect," said Harper Roy, "we might not have a Luck."

While Old Gwin washed and dressed the burned hand and the cut head, we examined our new Luck. We saw a tall, strongly made figure, like our own and yet not like. The proportions were different: heavier muscles, especially on the shoulders, like a porter. Arms shorter, head more round, face rather more flat, eyes more frontal and so on. This has all been detailed now and studied, but we were the first ones, so I believe, to make such observations.

The hair we could not believe: black as night, soft and curly as fleece; we all touched it as the Luck lay there, breathing strongly. We compared it with our own hair, all straight, of course, and fine, from Old Gwin's gray strands to the even brown of the grown-ups and the streaked blonde of myself and Narneen. Then the skin, paler than ours even in winter, pale and unmarked by the sun, the way grandees in Rintoul might be, if they took care and used sunshades.

"An Islander?" asked Brin.

The Luck wore a beautiful suit of rich, soft fabric, all in one like the body bag; a dark blue suit down to the feet, covered in white stockings after the heavy boots came off. Over the suit was a sleeveless vest covered with pockets and pouches, closed with that same interlocking fastening that had tried Old Gwin's patience. We took off the vest and laid it aside, then Mamor worked the fastening on the beautiful blue suit and drew it down over the shoulders, drawing the burned hand carefully from the left sleeve. More clothes—a shirt and long trunk-hose in fine white woven stuff.

"A quick look!" said Old Gwin. "We mustn't freeze the Islander to death!"

"It's not cold," said Harper Roy. "This is the Luck's showing!"

We laughed, and Brin stripped off the shirt; Old Gwin gave a sharp intake of breath.

At first I saw only those tantalizing marks of difference —like and unlike all together. The stripping made the Luck more slender because the suit gave shape and pad-

ding. The rib cage was the same, the muscles heavy like
an athlete or porter. The skin was utterly foreign in its
pallor and the pattern of body hair, thick on the chest and
descending onto the belly, was unlike a moruian.

"I think the Luck could grow that hair on its face!" said
Mamor.

"So much?" said Harper Roy enviously, feeling the
Luck's smooth chin. "You're right. It has hair scraped off
right up to the ears."

Old Gwin was amazed at something else: two circular
marks on the hairy chest.

"Great North Wind!" whispered Harper Roy, "what
sort of creature is this . . . to have teats on the chest?"

"They're not true nipples," said Brin. "Could they be
scars? Some kind of ritual cicatrice? Remember the legend
of the Branding."

Old Gwin clucked and made some crude remark to
Mamor, which he did not repeat. She made a sign to avert
threads of evil and reefed off the Luck's last garment.
There was no doubt, the Luck was a male person, and
below the waist his appearance was remarkably normal.
There was a round, sunken scar in the center of the body,
which we found puzzling, but the rest of him quite sound
and well-formed. Gwin covered the Luck and put back the
beautiful blue suit; Narneen, cheeky wretch, had slipped
off a white sock and counted the Luck's toes. Five of
course, rather squashed and flattened from their tight covering.

Gwin said: "Leave him be!"

"Name the Luck!" I said. "He must have a name."

"It will tell us," said Mamor. "Give the poor fellow
time."

"No," said Brin, "Dorn is right. A nickname would be
our gift to the Luck. Roy?"

The Harper ran a hand over the strings and pronounced
first.

"Nightbird."

"Starfall."

"Blackbird."

"Kind Star."

"Dark."

"Blueskin."

So it went round the circle until someone said "Diver . . ." and we knew this was the perfect name.

A diver is a bird with blue plumage, the color of the Luck's blue suit. Divers come to the Warm Lake for a while in spring, for the shrimp hatching. Diver! How we laughed!

"Perfect!" said Brin. "It gives nothing away." Narneen gave a squeak. We saw that the Luck—Diver—had opened his eyes, and they were blue. Not green or tawny or brown or hazel or any color but blue, bright piercing blue, an eye color unknown among the Moruia.

We stared and Diver stared back, taking in slowly the recesses of the tent, the glowing candlecones, the ring of faces. I heard the sound of the wind, thrusting at the edges of the tent. Outside was the glebe and beyond its wall the forest, the mountainside. We were perched high on Hingstull, upon the round orb of Torin, a small bead woven into the network of two suns. But the mystery of the spinning universe had been caught and held, for a moment, right here in our tent. I stared, on his behalf, at my own family. What could Diver see?

The looms that took up so much space, the brightly colored pieces of work drying or stretching up above us; the colony of spinners, all we had left, wintering in the fork of our tree. The wool sacks, the racks where Old Gwin kept food baskets. The hide bags for clothing, the sheafs of parchment and cypher threads and music skeins that Brin and Harper Roy had collected, Mamor's weapons.

Then the Family . . . the adults, who looked to me as well-worn and pleasant as the familiar objects we had made for our use every day. Thin brown faces, mainly hairless, though the Harper grew a lock on his chin. Heads of straight soft hair, plaited or tied, of a plain bear-brown; eyes widely spaced, long-lashed, all dark brown except Mamor, whose eyes, like my own, are hazel. Straight features, long upper lips, straight teeth . . . Old Gwin's were almost gone.

We were muffled in winter tunics and leggings and shawls, but Mamor's build was noticeably the heaviest; he had a scar on his left cheek. Brin's face was the noblest; she wore the vented robe and a copper amulet, very old, the only metal we carried in the house, besides four knives. Then the children, Narneen and myself, thin, straight and brown as the rest, our hair lighter.

Diver looked hard and raised his head. Old Gwin clucked and gave him another pillow. Then we began to speak, reassuring him. He spoke, in that surprisingly strong, guttural voice; his words seemed harsh, well-formed, dropping hard as graynuts into the murmuring pool of our speech. His teeth were as straight as ours; he curved up his mouth . . . we all smiled back. Narneen laughed, and Brin, picking up Diver's sound right hand, laced fingers in the sign that is called "Welcome." She said the word; Diver easily repeated it, and that was the first word he learned in our speech. We all made the sign with his hand or our own and repeated the word to him.

He greeted us, then became anxious; his words made us cringe a little. Harper Roy mimed the tale of the vessel landing in the lake and made zooming, splashing noises. Then we showed the Luck his body bag, the vest and the white tents that had supported him in the air. He was calmer. He took the vest, and from the first of those magic pockets dosed himself with two small orange globes of medicine. Then he opened another pocket and brought out a flat package of dark brown squares, wrapped in crackling metal paper. Old Gwin made an averting sign, not the first or the last; she was very superstitious. Anything to do with fire or metal frightened her.

Diver broke off a dark brown square and ate it. Then he broke off other squares and held them out in front of us.

"Go on," said Brin, "it must be fit to eat." She took a piece, then Narneen . . . always hungry . . . then the rest of us. It was indescribable. The sweetest thing I had tasted in my life to that moment was wild honeycomb, and not much of that. We devoured that first square of chocolate like Twirlers in ecstasy.

Diver had other rations, but we refused them and ate our blackloaf; we were positive now that our luck had changed. It was difficult to speak with Diver; but very soon he took from his vest a small sheaf of paper and a little, hard blue pen. With these he began his drawings. He was very skillful at drawing all kinds of simple things, and he could draw faces . . . our faces, his own. His work was clever as a tapestry tale-weaver. At the very beginning of his life with us, something was said that rings in my mind still, because it is so strange.

Diver listened to us very closely but he could scarcely repeat anything we said, at first, because our speech is fast and soft. But without prompting, he spoke up and said, "Moruia." We agreed, pointing to ourselves, and he said again, "Moruia of Torin." It could be argued that he caught the words from our speech or read our thoughts. This is not so. Diver had no magical powers in the true sense; he was "thought-blind" and could not use a Witness. I believe *his* explanation: that his ancestor spoke these names in a prophecy long ago, in the system of another star.

Our luck had changed. We slept late; and when we awoke, Mamor and Harper Roy had been to the lake. They had performed funeral rites for Odd-Eye and buried his body. I often thought of Odd-Eye in the days that followed, and sometimes in dreams I spoke to him and told him how well we were doing. I wondered if his soul-bird had flown with the North Wind, our Great Mother, or if it still hovered near us, watching, as certain brave souls are permitted to do. But I was a child and could not mourn long.

That morning my main interest was in food; Roy and Mamor had picked up a sack of mud-crabs, washed up on the lake shore out of season. Then on the way back Mamor shot a scrub deer. They saw certain other things and came back quickly to report. I left off threading the contrary little brute of a mat-loom and was unloading the mud-crabs.

"There's company!" said Mamor, jerking his head towards the lake.

"A search?" asked Brin.

"It will come to that."

"Armed vassals," explained Harper Roy, "trying to drag up Diver's ship in a net. It will go all the way to Rintoul."

"What was that crest again?" mused Brin. "Star and spindle. Do you know that, Mother?"

Old Gwin snorted and went on skinning the deer with her own shell-knife. "A branch of Clan Galtroy. That crest was quartered on a hanging by Roneen Tarroyan . . . may her soul-bird fly far . . . Galtroy are southern grandees. City-folk."

Mamor shook his head. "That was not the only crest we saw."

"What else?" asked Old Gwin, catching something of his tension. "Out with it!"

"Three knots," said Mamor. "The armed vassals in the patrol all bore this device." Brin looked for confirmation to the Harper, who struck three notes on his harp. I was filled with uneasiness.

"What crest?" I asked. "Brin, tell me, who is that?"

"We live on his land, child," she said patiently, kicking the changes on the great loom and running the shuttles through. "That is the device of the Great Elder, Tiath Avran Pentroy."

I blurted out the terrible nickname: "Tiath Gargan!" It was a name to frighten children; all the adults turned to me and laughed.

"Yes!" said Mamor, "old Strangler Tiath himself. This Galtroy visitor and a party of Pentroy vassals have been using the hunting lodge at Twin Peaks, beyond the lake."

"Will they come searching?" I looked at Diver, deeply asleep on a pile of bedding, within wind of our looms.

"They shall not have our Luck!" said Brin firmly.

"Maybe they'll be content with the ship," said Mamor.

"It was a fine sight," said the Harper, "roundish . . . silver . . . made all of metal." Old Gwin hissed and made the averting sign.

"Cook the food," said Brin. "If the weather holds we'll travel south tomorrow."

"After we eat," I said, "could we do the binding ceremony?"

They all approved, and I was proud to be taken into their counsel. So at midday we feasted on mud-crabs and venison, then we woke Diver, and Old Gwin fed him some broth. Afterwards we enacted the binding ceremony with a white cord. Diver was refreshed from his long sleep and watched everything we did; I think he understood it. We bound all our wrists together, chanted and clasped hands. Then Old Gwin drew out a message skein, and it went round the circle with each of us tying the knots that spelled out our names. Narneen and Brin guided Diver's hand, and there at the base of the skein was his given name, Diver. He was bound a member of our Family, Brin's Five.

After that we drank water and went back to our weaving. Narneen, lucky wretch, was permitted to leave off her carding and spinning and sit with Diver. He began at once to learn our speech, beginning with the names of common objects. He was especially quick and diligent in this study, copying what Narneen said in his penetrating foreign voice and writing in another small bound sheaf of paper. We felt his determination, his eagerness to know all things; we took things more steadily on the mountain before Diver came. He was of a different race; there was an edge of impatience about him.

The break in the weather did not last long enough; Mamor believed another blizzard was coming that would keep us on the mountain. As we were dismantling the looms that same evening, Narneen heard something. Old Gwin and Brin buried the Luck in a cloud of new work and blankets; Whitewing, that bird of evil omen, stood outside our tent.

"Peace to Brin's Five from Hunter Geer, their glebe neighbor."

"Peace in sad time," replied Harper Roy, lounging at the open flap with a bunch of red mourning threads.

"Sadness?" The albino peered boldly into the dark recesses of our tent.

"Odd-Eye is gone," said the Harper, making an avert-ing sign.

"May his soul-bird fly far," murmured Whitewing, run-ning a thin, blue-veined claw down the tent fabric so that the dry skin rasped against the coarse cloth. "Have you heard of the fire-ship in the lake?"

"I have seen comings and goings," said Roy cautiously. "A fire-ship?"

Whitewing hissed with pleasure. "There is a great re-ward for catching its devil!"

"A devil!" Harper Roy made an averting sign. "There was a devil in the fire-ship?"

"A devil . . ." said Whitewing, ". . . and Tiath Gargan will have it for his own."

"Great North Wind . . ." said Roy. "Is our Great Elder come to Hingstull as well as a flying devil?"

"He lies down river at Otolor; he has flown in a party of vassals to scour the mountains."

We shuddered now at Whitewing's story; Tiath Gargan had never come so close.

Roy probed a little. "Is it certain this devil did not . . . drown?"

"Tiath's hunters saw it flying down," said Whitewing eagerly. "The Great Elder will give land-title to any Fami-ly that delivers up the flying goblin, dead or alive."

"That *is* a great reward." Roy was cunning. "Perhaps Mamor and I might try . . ."

"What?" creaked Whitewing. "With no Luck in your house? Hunt a devil?"

"Why do you tell us then?"

"Out of friendship." Whitewing grinned like a wolf. "Hunter Geer will catch the devil. Tell us if you see any prowling thing."

"None," said Roy, "before you came."

Whitewing's pink eyes blazed. "Take care! If the devil is not found . . . who knows what Strangler Tiath might do in his wrath?"

"We need not fear him!"

"You must!" Whitewing took a step into our tent, but the Harper blocked his way. "Your Luck has died. You are accursed. If the devil is loose, your ill-fortune will keep us from finding it. Tiath Pentroy is a devout follower of the old threads."

"Our prayers for Odd-Eye's journey are not ended!" growled Roy, "leave us in peace . . . or you blaspheme against our Mother, the North Wind."

"Remember my warning . . ." Whitewing drew back, hovering for a moment outside our tent. Then through slits and watch-holes we all saw the creature run flapping through the snow towards Hunter Geer's tent, under the rock wall.

We doused our candlecones and talked in the dark. Poor Diver came out from the covers confused and still more confused by the way we clapped hands over his mouth to silence him. There was a terrible struggle to communicate, but he accepted that danger was about and sat mute.

"We must leave!" said Mamor. "This night, rain or snow. Our good fortune depends on it." He dug me in the ribs and rattled the mat-loom; I went on taking it to pieces. Brin was already packing her scrolls and skeins into one of the hide bags.

"Strangler Tiath . . ." quavered old Gwin, "will he come after us?"

"Not likely," said Brin. "We have more to fear from the weather."

"You don't know," Gwin whined. "You've not seen the Pentroy's handiwork. Trees strung with the dead, like rotting fruit!"

"We must leave, Mother!" urged Roy. "What if they searched this tent? Then we *are* in trouble with Tiath Pentroy, and our Luck is dragged into Rintoul as a devil."

"We must leave word for Hunter Geer," said Brin. "We have gone in order to leave him a clear field . . . to take away our accursedness."

"The Luck wants his pocket-vest," said Narneen. "He is patting about for it."

We gave Diver his vest, thinking he was hungry for more chocolate, but instead he performed another of his miracles. He produced something from a pocket, and

there was light . . . a marvellous cool circle of light, better
than a candlecone, coming from a small gray rod. We sat
in amazement; then Mamor began to dismantle the two
great looms while Brin and Roy rolled and sorted the
finished work. Gwin fussed in case there was fire-metal-
magic at work; but I tapped the case of the magic light,
and it was not metal. It was not wood either but something
like horn or crab shell. Wonder of wonders, Diver had two
of the magic lights, and he gave me one to hold. He
showed me how to work a sliding catch on the shaft and
turn the light on and off.

Then he gestured to me. "Why?" I believe he even had
the word. Why were we alarmed, packing up, talking so
urgently in the dark? So while the Family labored around
us in the familiar ritual of packing, Narneen and I labored
with the explanation. Danger! Armed vassals with spears,
ropes . . . ropes for hanging. Diver drew on his paper, we
tried to draw. New words crackled around Diver's head,
but he took it in. And all the while he and I held the magic
lights and spotted them in the exact place that they were
needed.

Suddenly Diver stood up, excited; I would have said
afraid. Of what? Our spinners, poor creatures, that Brin
was popping one by one into their sack with a few ends
of deer meat . . . they hardly ate in winter, they were
sleepy. We laughed and explained and showed him the
skeins of silk and a finished piece of work from Old Gwin's
lace loom. He understood and drew a picture of some
smaller variety of spinner. Yet he had a horror of these
harmless things. We brought him the largest one to stroke,
the one called Momo or Cushion, and it was all he could
do to place his hand on its soft hairy back and look at its
sturdy spinnerets. His face was stiff with loathing, like Old
Gwin come upon a pile of sharp knives beside a blazing
fire. Narneen made Old Gwin's averting sign for Diver
. . . and he understood; we all laughed again.

By the middle of the night, we were packed up; the tent
was an empty shell with all our gear shrouded in its center.
The weather was holding, just; a fine flurry of snow, but
no wind. Old Gwin believed her prayers were being an-

swered. We were wrapped and shod; Diver had a cloak muffled over his suit and vest, and his boots were excellent. Our heavy stuff—the folded loom boards, the work rolls, the wool sack—was packed onto the sled, and the way was clear. We stood in shelter, without light, while Brin and Mamor took down six panels of the tent. We would leave the other three between us and Hunter Geer as a shield. Roy was weaving a message skein; he gave me careful instructions. When the Family had passed through the break in the glebe wall and descended onto the track we had chosen, I, watching, would slip across to the Hunter's tent and leave the skein under the flap weight-stones.

So I stood watching as they all went over the edge. I stole along, crunching a little on the snow and thinking of Whitewing. I got the skein down under the weights and was on my way free and clear when a terrible sound rang out. A hunting horn at the western gate! Torchlights! Armed vassals! I ran blindly into the ruin of our tent, fifty paces from the breach in the wall, across a clear expanse of snow, marked with the tracks of our Five. The party had entered the glebe; voices were raised—there was movement in Hunter Geer's tent, and movement too in the breach of the wall. I longed to cry out to my Family, urging them to stay back.

When I thought I saw my chance, I dived across the snow. There was a cry; two vassals with spears came after me. I was hard held against a leather breastplate with the Strangler's device of three knots. I struggled, kicking and biting in blind panic.

"It's no devil!" panted one vassal. "Just a child!"

"Hold the brat!" said the other. We were halfway between the ruined tent and the open glebe. There was a frightening shout, and Diver came through the breach in the wall. He raised his hand, and a reddish beam glowed in it. The guard on my left was dashed into the snow. Again, with the same glow and crackle the other guard was struck, taking me down too.

"Dorn!" It was Diver calling my name. I jumped up and ran to the breach in the wall. Mamor was with Diver, and he dragged me through; we went slithering and bouncing

down to the track beyond. We did not wait to see what the
search party made of Diver's attack; in fact it had been
hidden from them. They would find two guards flattened,
that was all. The Family was waiting, and with hardly a
word we went down Hingstull at a breakneck pace. Old
Gwin rode on Roy's back; Narneen was lying on top of the
sled, like a package. We raced on down, driven by a rising
wind, pressing through the cold scrub and the snow-filled
hollows among the stones until at last Brin said: "We must
rest now."

"A few paces more," said Mamor, whose track it was.
"This is Stone Brook. I have a cave."

So we came to the cave, jolted and weary, and pressed
into it. We laid down the tent fabric and used the light
sticks to help settle ourselves. Everyone was bone weary;
Diver looked sick again and lolled against the wall of the
cave. I did not dare ask him, or try to ask him, what was
uppermost in my mind. Were the vassals dead? I asked
Mamor, and he thought not . . . the vassals were only
knocked unconscious. I was still shaken by the thought of
a weapon with so much power.

Brin sat in our midst, as usual, resting her back and
drawing great breaths.

"All right?" asked Roy. He was concerned for the hidden child; too much running could unsettle it.

"Fine," said Brin. "This one will have an early showing,
I think." As if to answer her, the child whimpered. We all
took this as a sign of good fortune. Gwin twitched back
Brin's vented robe to let the air come to the child. Diver,
in the light, had a look of extreme bewilderment. We made
signs to him . . . child . . . rocking it in our arms, but he
still did not seem to comprehend. He signed or said,
"Where?" and we pointed to Brin and said, "There, of
course," but he shook his head.

The child whimpered again, and Brin had to reach
down as mothers often did before the showing, to settle it
to the teat. Diver's curiosity overcame him, and he
crawled forward.

"Well, you are our Luck," said Brin, smiling, "so I will
show you."

"What's bothering the Diver?" asked Mamor. "Doesn't he know where children are nurtured?"

"Perhaps his people are different," suggested Roy.

"What difference could there be?" said Gwin. "Show the Luck quickly, so the child won't take cold."

So Brin, in the magic light, let Diver look into her pouch and see the hidden child, settled into its milky sleep again. She had already given Narneen a look, and I remembered seeing Narneen before her showing. It was the way we were taught.

Diver learned his lesson and drew back, shaking his head as if he had seen a miracle. He talked in his own language and laughed and shook his head and, for some reason, stroked his chest. Then he made signs to each of us in turn, and guessed, correctly as it happened, which we all were . . . female or male. I was certain, by this time, that Diver was different from us in ways we could not imagine . . . ways that concerned both life and death.

Our link with him was frail, yet already there was trust between us. We turned back to the Diver and he to us after each revelation. He needed us, certainly; what could he do in an alien place, for all his magical devices, alone on a mountain with hunters out after him? We needed him too . . . although this might be harder for city folk to understand . . . because he was our Luck and in spite of all his strange magic, not because of it. The bond that was woven was the simple Family bond that had brought all the Five together. Now Diver, whatever he was, had become part of it.

Presently we lay down to sleep in our cave while the snow came down. Next day it was so bad that both hunters and their quarry had to remain under cover. It was a holiday of sorts, because we could do no weaving. We sat and ate chocolate in the cave at Stone Brook, teaching Diver more and more new words, while he drew us pictures.

III

There is a road winding down under the cliff below Stone Brook. It meets up with the brook below the falls and leads down into Cullin, where the brook joins the great river, the Troon. On the third day we had made certain plans; Harper Roy and I set out for Cullin. We had come to a way down the cliff when we heard voices, a chant, drawing nearer on the road. The Harper looked through the snow-laden trees and whistled. "Diver must see this!"

I ran to fetch the Luck from the cave, then we crouched out of sight as the party of armed vassals came singing and chanting down the road below us. They were carrying Diver's air ship between poles in a huge transport net. It must have been heavy, for it took twenty Moruians to carry it, but I was surprised to see that it was such a small thing. Its shape was like a rounded fish, and it was patchy silver in color. The light bounced off it as it rode in the net; there were streaks of charred blackness on its surface as if it had come from the fire.

Diver watched it go by and we watched him, doubtful, in case the sight of its capture might make him restless or sad. He watched the procession with narrowed eyes, then asked, "Where?" The Harper told him Cullin, the place we were bound for, to spy out the land. I took Diver's arm and pointed again. A litter was being carried down after the air ship. A rich palanquin, with ruby-red hangings,

quilted with white silk cord—a ridiculous carriage for the
mountains. The crest was the one we had first seen, star
and spindle, which Gwin named as Galtroy; but the vassals, most of them, had worn the crest of three knots.

"Flitterling!" scoffed the Harper. "Some fancy-work
friend of Tiath Pentroy. That grand equipage will get
soaked if the bearers miss their footing." Diver wanted
badly to go after his ship. He could speak enough now to
say "Follow . . . follow . . ."

I begged him not to leave us, holding his arm in case he
should scramble down the cliff. He exchanged glances
with Harper Roy, the sort of glances grown-ups exchange
over the head of a child, and I felt foolish, but I knew he
did not mean to leave us. The Harper and I took him back
to the cave and we talked a great deal, quickly, about the
matter, with poor Diver looking on and occasionally
putting in a word.

"Danger . . ." fussed Old Gwin, ". . . the Luck will be
found . . . the vassals will carry him off!"

"Not so!" said Mamor. "You've bleached his hair,
Gwin. Muffle him up, he'll pass unheeded."

"Our main object was to consult Beeth Ulgan in this
matter," said Harper Roy. "Why not present Diver to her
in person? It would test a Diviner's art to describe our
Luck."

"Let him go with Dorn and Roy," said Brin. "Take the
skein I wove to the Ulgan, Roy, and show her the Luck.
She has, besides wisdom, all kinds of secret knowledge.
Beeth will know where the air ship travels."

Diver smiled and kissed her hand. She put her hand on
his head . . . bleached brownish-red by Old Gwin's white-
clay . . . and reminded him of his bond. He affirmed,
solemnly, in the way he had, one hand on his chest, one
lifted, palm outward. This is because his people consider
the heart, in the left side of the chest, as the organ of
loyalty . . . while we swear with our heads and eyes,
touching the forehead and blinking.

Old Gwin, still fussing, made Diver dress in mountain
clothes and leave off his blue suit. He would not be parted
from his pocket vest, but with a gray tunic, fustian leg-

gings and one of our enveloping frieze cloaks, with the black hood, he looked like a Moruian. His eyes and voice might give him away, but nothing else. Diver produced a pair of dark glass goggles, like the grandees wear in the snow, and Gwin drew out a blue knit scarf-mask and put it over the goggles. A tall weaver stood amongst us . . . with maybe a touch of snow blindness. So we were on our way again, less than an hour behind the carriers and the sprig of Galtroy in the palanquin.

We kept up a good pace once we had reached the slippery surface of the road. The weather had been holding so well for the past day that I began to believe, as I did every year at that time, that we had turned the corner; the numbered days on Brin's skein were reaching towards the spring. The Harper put a hand over his shoulder and struck a note or two to help with his singing. Then Diver began to sing, in a sweet voice, quite different from his usual growl, and the Harper tried to learn this foreign melody. It was the "Song of the Cheerful Walker," and Roy was just beginning to fit words to it, as he did later with many of Diver's songs. This is not so easy as it sounds, for though the notes of our two sorts of music are similar, the beat of our two sorts of speech is very different.

So we three went singing down the mountainside until there was a strange cry and the Harper drew us up short.

It came again.

"Hold!"

We came round a bend, and the road ahead was blocked by a great clump of snow. It had come from an overhanging cliff and landed squarely on the palanquin. There was no sign of the vassals transporting the ship—they had gone blithely ahead leaving their noble travelling companion who knows how far behind.

We rushed up and began digging with our bare hands. The Harper called out respectfully to reassure the entombed grandee. I began dragging out one of the bearers; Diver tried for another. Through a round hole, like a window in the snow, a penetrating voice . . . two voices . . . a whole pouchful of grandees besought our aid. It is strange that the more civilized our people become the louder they talk.

"Easy!" said the Harper. "The roof of the litter is just holding."

He managed to clear a space at the narrow end of the palanquin: he slashed the fine hanging with his knife and gently tamped down the snow to make a way out. Out they came, the pair of them: two tall personages, not much shaken by their ordeal. Their finery made me gape . . . I had never seen such furs and jewels and leather work. I knew the fine silk-woven wool of their cloaks had brought some weavers a year's food.

The taller one wore a black travelling wig and snow-goggles trimmed with brilliants.

"Thank you, brave weavers, a thousand times . . . Come along Tewl . . . where are those blistering wretches in the convoy . . . Rilpo Rilproyan Galtroy!" This was accompanied by a flourishing bow.

The Harper bowed too. "Roy Brinroyan, called Turugan, the Harper." Tewl was willowy, aristocratic, with hair blonded at the crown and curled up at the edges. I noticed the pallor of their skins, the movement of their long hands, like birds.

"Don't stare!" said Harper Roy. He helped drag my bearer clear; a sturdy vassal with a broken neck. Stone dead.

The Harper said to the grandees, "This bearer has taken flight, highnesses."

I stood dismayed in the presence of death, but Rilpo and Tewl knelt down in the snow examining the bearer tenderly. Hands fluttered, they talked aloud with no self-consciousness. Meanwhile Diver gave a muffled cry; his bearer was alive and unharmed.

Diver and the Harper drew out the limp form, feeling for broken bones but finding none. The bearer was short and sturdy with that breadth of shoulder that vassals get in their heavy work.

"Omor," said the Harper, "an empty one."

"Is it?" I had never seen one.

"Omor?" whispered Diver. The Harper and I were at

a loss to explain but we tried; an empty one is a female who deliberately bears no children. There are none in the mountains; they are usually vassals of the grandees in the capital or mineworkers in Tsagul, the Fire-Town. They have a reputation for being very strong, and this seemed to prove it.

"How is poor Tsammet?" inquired Tewl, striding round the heap of snow.

"Living . . ." said Roy.

To prove his point, the drenched omor took another heaving breath and sat up cursing. The name was a fiery one . . . with the hateful fire-sound of Ts . . . and Tsammet had a blistering tongue.

"Sorry Highness . . ." she growled, "couldn't duck that one."

"Glad you're alive, child," remarked Tewl. "Thank these mountain folk who were passing. Your stablemate Gwey was not so lucky."

We helped Tsammet up, cursing sadly for the loss of the other bearer.

"Thanks, gentle friends . . ." she murmured. "Where's the flaming convoy?" She caught the Harper's eye. "Get my lieges out of this trouble. It'll be worth your while."

"We'll help," said the Harper.

"What's wrong with your big sib here?" she said, peering at Diver. "Don't it talk?"

"Not much," I said. "Poor thing has a thread loose but quite gentle."

"Help me . . ." Tsammet tried to walk, but an ankle buckled. "Flaming hot blistering sprain . . ."

We helped Tsammet around the snow drift and all huddled there, grandees, two vassals, one dead, weavers and Diver, our newcomer, out of the rising wind. Rilpo, I saw, had folded the dead one's arms and laid a red mourning skein on the cold forehead.

"Highness . . ." said Harper Roy, "is there a convoy ahead?"

"A long way ahead by now," said Rilpo. "Any suggestions? Fit us a tune to this perilous situation, Harper."

"The child will run on down," said the Harper, who had

already worked things out to suit our own perilous situation. "Dorn can meet the convoy and send back strength
to dig out the litter and bring down your lost bearer."

"So far so good," said Rilpo. "I don't fancy a long wait
in the cold."

"By no means," said Roy cheerfully; "but one of your
highnesses must take turns with the other at riding on my
back. My sib, poor stupid Diver here, will carry Tsammet,
your wounded dependent."

"Fine! Fine!"

Tewl clapped long hands. "Anything we need from the
litter, Rilpo?"

"No!" cried the Harper. "Pray you . . . keep away from
the thing . . . it may collapse at any moment."

"Ah well . . ." Tewl was dissuaded.

"You're an idiot," said Rilpo fondly.

Diver drew me aside before the mounting up, and I did
my best to explain the plan. One thing bothered him. Were
Rilpo and Tewl male or female? I shook my head; frankly
I had no idea. "Who cares? They're grandees." I looked
again, as Rilpo helped Tewl mount on Harper Roy's back,
and indeed it was hard to tell. No question here of a vented
robe or a hidden child. Grandees were notorious for having more or less mating life than mountain folk . . . Their
adults were not called to the mating tents in the spring
only. I solved the problem by asking Tsammet.

The omor flared up, aiming a blow at my head. "Cheeky
brat! Tewl is the Galtroy's female partner. They have a
pair-family, city style. She has carried him two fine children, what more do you want!"

Diver took some of this in, grinning. He knelt down,
and I helped Tsammet onto his back. She weighed heavily,
but he was equal to it. As I went scudding off on my
errand, I heard her say to him slowly, as if speaking to a
child, "We've got a strange thing in the net, up ahead
. . ."

Then I was alone, running on down in the wind, with
only the plaited-rope soles of my boots to keep me from
slithering off into the valley. I ran and ran until I thought
I must be nearly down the mountain, but there was no sign

of the convoy. Then I paused, and over the side of the pass I saw the ship in the net far below, almost on the outskirts of Cullin. But the lack of the palanquin had been noticed; four vassals were toiling towards me up the next curve in the road.

I hailed them, still out of breath, told the tale and handed over Rilpo's message skein. They were all hefty and stern, with three knots on their tunics; any one of them could have been a bravo who seized me, back in the glebe. Their manners improved when they read the skein, and they went on, cursing, to dig out the litter. I sat idle on the roadside, watching the roofs and tents of Cullin and the cloud shadows moving over the Great Plain. The river Troon, behind its broad groves, flashed gray as metal in the wintery light. Presently there came a sound of singing, and there they were: Rilpo riding now on Harper Roy, Tsammet grinning from Diver's back and Tewl, striding along, strumming Roy's precious harp and singing an old mountain air, "Sweet Bird of the Snow."

So we all went on down. I walked beside Tewl and looked my fill at a grandee. There was a gaiety, a brightness about Tewl and Rilpo that was all of a piece with their finery. I could almost understand serving such persons, being a loyal vassal like Tsammet. I had an impulse to trust them, to ask Diver to trust them and tell his story and show them his magic and reveal his knowledge of the air ship. But I kept these dangerous thoughts to myself, and we came at last, in the darkness before the rising of the second sun, to the riverbank outside the town.

The Troon rises on the west face of Hingstull and passes through great falls and caverns, so that it is a sizeable river when it curls round the mountain's base and is joined by the Stone Brook. Then, beyond the joining place, it curves through the town and on into the Great Plain. We saw the convoy with the air ship in its net, drawn up on the Troon bank where the two waters meet. There was a paddle barge ready and a smaller passenger boat. As we made our way to the riverbank, the vassals in charge of the convoy were preparing to load the ship on the barge.

Diver was able to set down Tsammet at the landing

stage, and all of us pressed closer to watch the loading. No sooner was the air ship laid on the barge than it was covered with vast sheets of canvas and bound with ropes into a great bundle of ordinary merchandise.

"Secrecy," whispered Harper Roy. "Tiath Gargan will not have it borne through Cullin." Diver was restless and tense, but he made no move.

Rilpo Galtroy, who had been speaking to the vassals, drew us all aside. "Friends . . ." he said, "I must charge you all—explain it to your quiet sib if you can—never speak of what you have seen here."

"You mean that vessel?" asked Harper Roy. "Where does it come from, Highness?"

Rilpo and Tewl became still and silent. "You read those crests," said Tewl. "The Great Elder has expressed a particular need for silence."

"I will say this," put in Rilpo carefully. "It is believed that a foreign race has flown from the void and made a nest in the islands."

"But we charge you most solemnly. . . ." Tewl's eyes were luminous in the dusk. "Say nothing even to your nearest kin. Do not betray our trust."

"Believe me, Highnesses," murmured Harper Roy, "I speak for us all and say we will not breathe one word out of place in this matter."

"Highness . . ." I plucked Tewl gently by the mantle.

"Is it not possible that a foreign race might be our friends? They may resemble us in form? They may pass among us and join with us, like Moruians indeed?"

"I pray it may be so, dear child," said Tewl. Her voice was sweet and brittle. She took from her finger a little ring of silver, made like a rope, with a blue brilliant on the knot, and slipped it onto my finger. I blushed and kissed her cool hand.

Rilpo smiled. "Come, you have saved our lives and served us immensely. We can't repay that kind of service. I have had my eye on this poor fellow Diver, your sib. He is very strong, though simple in the head. I think Tsammet likes him. Let us pay you a consideration for his first year's wages and let him be our Luck and come with us to Rintoul."

"Oh yes . . ." cried Tewl. "Sweet Rilpo . . . you have such kind ideas. Let Diver be our Luck. We had a dear Luck, a dwarf, but she died, poor creature."

"Highness," said Harper Roy, "we would not disoblige you for the world, but in truth and according to bond we cannot part with Diver. He is *our* Luck, signed and sealed."

"Too bad," said Rilpo. "What Family? Brin's Five? Well, so be it. I am sure he is most valuable."

He reached into the furry sleeves of his tunic and produced, carelessly, a handful of pure silver credits and gave them to me, filling my cupped hands. It was politeness—giving the child a present rather than tipping the adult. So they parted from us and joined the vassals of Tiath Pentroy. The giant paddle wheel, turned by ten heavers in the bow, began to churn the dark water, and the barge with its shrouded cargo moved slowly from shore. Tsammet had been helped aboard the smaller travelling boat, and now the grandees joined her.

The two vessels moved on down river, and we were left on the shore, wrapped in our cloaks. Diver bared his face; we laughed together, rather shakily.

"Danger!" said Harper Roy. Diver understood.

"It is not over yet . . ." he said. In the light of Esder, the Far Sun, newly risen and moving towards its fullness, a detachment of Pentroy vassals were marching on ahead of us into Cullin.

"We must seek guidance," said Harper Roy. "Beeth Ulgan will help us."

It was a cold evening, and I was sorry we could not visit any of our usual haunts. There were blood kin and glebe neighbors wintering in their warm tents on the slopes above the town and on the edge of the fairground, down over the river. We went looking for a meal in the broad, swept streets of Cullin, between the fixed houses. The tall house of the Town Five hung in curving folds of plaster and bent beams on a mound beyond the circle. The only other buildings of any size were the wool and food store

by the main wharf and "Vanuyu" or the House of the
Four Winds. This is a hunting lodge built by some Pentroy
ages ago on the river, before the weavers bought out the
land and gained the title for a free town.

Vanuyu is a beautiful house—for years the only fixed
house I believed could be beautiful—and it is built partly
of brick, with curtain walls of plaster to either wing. It is
inhabited by some of our town grandees or climbing weavers—the Wharf Steward and the Fair Caller and their
fives. We showed these wonders to Diver by the bright
light of Esder, and I was impressed, as always, by the
lights used in the town . . . candles, oil lamps, rush-lights,
for the townees are far less chary of fire than mountain
folk. But it was still cold; we pulled into one food shop by
the wharf and found it full of Pentroy vassals guzzling
bowls of hot tipsy-mash. We moved on to another, near
the open circle, where we smuggled Diver into a dark
corner, back of the steaming cook pots, and Harper doled
me out a credit to buy our supper.

We ate delicious, hot tipsy-mash and venison stew with
flour dumplings, real town food, in glazed earthenware
dishes that had been hardened in fire. The spoons had
metal bowls, but the handles were safe wooden ones, to
cheer up superstitious country visitors.

"How do you like our town?" we asked Diver.

"Good!" he said, "A *town*."

We were pleased.

"Like the towns in your land?" asked the Harper, slyly.

"Like the towns in my land . . . long ago."

"Never fear," I said, "wait until you see Rintoul."

"Ah, Rintoul . . ." sighed the Harper. "The Golden Net
of the World!"

"My ship goes to Rintoul."

"Diver . . ." I was bold now, with the warmth of the
shop and the tipsy-mash rising into my head. "Are there
others . . . your Family . . . in the islands?"

"Yes . . . but not Family." Diver tried to explain.
"Friends, workers . . . helpers."

"How many?" asked Harper Roy.

"Three and myself. They will think me dead," said Diver solemnly.

"Females and males?" I thought of the strange shape of the female creatures in his drawings. "Will you make a Family?"

"Two males, two females," he replied sadly. "We came as scholars. To see what lived, what could breathe . . . on Torin."

Then a drunken townee from the front of the cook-shop saw Roy's harp and called for a song. He moved away cheerfully, leaving us in shadow, and began to sing, sweetly as ever, a whole string of his mountain melodies. I sat in the gloom, at Diver's side, growing warm and sleepy. The shop was no more than half-full with townees and some travelling Families; suddenly there was some sort of commotion by the round doorway that looked out on the circle. The Harper finished abruptly; customers were making a move. I stiffened, thinking of Pentroy vassals, then I heard the jingle of shell-bracelets and the thud of dancing feet. "Twirlers!" I whispered to Diver.

The shop emptied quickly; even the cook downed ladles and ran out. I gulped down my food and tumbled out into the dark street after Roy and Diver. A blue flame shot up in the center of the grassy circle—Twirlers' Fire. It is a cool, harmless flame, so they say, but it was flame enough to send a thrill through the crowd. The Leader stood in the midst of the circle, beside the flax-bound stake hissing with blue fire. A tall figure, brown and twisted like a burned tree, painted with clay and naked except for a long cloak of blue rag-bunches. Around the circle there danced ten, fifteen others, thumping the ground rhythmically with their heels, between leaping and prancing. The shell-bracelets on their wrists clashed and jingled and caught the light of the fire. Their blue rags were spattered with mud; they were sweating, and the dark streaks on their skin might already have been blood. The twirlers' shell-bracelets are sharp and they cut their flesh as they dance, until the blood runs down.

Every so often one dancer would advance into the circle and twirl on the spot, slowly at first, then faster and faster, unbearably fast, until there was a thin blurring column of blue and brown.

"Trouble!" whispered Roy, as we stood in the shadows. "Time we went to the Ulgan's house." The twirlers had drawn a crowd, even in winter. One or two of the Watch, employed by the Town Five, were lounging about with their staves, not expecting trouble. But the Pentroy vassals could be seen too, pushing their way through the quiet, hooded, clustering crowd. None came our way, and we did not make a move.

One by one the twirlers dropped to the grass like wounded birds, and the Leader, who had twirled and gestured close to the burning stake, began to cry out.

"Avert!"

The twirlers, in ecstasy on the bruised grass, took up the cry in echoing tones. "Avert! Avert! Avert!"

"Avert the Demon!"

Again the shout went round. "Avert the Demon . . . who comes from the Void . . . who flies on Hingstull . . . who flies in the night, encased in metal . . . with claws for hands!"

The crowd hissed with fear. The Pentroy vassals, I saw, had an officer, a grim figure in a leather mask-helmet, who was drawing them together.

"Avaunt!" screamed the twirlers. "Devil came down! Descended on Cullin! The devilish Silver Ship was shipped through the town! Here! Where is the Devil! The Devil! The Devil! The Demon with claws! The Devil is here!"

The Leader's voice was high and chilling; I wondered, how did the twirlers know? I shivered and clutched Diver's arm, to reassure myself that he was no devil. Roy led the way through the edges of the crowd, heading for Sidestreet Four, where Beeth Ulgan's house stood.

Suddenly the Pentroy officer made a booming blast on his roarer and the vassals moved in. The twirlers, disturbed in ecstasy, fought and screamed like mad things. A panic spread among the poor wintry citizens; a few ran to help the twirlers or beat feebly at the vassals who were hustling them out of the way. The burly members of the Town Watch waded into the fray, striking—I saw—mainly at vassals and calling aloud for the townees to clear the streets.

Through an opening in the crowd came two vassals struggling with a poor naked twirler, wide-eyed and streaked with blood. I tried to dive out of the way, but a movement of the crowd bore me to the ground. I remember flailing about and screaming like a twirler myself before Diver hauled me up again. We tried to continue on our way, but the vassals and their prisoner were behind us, pressing against the frightened, angry bystanders. Some of them, including the Harper, set up a shout.

"Let the twirler go! Shame! Set down the spirit-warrior! Out Pentroy! To blazes with the vassals!"

The vassals came on, grim-faced.

"They'll dump the twirler in Street Four," said the Harper, in my ear. We struggled out of their path; and when the crowd drew back, we followed the vassals and their shrieking burden into the dark mouth of the street.

Diver had taken the lead. My heart was pounding; I thought I knew what he was about to do, but I was wrong. He had no need for a weapon. When we were out of sight of the crowd, he threw back his cloak and downed one of the vassals. Diver had an extraordinary way of fighting. I have seen no one to match him save Blacklock himself. He chopped the vassal across the back of the neck with the side of his hand, and the creature dropped like a stone.

"One for you!" he shouted to Harper Roy.

The Harper, nothing loath, did a hip roll on the other. I got into position, crying, "Tree trunk," and together we took the staggering vassal by the arms and ran it headfirst into the nearest wall. The tree trunk, which is the oldest mountain wrestling trick in the skein, works even better in a town, there are so many walls. I was trembling with excitement and fear; the experience of using the tree trunk to bring down a person, instead of practicing it in sport and stopping long before the head hit the tree, was too much for me.

We turned to the twirler, who was propped upright against a wall. The Harper moved in, uttering soothing words, but the twirler was still mad. A hand laid on the shivering brown arm caused more shrieks, more kicking. Already the mouth of the street was full of townees.

"Come on!" said Diver. He seized the slight figure of the twirler, trying to pinion those flailing arms and sharp shells.

"Quiet!" he said in his clumsy Moruian. For an instant the torchlight rested on Diver's face: then with one shriek —at the sight of those blue eyes—the twirler fainted away.

Diver hoisted the limp body, and we ran off into the shadows. Round two corners, with the sound of the riot fading, and Harper Roy was hammering on the door of Beeth Ulgan's house, beside the weathermaker's shuttered booth. We stood shivering until a deep voice answered.

"Who?"

"Brin's Five!" cried the Harper. "Dear Ulgan, open to friends in need!"

There was the sound of the door-pole being hastily drawn, and on the threshold in the dim light stood the tall, sagging figure of the Diviner.

"Great North Wind!" cried Beeth Ulgan. "Harper . . . and your eldest . . ."

"Refuge we pray . . ." panted the Harper. "Pentroy vassals . . ."

"I'm not surprised. Come in."

We pressed on into the house, where it was beautifully warm, warm as a proper tent. The outer room had a metal stove that scared Old Gwin to death when we visited. Beside it lay the Ulgan's apprentice, a young townee, a male, not much older than myself. Diver laid down his burden on a pile of mats in a corner, and the apprentice went over curiously to attend to the twirler.

The Ulgan held up a candlecone. "Let me look at you . . . What have you got there . . . a wounded twirler? And an outclip? An extra member for Brin's Five? Winds forbid! How's Brin? How's the hidden child? How is Eddorn Brinroyan?"

"Odd-Eye is dead," said Harper Roy, standing like a child, with bent head, before the Ulgan.

"Alas . . ." Beeth Ulgan stood clutching the candlecone and murmured a prayer of departure.

The Diviner surprised me every time I beheld her. For a start she was fat, the only fat person I ever beheld before we went to Otolor and to Rintoul, and she was also very tall. Beeth Ulgan had a long, drooping face, very smooth and brown, with thick handfuls of white hair, plaited into great curtains and baskets around the head. The Diviner's robe was of soft wool, of our own weaving, thickly embroidered, with loose sleeves full of magical trinkets, sweets and nuts and message skeins.

"You come in sad time," she said, laying a gentle hand on my head, "but I must ask you again. Has my old teacher's prophecy been fulfilled? How is the destiny of Brin's Five?"

"You have asked that question for years now," said Roy, "and at last I have an answer for you . . ."

"We are blessed with a New Luck . . ." I babbled.

"Hush!" said Harper Roy, pressing Brin's message skein into the Diviner's hand.

"Beeth Ulgan, you were ever our friend and guide. What we show must be secret—"

"Secrets?" The hooded eyes flashed in the dim light; Beeth Ulgan stared at the Harper as she fingered the message skein.

"Diver," said Harper Roy. Diver, rearranged in his cloak, stepped forward.

"New Luck . . ." whispered Beeth, "from Hingstull. Oh great earth and sky!" She seized Diver's hand and led us all into the inner room, a wonderful bright place, full of tapestries and cushions.

Diver stood erect before her, and his hood fell back. We had lived too much in shadow. Now the bright light of a dozen candlecones and two lanterns showed Diver for what he was. Utterly strange, a creature of essential difference, bred in the body's weft. By comparison the grandees, whose fine trappings had made me gape, were like our very blood kin. A pale face, blunt-featured, a round head, curling hair with its true darkness still visible at the nape of the strong neck. Keen, round, frontal eyes of bright blue.

Beeth Ulgan drew breath steadily, holding Diver's gaze.

"Who . . . what . . . are you?" she demanded. "What sort of being do you call yourself?"

And Diver answered formally. "I am a man. My name is Scott Gale."

"Where do you come from?"

"From another world."

It was an odd formula we had worked out while teaching him our language. Diver went on to repeat his identification in his own tongue. By now I recognized it pretty well. The learning went in two ways—we all had a few words of his speech.

"Scott Gale 20496, Lieutenant Navigator, World Space Service/Satellite Station Terra-Sol XNV34, Biosurvey Team One, Planet 4, 70 Ophiuchi A."

Beeth Ulgan peered heavily at Diver. Finally she turned away, shaking her grand loops of hair as she flicked through a bundle of silk scrolls and fixed one on the rack. I could see that it was a chart of some kind, finely woven, like all the Diviner's scrolls, and overstitched in black thread on the cream and gold body of the work. Diver stepped close and looked very hard, turning his head to find a direction. Then he pointed. I saw with a thump of excitement that it was a star chart with the constellations traced out in black, and red points inwoven for the stars themselves.

There was the Sun and the Far Sun. There were the sibling worlds of Torin: Derin or Far-World and the twins Thune and Tholen and the strange distant world that we called Derindar, Even-Further-World, but which astronomers call Veer. Beyond our web of worlds were the constellations: Eenath, the spirit warrior, with her bow; Vano, the great bird; the Spindle; and the Box-Harp. There was the great constellation of the Loom; Diver had pointed to a star in the loom bench, where the great weaver sits.

He brought out a chart of his own and other objects from his pocket vest and laid them on the Diviner's worktable. Beeth Ulgan examined everything with an intense concentration, poised over the worktable with a solemn face and hands hovering, as if she were working a conjuration for some grandee. Roy stood by and acted as interpreter, although Diver used the words that he had pretty well. He displayed and demonstrated his wonders; we knew some of them already. There was the flat box, no bigger than the palm of my hand, that tells again what is spoken into it. There was a thin, fine apparatus like a silkbeam . . . and Diver was surprised in his turn when the Ulgan showed him a box of silkbeam copies.

There was the terrible weapon that he had turned on the Pentroy vassals in our glebe. He aimed it at a tall vase, and I cringed, but the vase toppled gently onto a cushion . . . the power of the thing could be altered from a stunning blow to a feather touch. There were the lightsticks and a set of metal tools and the tiny buzzer that Diver used to shave his face and something called a recharger to make all the marvellous engines well again when their power diminished.

While the Ulgan marvelled at all these things, Diver asked for a map of Torin, and she gave him a colored "Fortune Map" on good willow paper, the kind she had made up by the printmaker two doors away, to sell in her booth. He stared at it sadly and compared it with a map of his own. Then Beeth Ulgan produced larger maps, one on silk, one on parchment, but on these maps also the islands were no clearer, and the distances, though vague, were just as great.

The Diviner looked at Diver's map and shook her head. "As I thought," she said. "We know nothing about the islands."

The islands on her maps, beyond the western edge of the land of Torin, were huge patches of green, coastlines unfinished or fantastically drawn into bays and sounds. On the old silk map there were the sea sunners, giant water beasts embroidered, and strange beasts on land too. There were five mountains breathing red fire that had split the world asunder in ancient times. Diver could still hazard a guess. He pointed on all the maps to a place on the largest island, the one called Tsabeggan or Nearest Fire.

There were his people—three of his own kind—and they might as well have been on a distant star. Whatever way he chose to reach them—and by contrast the land of

Torin, with its plain and rivers and mountains and the desert, was all finely mapped—he must cross a continent and sail the ocean sea. He turned to Beeth Ulgan with a look of despair and spread his hands in a gesture that said plainly, "What shall I do?"

The Diviner took one of his hands and looked at the palm lines, then turned it away from her, as if it were a scroll in a strange tongue that she found too fascinating. "Are your people safe in the islands?"

"Yes."

"Is their tent strong?"

"Yes."

"Is there food and water?"

"Yes."

"Are you the leader of this Family?"

"No."

"Have they another air ship?"

"Yes, a larger one."

"Then they will come seeking you!"

"No," said Diver sadly. He explained, and finally we grasped his meaning. His people must follow certain rules; they could search around the camp and the sea nearby, but the larger air ship was of no use in the search. It was not an *air* vessel at all, but a ship for the void where there is no air. It was for taking the man Family back to the space station or larger sky town around Derin. Diver explained that he had done his people a terrible wrong in depriving them of his little ship, which went in the air or out of it, and was meant for short journeys. His people must continue their scholarly tasks, testing the air, numbering the flowers and the creatures, until their time of two hundred days had elapsed and they would return to the space station.

I found it difficult to believe that they would obey such harsh rules; surely they would continue searching for him and go further afield. His instructions were equally harsh and plain: if he could not return to the party, he must shift for himself.

Beeth Ulgan stared keenly at Diver. "Your people have flown around Torin. You must know there are cities."

Diver nodded. They had reports of inhabited places made some time ago from a great distance. But his people . . . the Biosurvey Team . . . were not envoys; their duty was only to discover how well man might live on Torin.

Harper Roy laughed aloud. "Great North Wind! You have picked a bad spot. The islands are choking hot, full of fever and poison stings."

"Perhaps that's another Diviner's tale," grinned Beeth Ulgan.

Diver smiled and sawed his hand as if to say, "more or less." "It's hot."

"Are you under rule *not* to find other beings?" asked Beeth. Again Diver sawed the air.

"I flew too far," he admitted sadly. "I hoped, always, to find . . . others. The ship failed on my second journey."

Beeth Ulgan was pacing now, with her long hands pressed together in an attitude of thought. "Escott Garl Brinroyan," she said formally, translating the name or at least making it easier to pronounce, "what have *you* in mind?"

"To find my ship."

"Will it fly again?"

"Maybe not," said Diver, "but it has 'radio', to speak with my friends in the islands."

"Ha!" said Beeth, "I think this magic is known here. It resembles the voice-wire."

"The voice-wire is forbidden in Rintoul," said Harper Roy.

"Still used in the Fire-Town," said the Ulgan, "and I could do with one now, though the Winds know it would take a long wire to reach from here to Rintoul. How does your speaking device work, Diver?"

"The words travel through the air . . . no wire is needed."

The Ulgan held up her hands as if she would cry out all the way to Rintoul.

"Oh, these things will be known!" she cried triumphantly. "This will indeed be what the charts proclaim . . . a three comet year. There are others; there is a great one in Rintoul who must know these things."

"The Great Elder?" asked Diver innocently. "Should I go to Tiath Pentroy? To the Elders in Rintoul?"

For the first time Beeth Ulgan made an averting sign. "No! Winds forbid!"

"Why not?"

"It might mean your life and the life of Brin's Five."

"This Elder would take our lives?"

"If he could do it secretly," said Beeth Ulgan.

Harper Roy protested. "Even the Great Elder is bound by law; he must follow the old threads. . . ."

"That's true," said Beeth, "but very often he may weave those threads in *his* pattern."

"But why kill us?" burst out Diver. "From fear? Why should he fear a lone man? I come in peace. Why should this grandee kill a stranger when simple folk have shown me nothing but kindness and love . . . when Brin's Five has adopted me without a trace of fear?"

"You bring power and skill!" said the Ulgan. "You bring fire-metal-magic. We might have had all these things ourselves from Tsagul, long ago. But the Elders, the clans, will brook no change in their power. They cannot see the way the world must go."

Diver studied the maps and traced on one the course of the river Datse down to the sea. "Should I go to Tsagul?" he asked.

"No!" said Beeth Ulgan sharply. "If you found friends there, it would split the world like the blast of a fire-mountain."

"Besides," said Harper Roy, "it is a bleak place. Mamor was there once and did a stint in the mines. Mountain folk do not care for the place."

"Do not be too sure, Roy Brinroyan," smiled the Diviner. "There may be one of your kin well-known in the Fire-Town."

The Harper shook his head and began numbering our kin on his fingers.

"No," pronounced Beeth Ulgan, "be ruled by me, Diver. Go with Brin's Five, be patient."

"Where shall we go?" I asked.

"To my fixed house at Whiterock Fold," she said. "And my own barge will take you all downriver."

"Very well," said Diver, "if Brin will go there . . . if it serves all the Five well . . ."

"There is one in Rintoul who will weave all these threads into a safe web," said the Diviner.

"But who, Beeth Ulgan?" I cried. "Who will save us? Who is more powerful than Strangler Tiath? Is it . . . is it *Blacklock?*"

Beeth Ulgan laughed aloud. "Well, you are not far from wrong, child. I will not say the name, but it is the one who gives Blacklock—young Murno Pentroy—his wings to fly with."

I had to be satisfied with this. In fact it was many days before any of us heard the name she would not utter . . . but from this time we were aware of the presence of this subtle magician, this Maker of Engines.

Beeth Ulgan clapped her hands and went bustling into the other room again. "There is much to be done!"

We followed and found her kneeling beside the twirler. The apprentice had sponged down the poor creature and covered the thin body with a blanket, but still it had not awakened.

"What are the twirlers?" Diver asked softly.

"Outcasts," said Beeth Ulgan, "vagabonds. They fly from a sad fate that haunts all Moruians. Do you know what that is?"

Diver shook his head.

"To be alone . . ." said Harper Roy, making an averting sign. "How is it with your people, Diver?"

"Some bear it pretty well," he replied.

I was stricken with fear in case poor Diver felt alone . . . far from his own people. It was such a dreadful thing.

"Cheer up!" I whispered. "*You* have a Family."

"I know it!" he said, smiling.

Beeth Ulgan was stroking the face of the twirler in a certain pattern; the apprentice crouched beside her, watching keenly. "Our legends tell of a few spirits, neither good nor bad, who lived among the Moruia," she said.

"Name us some names, Dorn. Show your mother's loom teaching."

"Eenath, Vuruno, Ullo and Telve . . ." I parroted gamely. "All were great spirit-warriors and made Families with the clans long ago. Eenath for Pentroy, Vuruno for Dohtroy, Ullo and Telve for Tsatroy, the fire-clan that is no more."

"Good child!" smiled the Ulgan. "The legend tells that these spirit-warriors, especially Eenath, still inspire these twirlers. A Leader, once inspired, gathers poor outcasts into a skein. Those whose families have been broken by death or misfortune, runaway vassals, disgruntled townees or miners. They roam about begging alms and doing their spirit dance. Simple folk are kind to them."

"What will you do with this one?" asked Harper Roy.

"I must put the poor wretch to use," sighed the Ulgan. "I know the leader of this twirling band. He's a wily one, who plays politics."

She motioned us back behind the curtains of the inner room and, raising her arms, began a crooning chant. The apprentice, who divined her will, took over stroking the twirler's face. Presently the twirler sat bolt upright, and I saw that it was a female, no older than Brin, but scarred and undernourished. As the Ulgan crooned, all the harsh lines left the poor face and the twirler spoke its name, like a sleeper. "Mooneen uto Vilroyan. Mooneen, once of Vil's Five. Now roaming with the spirit warriors."

"Your Leader?" asked Beeth Ulgan.

"Petsalee, host of spirits."

"You will bear this message to the Leader, with a gift of silver," pursued the Ulgan.

"Surely . . ." sighed Mooneen, in the same eerie tone.

The Diviner spoke quickly and earnestly: "Tell Petsalee that he will earn praise and riches from the Maker of Engines if he goes straight downriver and plays all towns and villages between here and Otolor. The burden of his teaching shall be: no devil came down from the void but a true spirit warrior, who will bring glory and peace and honor to the land of Torin."

Diver could not follow all this; but as I peered from the

light into the darkness, I was struck by the cunning of the Diviner.

When the twirler knew the message, she was awakened. We saw her dressed in a cloak and given silver, then sent out into the night-light. Beeth Ulgan called us back and for the first time introduced the apprentice, whose name was Gordo Beethan—Gordo, Beeth's helper. No Five-name, or if he had one he did not use it. Again, I wondered about living with a teacher instead of a family. The Ulgan was explaining: "Gordo is a Witness," she said. "The only one registered in Cullin. Ask Diver if such things exist in his knowledge."

We had already tried to explain this way of sending messages to Diver. He understood fairly well what we meant but seemed to doubt if it would work. He admitted he was thought-blind himself but not all his folk were so. A few had the power to link minds. He asked now, could it be shown?

The Ulgan could not do it. "One must believe," she said. Gordo looked smug; he valued his powers. I was sleepy and jealous.

"I will link minds with the Witness," said Beeth Ulgan. "Then, when he calls, far off, at an appointed time, I hear and speak through him, while he is entranced. His hearers hear *me* speak."

At that moment there came a musical rapping sound from deep inside the house; Beeth Ulgan's big silk and wood clock was striking in her clock room. Long before its echoing wooden notes had died away, Diver knew what engine it was and asked to be shown. The clock made me sleepier than ever; I had lost all the hours of total darkness, which the mountain folk use for their best sleep; the Far Sun had been hours in the sky. The apprentice, Gordo, began curling up by the stove in the outer room in an old blue sleeping bag that might have been one of our own weave, for we supplied the Ulgan with much of her furnishing. I went back into the inner room and fell asleep on the fine cushions.

Suddenly I was wide awake; Harper Roy had gone. I felt a stab of alarm although the place was warm and beautiful; I was alone. Then I heard a murmur of voices and saw Diver, quite close, talking with the Ulgan. One of my family was there . . . I was safe. The Harper, I knew, had gone to fetch the others from the cave at Stone Brook; they would join the Ulgan's barge outside the town at the river junction, according to the plans we had made. So I went back to sleep and half woke, once or twice, to hear Diver and Beeth Ulgan talking away, companionably, about stars and engines, like two ancients, yarning over their lace-looms at a spring fair.

The two suns were shining and the sky was so clear that it seemed to stretch all the way to Rintoul. The cold ate into our bones as we crouched on the wharf; the weather was clear and cool as the Ulgan had predicted. We shivered in our cloaks and waited, behind a stack of wool bales: Diver and Dorn, alone. The wharf was not busy. We had just seen Petsalee, Leader of the twirlers, bundling his bedraggled flock into a shabby old bird-boat, all lime and old cages, for the journey downriver. The Pentroy officer was there and a couple of vassals to hustle the twirlers out of town. Now these vassals hung about, two hundred feet away, chewing bara seeds against the cold and spitting out the rinds.

There was a step, and Gordo loomed up beside us. He spoke without looking down. "Barge coming. Be ready."

There was a churning of water and the Ulgan's barge, a cheerful, flat-bottomed fool of a boat, painted in bright colors, swung slowly up to the wharf. Diver, struggling with his cloak, muttered, "Hope this works."

"Have no fear," said Gordo. He stared at me boldly and said: "Are you strong enough, hill-child?"

"Strong enough to break your magical head!" I snapped.

Gordo and I picked up the prepared bale, which weighed as much as a tree trunk, and walked towards the barge. Far to my left I saw the vassals staring; I concentrated on my load. Then, just as I was sure they were coming to investigate, Beeth Ulgan in a gorgeous robe strolled onto the wharf with an entourage of town grandees. This party captured everyone's attention, Gordo was on the low gangplank, so was I; the load was crushing me to death, but I breathed out hard and lasted until the clear deck space was reached. The wool bale lay at our feet, and the muscles of my legs were twitching with relief.

Gordo grinned; he did not seem such a bad fellow. "Good luck!" he said. "See you at the Spring Fair."

I sat down on the deck, and he skipped back onto the wharf. He flicked up the gangplank and shoved it aboard. The barge heaver, a sturdy figure in a checked sailor's hood, pushed off with the pole and went back to working the paddle wheel. Beeth Ulgan raised her staff in a gesture of farewell, and I managed to wave back politely, like her deckhand. The barge swung out onto the broad blue gray waters of the Troon and went slowly, easily, towards the south. I sat there feeling for the first time the sensation of floating on water in a boat. The water spread between the barge and the wharf; there was a sundering, a breaking of ordinary ties. The figures of the Pentroy vassals looked smaller already. Then, with a slight curve of the bank, the houses hid the wharf from view.

The flap of the stern tent flew up, and I was embraced on all sides. There they were . . . Brin, Old Gwin, the Harper, Narneen dancing about like a mad thing. Diver crawled out of the wool bale. We stood all together on the deck and shouted with triumph. The Great Sun blazed in the east, and the Far Sun shone overhead; we were setting out on our journey under a clear sky.

"But where . . . ?" I cried.

"Here, of course!" said a familiar voice. The barge heaver threw back his hood, and it was Mamor.

IV

Brin set up my enemy, the mat-loom, on the open deck,
but I doubt if I completed ten rows of leaf pattern in all
the time we went downriver. It was just so good, so new,
to be moving on the water. I fell into my sleeping bag the
moment Esto went down and woke early, with Esder's
thin light silvering the broad stream. Mamor let me be
tillergrip; Diver and Brin took turns at the paddle wheel.
Old Gwin and the Harper turned to and washed our linen
as if it were already spring. We were travelling light: most
of our new work had been left in the cave at Stone Brook
for Beeth Ulgan's factors to collect and market. Narneen
sat in the stern catching fat water flies for our spinners and
chasing the flatbills from our fishing nets with a green
branch.

Down in the city I have seen plenty of tame flatbills in
ponds and watergardens fed every day on cultured worms.
But they cannot match the marvellous wild creatures who
live in the Troon north of Otolor. The big ones, the To-
tofee, are golden brown with dull green webs; they roll and
play and chase each other from morning to night. They
thought nothing of taking locusts from our fingers over the
side or chasing across the deck, two or three at a time,
with a peculiar snuffling noise from their broad bills and
their tails slapping on the boards. Then there are two
smaller varieties, the common Narfee and the striped Uto-

nar. We saw them swimming in lines, their heads just breaking the surface of the water.

Diver came across the box of wood paints for decorating the barge and painted a frieze of flatbills on the lid of the cargo locker. His artwork was to spread over the face of Torin too quickly for our safety. It must have been about this time that one of the townees in Cullin found his drawings in the cave at Stone Brook and had them copied, with notes in Brin's own written script. Perhaps Beeth Ulgan had a hand in this; she has never denied it.

Mamor was the only one of our Five accustomed to boats; he was the child of river people, far away on the Datse, the river that leads to the Fire-Town. On the second day he and Diver broke out the mast from its long slot on the deck and raised sail. The barge lumbered along faster, but it was very clumsy. It was a matter of watching for channels, shoving off from banks and shoals, shouting a warning to other craft; there were not many at this time of year. We passed villages and hamlets on either bank where we had made spring and summer camps in other years. What a pleasant thing to sail past a track you trudged on, once before.

Diver sat with me at the tiller, and we saw a herd of wool-deer, outside Nedlor, where the banks rise up and there is a hanging bridge over the river. The shepherds were having a hard time cramming the silly creatures into their high-walled fold. Every so often a wool-deer broke free and went leaping and bounding to the edge of the cliff overlooking the river. Then the shepherds moved in with their catch-nets on long flexible poles and brought the straggler in by catching its "hands" and its strong tail. The wool-deer were unshorn; their coats become so thick you can sink an arm up to the elbow in the lovely fleece. This was a herd of pied cross-breds, and their colors were black, white and tan. Diver laughed and told me some more about a strange place on his world where the wool-deer leap about with no wool and the fleece comes from a more docile species.

It was that same day, in the evening, as I rode in the

bow, going tillergrip for Mamor, I spotted a boat ahead of us. It moved oddly in the water.

"What is the matter with that craft?" I asked Mamor.

"Stuck on a sand bank!" We were under sail, so he had Brin reef it in a little as we steered closer. The river was broad and shadowy at this point, with a clear, deep channel between two bars of sand so high and dry they were like islands.

The water flowed swiftly through the channel, and I fought with the tiller. The stranded boat was not a barge but a keel-boat, old and brown. It was caught up by the stern, and the bow swung free in the channel. As it moved, the keel scraped from side to side across the bar. Mamor hailed and hailed again, but there were no signs of life.

I caught sight of Narneen, crouched by the door of our tent, hands to her mouth in fear. I shared her fear; there was something dreadful about the quiet old shell of a boat, swinging lifeless on the bar.

"Dorn!" It was Diver coming to help reef sail.

"That looks like the twirlers' boat."

I recognized it then: the filthy old bird-boat that the twirlers were hustled aboard at Cullin. I slackened my grip so that we entered the channel badly; Mamor seized the tiller and gave me a shove. "Watch out!"

He maneuvered more skillfully, and we drew level, away from the swinging bow.

We could see aboard now; the deck was empty ... a tangle of broken cages scraped and rattled as the boat moved with the current. Not a sign of the twirlers or the boat's crew. We were all watching now, crowded to the low rail.

"What crew was aboard?" asked Brin.

"Captain and one or two sailors . . ." said Diver, "old fellows in whitish clothes. Do you remember, Dorn?"

"No . . ." I whispered. "Two sailors helped the twirlers go aboard."

"Na-hoo the bird-boat!" Brin hailed them in her fine, mellow voice, seldom raised. Then we joined in, piping and calling, with the Harper making a melodious descant.

"Na-hoo the birder . . . Brown Keel . . . you there, the bird-boat!"

"Vano deg!" boomed Mamor, and we laughed uneasily at his joke . . . it means something like "big, cross, old bird."

Then Diver filled his lungs and set the whole river ringing from bank to bank with his strange cries. "Coo-ee! Ahoy the bird-boat! Ahoy there!"

There was no reply; the boat was derelict, deserted. Night was coming down, and we all felt the same uneasiness. Old Gwin urged Mamor to move on and made the averting sign.

"We must search," said the Harper. He cursed the twirlers under his breath and Old Gwin rebuked him, saying they were holy creatures. No one wanted the task of searching the bird-boat. The Harper gritted his teeth and gave me his instrument, but Diver laid a hand on his arm.

"I'll go and take Dorn," he said, "in case I need an interpreter."

I looked at Brin, and she questioned with her eyes: was I afraid? "I'm ready." I was afraid, but game enough with Diver for company.

Mamor timed it nicely; he inched his barge pole along the left sandbank and slewed the barge around as the bow of the bird boat swung towards us again. Diver and I leaped across the thread of water and landed in a heap on the limed deck. We picked our way across the boards, slipping over old tackle, a leather boot, a bunch of blue feathers . . . from a twirler's cloak? Diver paused, head erect; even one thought-blind could sense it. He gripped my arm.

"Don't come any further . . ."

"I know," I whispered. "Death . . . dead persons. Go on." Slowly he bent down and lifted the worn leather curtain that covered the wooden cabin housing. He shone his light down into the blackness.

The cabin was larger than I had expected, a bare, brown hold, with the ribs of the vessel showing through thread-bare hangings. No twirlers, alive or dead, only a torn blue cloak to show that ten or fifteen passengers had been aboard. Then the circle of light rested on a tabletop, a rough thing made of a wicker bird cage upended. There were three of them, two slumped forward, one upright. Diver drew in his breath. The captain and the sailors were dead, dead as tree stumps on their wicker stools; three ancients, all female, old as Gwin.

They were still, their faces hidden, their limp bodies moving a little with the motion of the old keel boat. And I saw why the sight of them, strange and terrible as it was, moved me to pity rather than terror.

"It is a death-pact," I said. "See . . . their hands." The wrists of the three old persons were firmly bound with a red cord.

"How?" whispered Diver.

"Poison. It is an old thread we follow. See the cups." Two cups and a cracked beaker rolled about on the table top.

"Come away," said Diver. "Poor old creatures . . . Aren't they female?"

"Yes," I said. "We must go down."

"No need."

"Yes!" I was urgent. I did not dare look back to the friendly shape of the barge in case my nerve failed.

"Please, Diver. We are the first finders of a death-pact. We must pray and take their message skein."

Diver nodded, and we went down the slippery ladder into the hold. I began the prayers as soon as I came to the foot of the steps, stumbling over the words in my haste. I picked at the fringe of my tunic and drew out a red thread; this was going to be the hardest part. With Diver, solemn-faced, watching me and shining the light, I drew back the captain's leather coat and laid the thread to her forehead. It was not terrible. She was old, wrinkled, pale; now she slept. The same with the other two. Three old sibs, most probably, or relicts of some five with a new bird-boat in happier days.

There on the table lay a long message skein in yellow flax fiber, teased from a rope. I finished my prayers and took it up, with the required response, near as I could recall. Diver saw that I was ready. He flicked the light around, examined the piece of the twirler's cape, then flung it aside. We hurried away, catching our breath.

"Anything else?" asked Diver, on the deck.

"We must show Brin the skein."

It had grown much darker, and the crossing from one vessel to the other was more difficult. Coming back to my Family, even so short a distance, was enough to make me shudder and sob with relief.

We sat in the tent, except Mamor who kept watch, while Brin read the message skein again and again. Her eyes flashed golden in the light of Diver's torch.

"What's in the wind?" asked the Harper.

"Evil . . ." said Brin in a fierce tone.

"What became of those spirit dancers?" demanded Old Gwin. "Child, tell us. . . ."

I looked at her and saw the three pale faces in my mind, in contrast to her lively brown wrinkled face. Brin read the skein:

"Our birds have flown.
Our sweet singers have been hauled from the hold.
We plied our trade honestly and gave shelter to
    travellers,
But now our good keel is dishonored.
Mother North Wind accept all we can give,
Ourselves compacted in death.
Mother North Wind bring deepest ruin
Upon the hand that strangles the Spirit Warriors.
Spirit of Eenath, his own kin,
Be stern upon the Elder Tiath.
First finders, remember your charge.
Be blessed if you be not accursèd.

                              Itho, Lanar, Meedo.
                    Bird Carriers out of Cullin."

She read the message aloud several times until even Diver understood, with our prompting. Harper Roy went out and told it to Mamor.

"I have put too many in danger," said Diver. "The twirlers were speaking about my ship. . . ."

"Not you . . ." Old Gwin flashed her favorite finger sign before her eyes like bone scissors. "Not you, young Luck. There's only one hand at work here and a bloody one. Strangler Tiath has dishonored these poor old bird runners."

"Dragged the twirlers off their boat!" said Brin. "That means he may not be far away. I could wish we were all safe at Whiterock Fold."

"Does this mean Tiath Gargan killed *all* the twirlers?" I asked.

"Who knows?" Mamor had come to warm up and talk. "They're hardy outcasts. Perhaps some escaped."

"What is the first finder's charge?" asked Diver. No one liked to tell him.

Brin sighed. "Dorn," she said, "you were very brave, but the charge may never be complete." I agreed.

"The first finders are charged, according to the old threads, to deliver any curse or blessing in a death-pact skein," she explained.

"To blazes with that!" said Mamor. "The child has done more than enough. Don't put ideas in his head."

"Don't worry," I said. "I hope I never get within offering distance of Tiath Gargan."

The full darkness was slipping away, and I was suddenly bone weary, as if I had climbed Hingstull. I fumbled my way into the sleeping bag and fell deeply asleep before Old Gwin had finished brewing me a herb drink. I dreamed that a brown bird, a night-caller, sat on our tent by day, and I knew, in my dream, that it was Odd-Eye, our old Luck. I told him all was well with us and the new Luck he had found for us was the best in all the world. Then the dream dissolved; I woke once, and the barge was still not under way. Narneen, half in the sleeping bag, was peering through a slit in the deck tent, and I joined her. Outside in the silvery light of the far sun I saw figures moving on the west bank; Mamor and Diver and the Harper were digging in the sand, laying the dead to rest. I slept again and did not dream; by the time I woke, we were far downstream. The bird-boat had been towed out of the channel and moored in a marshy inlet, among the mud-trees.

The broad stream stretched before us; it was the third day, and I felt as if I had spent all my life on the river. Yet I was troubled, and so were the rest; I could not get the image of the death-bound ancients out of my mind. The looms clacked slowly in the tent; Narneen had fits of weeping; Mamor cursed invisible shoals. Diver sat amidships with the Harper, trying to master the knots of the woven symbols with a practice skein. The fine weather that had echoed our happiness turned round now that we were downcast. It was gray and chill at midday; we passed one or two small craft travelling upstream.

In the distance, on the west bank, there was a break in the thick groves of willow and mud-trees: a larger town, Wellin, the last place we must pass before Whiterock Fold. Idly, at the rail, I lobbed a fish spine at an odd blue piece of flotsam, then felt my skin dimple with cold as I realized what it was. I shouted, and Mamor held down the sweep. I crossed the deck to stand with Diver and the Harper as the body of the dead twirler was borne slowly past.

"Great Wind!" breathed Roy. "There was some sense in that death-skein."

Diver brought out his glass; it looked like a light-tube, but he could draw it out to twice the length. It had a lens inside to make distant things look closer; Mamor said that such things were made in Rintoul and the Fire-Town to guide sailors on the Great Ocean Sea. Diver scanned the stream ahead and the landing stage at Wellin, his face darkening. He handed the glass to the Harper, who took one look and went to Mamor.

"What is it?" I tugged Diver by the sleeve. His blue eyes rested on me.

"A black barge," he said, "moored at this place ahead. Some grandee . . ."

Already I knew which one. "Pentroy?"

"There are three knots on the sail."

Mamor altered course to the east bank and presently, when we saw a little wicker crossing-boat approaching, he sent us all into the tent. We heard him hail the solitary rower.

"What doings in Wellin, friend?" We were huddled together, beside Brin, at the loom; the voice came thinly over the water.

". . . assize . . ."

"Great Wind save us!" Mamor was shocked, or pretended to be. "Thought I saw a drowned spirit warrior?"

The voice of the passerby became urgent, telling some long tale; then as the coracle was rowed closer, we caught a few words.

". . . no friend to the twirlers . . . the river or the rope . . ." There was a cackling laugh. We heard Mamor wish the rower a surly good-day and felt the vibration as he began heaving on his capstan to turn the paddle wheel.

We could guess the story Mamor had to tell. "Tiath Pentroy lies at Wellin wharf. He held assize there yesterday. The Town Five went along with him, threw in some local troublemakers—a thief, a bush weaver who killed a cook-shop servant in a brawl. Ten persons hanged, most of them twirlers that the Elder had chained on the deck of his barge."

"Where did he capture them?" asked Brin.

"On the river itself . . . the twirlers made good speed to Fanne and Nedlor, so I gather, and danced in these hamlets."

I seemed to hear the thud of bare feet on packed earth and the jingle of shell bracelets . . . with a new message. Beeth Ulgan's words had told of "a true spirit warrior, bringing peace and honor."

"The Strangler caught up with them at Nedlor," said Mamor, "as he bore downriver on that black palace moored up ahead. His vassals went to watch the twirlers dance . . ."

"He seized them in Nedlor village?" asked Old Gwin.

"Not he! The Great Elder is cunning as a honey-stealer. His dark craft lay off Nedlor, and when the vassals brought back word to him, he decided to put down the twirlers. Or so I read this fellow's skein . . . his family have to do with a bean plot in Nedlor. The twirlers set sail in the bird-boat after their dance, and Tiath pounced. The villagers saw it by Esder light, just about the rising of the Great Sun. The grand barge grappled the bird boat, vassals dragged off the twirlers . . . some were drowned, some put in chains. I reckon that some escaped too . . . maybe the villagers got them to safety . . . this bean-grower knew more than he was telling."

"Cunning is the word for the Great Elder," said Harper Roy. "Twirlers have no fight in them once the dance is done."

"But the old persons on the bird boat . . . who witnessed his crime and were carrying the twirlers . . ." Diver was puzzled. "Why did he let them go free?"

"Tsk! No crime, young Luck!" chuckled old Gwin. "When will you learn? Tiath Pentroy commits no crimes. He is first of all a judge, who may hold assize at request, in any place on these his lands. He works by the old threads. He had no quarrel with the bird carriers . . . they are bound by custom to carry passengers."

"He arrested the twirlers . . ." put in Mamor. "They were brought up at Wellin assize for 'poisoning the river.' "

"Old stuff . . ." sighed Gwin. She rocked her body to and fro, chanting under her breath for the departed twirlers.

"A false charge!" said Diver.

"Of course," said Brin. "It's an old slander against the twirlers. Town Fives and shepherds use it to move them on. They carry herbs for their ecstasy . . ."

"The bird carriers were so old and helpless," I said, "that the Elder gave no thought to them or their poor honor."

"*U tsagara neri fogoban,*" said the Harper. "Can you make anything of that old skein row, Diver?"

"I know fire and 'goes on burning,' " said Diver.

"One fire-seed, one spark, goes on burning," said Brin. "We are peaceful people, here in the north, but very stubborn. A seed of injustice, of dishonor, settles behind our eyes and may drive us to death in order to put it right. So it was with the bird carriers . . ."

The boat scraped against a tree, and Mamor, who had propped the sweep, ran out to steer clear. We came out of the tent fearfully into the gray noon light. The smooth surface of the Troon was choppy with wind-waves, and the trees lashed about over our heads. It was decided that we would lie over all day, where we were, a mile or so short of Wellin, and on the opposite bank. Come the last light we would make haste downstream and slip through the deep channel by the wharf. We had to pass close to the Elder's barge because the river narrowed at this point— there were snags and sandbanks to the east.

I thought the darkness would never come; my insides were knotted like an ill-threaded loom. I sat apart on the deck, clutching the long, loose message skein woven by the three bird-carriers. Presently Diver came and sat beside me.

"Those names . . ." he said, "let me see if I can read them." He felt his way through the final grouping of the knots, consulting the learning skein that Roy had twirled up for him.

"Itho . . . La-bar?"

"Lanar," I said. "Itho is right. Then Lanar and Meedo."

"Poor old women." He used the word from his own tongue, and I wondered if there was much difference between women and female Moruians. I am still not sure of the answer; when first I saw a "woman," I only knew that she was of Diver's race. She was wrapped up in her clothes, sexless and strange as a female grandee.

Diver went on to tell me a strange tale, a spirit legend from his own world. It seems there were three ancient spirits who were said to rule over the lives of humans and control their destiny. They sat in a cave, and two spun the thread of life while the third sat by, ready to snip it off. I labored over the names as he did over the woven symbols: "Clotho, Lachesis and Atropos."

"When I saw the ancients," said Diver sadly, "they put me in mind of that tale."

"I wish it would get dark."

"What are you thinking?" Diver caught my eye: he saw

too much. Thought-blind maybe, but quick in his understanding. "You are thinking of the first finder's charge
. . ."

"We will pass so close!" I whispered, half-fearful that
Mamor or Brin might hear me. "Diver . . . couldn't we?
. . ."

"Maybe." His blue eyes were hard. I trusted him then
against the might of Tiath Gargan.

"Give me the skein."

"I should be the one to throw it."

"No!" He was firm. "Leave it to me. This Great Elder
is too dangerous. We'll do it from a safe distance."

"Don't tell!"

"I must," he said. "Only wait until dark."

So I thought my plan—one for hurling the skein aboard
the Elder's barge as we slipped through the channel—was
quite lost. I trusted Diver, but he was, after all, a grown-
up. I expected a bit of chiding from the Five.

We reefed the sail but did not stow the mast . . . Mamor
planned to use all speed. When the Great Sun was down,
we swung back into the current in the wake of a small gray
fishing boat. Their riding flare bobbed ahead of us; there
came a soft hail.

"Na-hoo the barge . . ."

"Na-hoo the fisher . . ." boomed Mamor softly. "Are
you bound for Wellin?"

"Beyond," came the faint answer, "fishing the reach by
Whiterock. You going to Wellin Wharf?"

"Not this time . . . too crowded."

The fishers laughed. "Too many ropemakers at Wellin
. . ."

We went on as swiftly as the current would take us; the
lights of Wellin shone out over the river. We saw the fisher
slip into the shadow of the grain store then out again, past
the great, lighted shape of the Elder's barge, and swiftly
on again into the darkness beyond. No one hailed from the
wharf or the barge; Wellin lay like the dead. I thought of
the trees of Wellin hung with dead twirlers; the hand of
the Great Elder lay heavily over the place.

Then we were in the channel; with Mamor working the

paddlewheel as fast as he dared, to keep up our speed, and
Harper Roy acting tillergrip. I crawled out of the tent and
went on crawling right to the rail. Little eddies of sound
came out of the night; we were in the shadow of the grain
store. I lifted my head and saw white water churning at
our bow. I realized that voices and music were coming
from the black barge.

We were abreast of it now, and still had a scrap of
shadow to cover us. I saw that Diver was lying on the deck
with his light stick shaded, looking at some magical engine. I looked right onto the deck of the Elder's barge; I
could not look away. We passed in a few heartbeats, but
the scene caught and held me and has lived in my memory
from that time.

The barge was enormous, with a tent the size of a fixed
house, all draped in fine, black hangings, of outdoor
weight, with swags and pelmets woven and reworked in
green and gold. There were vassals and their officers
drinking and gaming round a huge red mat at the bow. At
the stern was a lofty platform and steps, thickly carpeted.
The Elder's people were in attendance, so many that it
could be called a court, and dressed so fine they could all
have been grandees. I looked for Rilpo Galtroy and Tewl,
but did not see them.

The courtiers sprawled on the steps or clustered beside
tub gardens and a flowered trellis. Some were wrapped in
fur-trimmed cloaks, but others wore light robes; their bare
backs and legs made me shiver. The colors were bright and
rich: flame, purple, blue green. The musicians played on
a harp, a box-harp and a matched set of pouch pipes. In
the open space before the scrolled wicker throne, a dwarf
was dancing.

In the great scrolled chair there was a silent figure. He
was past middle age but not yet an ancient. His dress was
very plain: a black tunic, leather boots like his own vassals.
A single yellow jewel the size of a fist was strung round
his chest crosswise, on a thong; a fur-lined cloak of black
and gray flowed over the chair back. His face had the
pallor of a grandee, and the features were strongly
marked. I could see the deep grooves cut in the firm, pale

skin of the Elder's shaven cheeks and the fine carving of his lips. He filled me with fear and loathing. His nose had a high bridge and his eye sockets were so long that they appeared to join into a single slit, under the jutting line of a single dark brow. It is the look we call yadorn or three-eyed.

The Great Elder sat in his chair, still and brooding, with his hands lightly clenched upon the wings. I was convinced that I saw him now, once for all, *as he was.* He was fixed in my mind forever as cold, watchful, cruel, immensely powerful . . . silent among the jangling throng of courtiers, who went in continual fear of his presence. Then we were past the black barge, churning our way into darkness, with Mamor and Diver heaving up the sail.

Brin stood on deck, and I clung to her. "Yadorn," I whispered. "Did you see him?"

"I saw."

A soft wind thrust at the sail. My eyes were accustomed to the night again, and the great barge at Wellin wharf was, by now, a glow of light astern. I saw that all of us were on deck, even Old Gwin, muttering a continuous chant and Narneen with her teeth chattering. We had all come out and were standing close together, under the stars, in some sort of defiance.

Mamor said: "Far enough?"

"Fine," said Diver. He was working with a lightstick on the deck of the barge. "What do you think, Brin?" he asked.

"Worth the risk!" growled Mamor. "That three-eyed devil!"

"Do it!" said Brin. "Dorn? Where is the death pact skein?"

"Diver has it." I was still mystified.

Harper Roy, at the tiller, sent a breathy whisper. "Where's your star-gun, Diver?"

Diver drew out the skein, and I saw him wind it round a pointed tube, fitted to the firing end of his weapon . . . he called it a stun-gun. Then he went aft and balanced on the rail, aiming high into the air. There was a light thump, a pulse beat or so, and suddenly the air far behind us was filled with green fire. A green star, brighter than any light I had ever seen, brighter than Esto, the Great Sun itself, blossomed in the dark air above, directly over the black barge. We heard the shrieks and cries of the Elder's people. We saw, or hoped we saw, the death pact skein falling down like smoke, carrying the ancients' curse to the very lap of Tiath Gargan.

We sailed on into the reach and saw that this part of the river was dotted with fishing boats. Diver kept a close watch astern, but there was no pursuit. How could there be? No one on the river besides ourselves had the least idea of how this green star came about. Even Old Gwin, who saw Diver fire the flare, but was ignorant of our plan, had difficulty in grasping the notion. The Great Elder and his armed vassals knew about missiles—arrows, spears and catapults that hurled stones. They knew more than the old threads allowed about fire—flaming arrows and the terrible firestone clingers that assassins hurl from a metal cup. But Diver's stun-gun and the flare rocket were far beyond their knowledge.

They saw what we all saw and what was seen and wondered at by all the people of the river: a green star fell from heaven over the Great Elder's barge. We heard it from the fishing boats, minutes after the flare, and we heard it again, exaggerated, at Whiterock and all the way to Otolor. Tiath Pentroy had drawn down the wrath of Eenath, his immortal ancestor, for killing her spirit-warriors.

So we sailed on unharmed and came in at dawn to tie up at Whiterock Fold. An ancient shepherd came down to greet the blue barge, expecting Beeth Ulgan or her factors. We were escorted to her fixed house near the landing; our time on the river was over.

V

There are plenty of jokes about rough bush weavers moving into a fixed house, and I dare say we could have been the models for them all, at Whiterock. If it wasn't the cold, the cooking hearth, the earth closet or the cupboard locks, then we were complaining about the stuffiness and the way the walls did not give. We adapted pretty quickly, and the Ulgan's small white house became dear and familiar to us. But there were nights, as spring approached, when we couldn't stand it another moment and slept in our bags on the lawn or on the flat roof, under the stars.

Whiterock Fold, never more than a stopping place, was almost deserted. There were seven shepherds—one family, with two grown children as outclips—tending the fold itself, a mile away behind the outcrop of rock that gave the place its name. Half the hundred wool-deer belonged to Beeth Ulgan, the rest were divided among the shepherds and a town grandee from Wellin. Come spring they would be shorn and turned into the wider pastures round the rock, where they already grazed on fine days. The wool would be shipped up and down the river, some back to Cullin, some down to Otolor Spring Fair. Beeth had promised us a first-class bale in payment for our new work left at Stone Brook.

When our work was done, or when the weather was so bright we could persuade the grown-ups to set us free,

Narneen and I explored the glebe of the Ulgan's house. Eventually we grew bolder and crossed the grazing lawns to scramble on the tall rock and look down on the shepherd's fold. There was no need for Diver to hide . . . although he could have: the fixed house was full of deep cupboards in the curtain walls, as well as a cellar underground. He walked free and went on fishing trips with Mamor in a wicker crossing-boat from the landing. On one of these journeys they learned from a shepherd that the barge bearing the air ship had passed Whiterock a full five days ahead of us. It met with the Great Elder's barge, coming down from Otolor, and Tiath Gargan had gone aboard in midstream to examine the cargo. There was no shortage of gossip up and down the river. The shepherd even volunteered her own idea of what might be on the barge under the covers: a great hoard of silver treasure, fallen from heaven.

Diver was restless, but he was in a land that was all new, and every day he found new things to interest him. He made a folder of dried leaves and plant drawings; he collected rocks. Ten days, fifteen passed, and the suns moved ever closer, to mark the year's end. The weather was so fine that it brought the sunners out onto the rocks; the early-eyes and red-bells were opening. In the air and on the river, the bright two-sun days brought out the "deedeenar" or "flitterlings." One or two small pleasure boats with painted sails flittered past on the Troon; and one day, as Diver sat with us on the rock he gave a cry. The first balloon of springtime went past overhead, and not far behind it was a glider.

It was a fine sight: Narneen and I loved flying machines and looked for these flitterlings or spring visitors every year.

"Grandees?" asked Diver. He had moved into the shadow of a boulder and drawn out his spyglass.

"That's right," I said. "No one else has the time or the credits. Well, maybe one or two rich townees." I tried to explain about the air currents and the air races, the landing platforms and the catapults in Rintoul, Otolor and the

Fire-Town. And the greatest race of all, the Bird Clan at Otolor.

Narneen broke in, "We see them better here. At Cullin they land on the fairground, and on Hingstull they fall, poor dears, if the wind is wrong!"

It was true. On the mountain we got too many unskillful flitterlings who dashed their expensive craft, and sometimes themselves, all to pieces. Diver handed me the glass, and as I trained it on the flame and silver balloon, he laughed to himself and hummed one of his tunes.

There was something brave and comical about the party of grandees in the basket. They wore furs, because it was chilly, and seemed to be eating and drinking enormously. And one—I gave a yelp of laughter—a personage in a green cloak was looking back at us on the rock with another spyglass. Diver looked again, and Narneen took a peep. We could not stop laughing; we rolled about on the rock while Diver took back his glass and examined the glider, bearing away to the other side of the river. Then he sang us his song of the flying machines, and I gave him the first words, "Ototo Deedeenar . . . Great, great flitterlings . . ."

We lay on the rock hoping for more machines, but none came and we went back to the house, laughing and adding pieces to our song.

Diver could not hide his excitement.

"We told you," said Brin, after supper. "Did you think those were hill yarns?"

Diver shook his head and laughed; he was rather shame-faced. "The flying is more advanced than I expected." We sat in comfort in the midst of Beeth Ulgan's house, on cushions and our own mats laid down. When I saw our hangings on the white walls and looked round at the familiar faces, I could hardly believe that we had become so grand . . . like city-dwellers.

Diver asked about the use of gliders and balloons. Mamor chimed in; he had flown in a glider. Some distant sib of his Five had been a glider pilot, who carried messages and passengers about in the Fire-Town.

"There is the difference between Tsagul and the rest of

the world," said Brin. "Flying is a sport for the rich every-where else. In the Fire-Town it is put to hard use."

"Ah . . ." said Harper Roy, who was quiet and thought-ful this night. "Many others would fly if they could. Re-member Antho the Bird Farmer."

"Remind us," said Mamor. "Diver has not heard the story." So Roy took his harp and accompanied his tale, half-sung and half-told, in the manner that is called "man-tothan." I cannot set it down as he delivered it, but the story is a simple one:

"Antho the Bird Farmer was not a clansman; he lived on the outskirts of Rintoul where there are bird farms and market gardens to serve the needs of the great city. He followed the old threads, but he suff-ered a great loss . . . his Five and their children all were killed in an accident on the river, and Antho, who had been proud and rich, was left alone. He became mad, so it was said, with his solitude. One day he set free all his caged birds, even the scratching fowl who cannot fly, and wandered into the wilder-ness.

There the winds took pity on him and blessed him with the power of flight. He made a marvellous craft from bentwood and a bolt of silk he found floating down the Datse. It was launched from the roof of a ruined temple, with the aid of two hermits, male and female, who lived in the desert. Then Antho caught every current of air and flew better than the grandees. His glider took him home again and was a wonder to behold. No other craft could match it, and the design was widely copied. In the end Antho flew away on another of his journeys and did not return. It was said that the winds had taken him."

We applauded when the tale was done, and the Harper repeated his last notes . . . Antho flying into the setting of the suns.

"Is this tale very old?" asked Diver.

"By no means," said the Harper. "Antho has been gone no more than twenty springs."

"He could be still alive!" I cried. "An ancient—"

The grown-ups all laughed.

"Hush child," said Gwin, "you heard the Harper. The winds took him."

"I wonder?" said Brin. "Who is this liege of Beeth Ulgan's . . . the Maker of Engines."

It was past the time for our best sleep, and we were folding our clothes into their bags, ready to crawl into our own.

The Harper sighed and hung up his beautiful harp upon the white wall. "Diver," he said, "I have been talking with the shepherds . . . Varb's Five."

"What do they say?" asked Diver.

"Last spring there were grandees at Whiterock. They left behind a treasure that none could put to use."

"A treasure?" I asked.

"Their glider came down about half a mile north east of the rock," grinned Roy. "It lies there yet, covered with hides and branches."

"A glider!" Diver's eyes were shining with excitement. We knew why the Harper had been unwilling to tell about this treasure.

"We must look at it tomorrow!" said Diver.

"Will you . . . will we all go flying?" asked Narneen. Diver looked at us, sensing the tension.

"If your Luck can fly," he said, "then so can you all." It made me sleep easier.

When I woke up, in brightish Esder light, before the Great Sun rose, the Harper and Diver had already gone. I ran up onto the roof, struggling with my tunic, and caught sight of them, clear of the glebe, two dark figures striding across the grazing fields. They passed into the shadow of the tall rock. I dared not go back down the ladder for fear of waking the others. They would soon be stirring anyway, it was only the darkness of the fixed house that kept them asleep. I looked over the edge of the roof and found more handholds than there were on Hingstull. Down I went, by rain pipe, window edge, and a tree branch. I ran through the glebe and across the grass in the flat light of Esder, overhead. It was a near thing, but I glimpsed Diver and Roy passing into a grove of trees off to the northeast, away from the fold. The wool-deer thumped and chirruped in their stockades; I thought I heard Varb's Five stirring in their tent.

I could have run on and caught up; but instead, out of mischief, or shyness, or because I wanted to go back to the fixed house for breakfast, I decided just to watch. I turned back and climbed the white rock. It made a comfortable vantage point. There was soft grass growing in the hollows of the rock, young flax plants and berry vines, thick with buds and flowers, the promise of summer fruit. I settled in a warm hollow, closed on three sides with boulders, like a room in the top of a tower.

Diver and Roy were walking through open country now; all that lay before them was a fallen tree with some kind of lean-to against it. The glider must be there. The morning was so still that I could hear the sound of their voices, as they came up to the lean-to and began stripping away hides and dead bushes. Off towards the riverbank a wind flattened a clump of tall reeds, snaked through a patch of scrub, made a clump of trees and their shadows waver. But there is no wind, a voice whispered inside my head. "Look child, there is no wind."

What then? I whispered in thought, scanning the clump of trees. There, yes, I see now. A watcher. Only one? I cannot be sure. . . . there. . . . now it is clear. The Great Sun, rising to meet Esder, sent long, golden fingers of light across the land to the east. My eyes were fixed on the spy, the stranger, crouched in bushes, only fifty paces from Diver and Roy as they cheerfully uncovered the glider and walked around it.

I was afraid, uncertain of what to do. What I saw was like a dream and I was in the dream and out of it at the same time. If I shouted a warning, would the cry hang in air and never reach Diver and Roy? Would the watcher be alarmed, angry.

The voice in my head asked: "What would you do on

the mountain, child?" and I answered; I spoke the answer
in a low voice.

"I would high-call to Roy. . . ." And I knew the strang-
est thing of all: *I was not alone on the rock*. There was one
who stood at my back, shedding a mild radiance, a feeling
of warmth all round me. I was linked in thought, guided,
as Beeth Ulgan had guided Mooneen, the poor twirler.

I rose to my feet and high-called with all my skill to
Harper Roy. The trick is to produce a smooth flow of
notes, between singing and calling; I knew it was done
right when the back of my throat tickled. The high-call
flew out, straight to Roy's ears, like the call of a morning
bird. I called, "Danger . . . danger . . . danger" and then,
"Tree . . . tree . . . tree"

I saw Harper Roy spring back and lift his head, then
give the returning call, "Heard . . . heard . . . heard."

A figure leaped up from the bushes, and Diver gave a
shout. He ran forward a few paces, and I was afraid he
might use the stun-gun. But the watcher was very quick,
racing away now, bent double among the scrub.

"Have no fear, child; the creature is not worth your
Luck's weapon."

I sank down again and, still deep in the dream, I turned
my head. The fire of Esto was in my eyes. A tall figure in
black and green, not ten paces away, on the uneven summit of the rock.

"Who?" A bordered robe, long hands, but not the restless bird hands of a grandee. A glint of metal, dull gold,
green gold, in one hand, and I knew. I thought the words:
"Maker of Engines . . ."

A low chuckling laugh. I put up my hand to screen out
Esto's light. The words were spoken this time: "Guard
your Luck, Dorn Brinroyan!"

There was a first light gust of wind, stirring the vines,
and I was alone.

I climbed down from the rock and ran without looking
back through the trees and across the open spaces. I was
out of breath when I came up to Roy and Diver.

"Now what's this?" said Roy sharply. "Why are you
out after us, watching from the rock, high-calling?"

"The watcher . . ." I gasped, pointing towards the place.
"You did warn us, I suppose."

"But what was it?" I begged. "What sort of a person?"

Diver shook his head. "Tall, wild. A male. I have a feeling I've seen that creature before."

"Some outcast," said the Harper, "some wretched berry-picker scavenging for a poor broken Five."

"Well, what do you think of her?" asked Diver proudly.

He meant the glider. It sat on the grass, free of its coverings, like a fallen insect, a poor flitterling indeed. I had never examined one so closely before, although I knew they were made mostly of bentwood, covered with oiled fabric. This one was large—fifteen paces long and the wings a good twenty paces if one had not been broken. Yet it seemed a frail thing to sit in, above ground. When I looked more closely still, I saw that the bentwood was very finely worked; two lengths came from the tail in a swooping curve and arched over the pilot's chair. The wing, scalloped along its backward edge, fitted through this arch and was ribbed with short lengths of tough silken cord, most still unbroken. The fabric was a silk-weave, fine flax of a pale, clear yellow, mottled and torn in places, or stained with berry juice and bird droppings. The whole contrivance rested lightly on bentwood runners.

"It is beautiful," I said at last. "But can you make it fly again?"

Diver laughed. "Better than before!"

Then he and Roy began to examine the craft again, walking around it, flexing the broken wing, getting down on their haunches to peer between the curves of bentwood. I was impatient with them and still afraid. There were times when grown-ups had no sense and not enough fear. I sat on the fallen tree, staring through the bushes to the river reeds, the path where the watcher had come and gone. Had he used a boat? I carried the memory of that other watcher, the presence on the rock; the certainty of the experience was not fading but sinking deeper into my mind. If I did not speak soon, I knew I would never tell them, I might never tell anyone.

I had never in my life kept an important thing from my

Family. I had scarcely covered up the least mischief, had not bothered to lie about trifles: snatched graynuts, dropped stitches, time spent tree climbing instead of gathering food or dye-herbs. Should I turn away from them now and not try to explain that the Maker of Engines was protecting our Luck?

Diver and the Harper had hitched ropes to the head of the glider; we cleared the runners and swung it round. Roy called me, and I ran to lift the broken wing off the grass; the glider swung easily in a half-circle.

"Back to the fixed house glebe?" asked Diver.

"We could work on it here more secretly," suggested Roy.

"No!" I cried. "No, by the fire that burned the world! There is danger . . . the watcher . . . the outcast!"

They smiled but not scornfully. Suddenly Harper Roy gave a click with his tongue and strode towards the watcher's low tree. I stiffened, wondering if the creature had returned.

"Easy now. I had a flash that we do know that watcher," he said, tugging his chin-lock.

"Yes . . . but from where?" asked Diver.

The Harper made the sign that means "Discovery!" "The twirler! The Leader . . . what was his name?"

"Yes!" said Diver. "The twirler . . . I never got his name!"

"Petsalee, Host of Spirits!" I cried. I thought again of Mooneen, the poor crazed wretch that Beeth Ulgan had enchanted.

"Poor devil. At least he escaped Tiath Gargan," said Diver. But now the Harper was thoroughly alarmed, and I understood why. We tried to make Diver understand.

"He was a spirit warrior, an outcast, that's true . . ." said the Harper, "but he was also the Leader. Maybe he had a little substance, a bag of offerings, or a gift of fortune telling. And we know he fell into the hands of the Pentroy!"

"You mean he was hanged? That was his spirit?" teased Diver.

"No! But did he *buy a life?*" said Harper Roy.

It was an alternative to death, shameful, so it was said, but possible. A condemned person was sometimes permitted to buy into vassalage . . . become a lesser servant, like the clan slaves in ancient times. Diver understood.

"So Petsalee might be Tiath Pentroy's vassal?"

"His spy! His telling-bird!" I whispered.

Diver took it more seriously. He and Roy picked up the ropes, and we went back through the morning fields. We took a wide detour around the fold and the rock, then pushed and dragged and slithered the glider right under the spreading trees of the house glebe. We went straight indoors and told of our adventures.

Brin and Mamor joined with Roy to convince Diver of the risk. Petsalee was deeply suspect and a real threat to our security. He was one of the few who could weave the threads between Beeth Ulgan and our Luck. Mamor was all for scouring the riverbank and capturing the wretched "spirit-warrior," but we restrained him. Old Gwin still held firmly to the old threads; she could not believe that such a holy person could "buy a life" or turn traitor.

We settled down late in the day to our ordinary routine, if life in a fixed house could ever be ordinary, of weaving, cooking, playing, sleeping. Diver began searching up and down for wood and fabric to mend the glider. I was so quiet and worked so well at the mat-loom that Gwin felt my chest to see if I had a fever. I was still clacking away in midafternoon while Gwin dozed and Roy turned aside into another room to change a harp string. Narneen had run off to watch Diver and Mamor working on the glider. I saw Brin leave off her beautiful hanging on the great loom and climb the stairs to the room of evening. I went after her, and we knelt together by the bundles of new work and bedding.

"What ails you, Dorn Brinroyan?"

"Will you believe I speak the truth?"

The story was a burden to me; it had become false, as if it had happened to another person. There sat Brin, round, soft and tall, in the golden tan vented robe; in the warm light of afternoon I saw her too in the special way I had seen Tiath Gargan on the black barge. I saw her

forever: Brin, my pouch-mother. We were not quite alone
together, for by this time the hidden child was nickering
and stirring in its place. She heard me out and looked me
in the face:

"I believe you, child." She went on with her sorting for
a few moments then asked, "Do you think this is the
power of your thought? Are you marked for a Witness,
like young Gordo?"

I shook my head, a bit regretfully. "No, it is all outside
myself. Or maybe it is the power we all have as children.
The Maker of Engines works this will. It could have been
performed on any one of us . . . except Diver maybe."

Brin sighed. "Gwin waits for a Witness to be born of the
Five. She points to Narneen."

I felt a shock of envy, but I remembered certain things.
"Narneen could be a witness. She feels things before any
of us."

"Well, we won't put ideas in her head."

We smiled at each other, and the burden was lifted; I
felt comfortable again. I saw for the first time what it was
that Brin had been sorting from our bundles. It was the
beautiful showing cloth, five yards square, embroidered
with birds and flowers.

"Yes," said Brin, "it is time. Your sib is too heavy for
me."

I was filled with such excitement that I broke the silence
of the golden afternoon; I rushed from room to room
telling everyone.

The child had his showing that evening after supper.
We asked Diver to find a name. He sat at the edge of the
showing cloth, watching our new sib flex its limbs and
make baby sounds. He admitted that children of his race
were different: fatter, he said, and not so wide awake. He
uttered many strange names, searching for one that went
as well in one tongue as another. Roy is such a name. He
spoke a name To-mas; Gwin and Brin smiled.

"Tomar," chuckled Old Gwin. "Tomar . . ."

It is a good name because it has two meanings: "great
courage" or "great mischief." So there it was—the new
one became Tomar, and Brin wove in his name on her

skeins. He was measured, exercised, wrapped and put into Narneen's old swing-basket, with the green silk ropes at his hands and feet, so that he could pull up and stretch as babies do.

"When will he walk?" asked Diver.

"No hurry," said Brin, "ten days or twenty. He may take his time."

"When do your children walk?" asked Mamor.

"A newborn child cannot walk," said Diver.

"Not newborn," said Gwin, laughing. "New shown! Hark at the Islander."

"That's the difference," said Diver.

Now the year was far advanced to the spring; and by the time the two suns spent together in the sky, we knew it would soon be New Year's Day. I do not know how the next plan was made . . . it seems reckless now. Probably it came from Diver and Mamor, smoothing their pieces of curved wood and drawing in the dust. There is at Otolor Spring Fair a flying contest called Vantroy or the Bird Clan. There is a great prize of silver credits and woven stuff. Brin and Roy, who had gone to the fair as children, had often told us of the strange craft entering, the admiration and laughter, the winners . . . One they recalled was a sprig of Dohtroy who stood on the seat of her golden glider and flung pearl-shells to the crowd. Perhaps it was this glorious memory that persuaded Brin to agree that Diver should enter and try his luck. Perhaps she agreed to please Mamor and Diver, thinking, as I did secretly, that the poor glider would never fly.

Diver was not troubled by any such doubts. He was out all day by the machine, bending, patching, smoothing, or carving with Roy's knife or his own sharper one, on those curious spin-toys of curved wood. He had me cry out every time a flitterling went by, and we examined its design through his glass. I became familiar with the designs and would cry out, "Green slot-wing" or "Antho broad-tail" or "Pedal fan." The pedal fan models pleased him most, though his glider would be truly "an engine," and he could not believe that this was quite fair. We assured him that it was. In fact the Bird Clan was the very place

where "engines" came into their own. The prohibition
against "fire-metal-magic" did not work against the young
clanspeople who supported the contest. There were machines that flapped, flopped, buzzed, clanked, and gave off
sparks and clouds of steam. One promising craft that Roy
remembered had a sort of metal pot-stove aboard and flew
very well until it exploded in midair. Blacklock's entries
were notorious for their magic and their complexity.

I used to sit in the grass beside our glider and shiver
with excitement. We were going to Otolor, to the fair, to
race in the Bird Clan, and I should see Blacklock at last.
Tomar was brought out, for Gwin insisted that a weaver's
child must roll in the sun to get rid of its first-fur. He was
an exceptional child, I decided; anyone could see that
from the way he tugged his swing ropes and smiled and
tried to eat grass and hauled himself up onto his little,
gripping tree-bear feet. Diver saw it at once and made his
silkbeam pictures of the baby, which he could do, now
there was plenty of sunshine.

Fifteen days from the showing, Diver had his spin-toys
in position on the nose and on the wings of the glider; he
set them in motion with the engines from his vest, which
had worked his magic equipment. The only things he did
not take to pieces were his shaver and his stun-gun. He
was pleased with the result; the spin-toys buzzed and spun
so fast they were invisible. At this sight Tomar cried out
and took four steps. Diver had been busy with his paints
from the Ulgan's barge, and there on the glider's side was
its new name TOMARVAN. We were delighted, because it
meant so many things: Tomar's bird, his wing, his flying
machine. Or perhaps it stood for the bird of great courage,
the flying machine full of mischief.

Brin had laid aside her vented robe for a short spring
tunic; there was that springtime cheerfulness in the family.
I knew what would come next . . . a round of spring games
with Old Gwin. There are special games that the ancients
play with the children in the spring. For the first time I
was conscious of what it meant, but this year all had
changed. Diver joined in our games, and at night we slept
on the roof. The green and yellow mating tent that used

to be pitched for the adults some way off in the glebe was hung to the doorway of an extra sleeping room. Diver understood; he joined in our games of flying sticks and holdstone and bean-bean with perfect good humor, but I expect he was lonely. He looked out at the stars from the roof. We asked him to sing, and I took it for granted that some of the songs were about springtime among his own people.

One night Narneen said to Old Gwin: "Tell us how it was when you came to the Family Fair." This was one of our favorite stories; it was not respectful to ask a pouch-mother about her adventures at the Family Fair, but an Ancient could tell such tales.

"Oh, dear wind," sighed Gwin, "it is such a long way off!"

"Tell us, Gwin," begged Diver. "I would like to hear."

"Well, if the Luck asks . . ." she said. It was a mild and beautiful night on the roof; Tomar was fast asleep.

"I was sixteen," said Old Gwin, "the eldest child of my family and the only female child. We lived east of Cullin in a fine glebe and Felm, our leader and pouch-mother, ruled us all closely, so that we grew rich."

"Is the leader of a five always a female?" asked Diver.

"Great wind, no!" I said, "have you forgotten Hunter Geer?"

"I was never far from my lace loom or from herb-teaching," said Gwin. "Felm, may her soul bird fly far, would have been pleased to see me in a fixed house among the town grandees of Cullin. The choosing at a Family Fair is supposed to be done under the blessing of the North Wind, but I must tell you, young Luck, there is plenty of arrangement that goes on beforehand. Felm was always pointing out to me the advantages of this or that young person who might 'stand forth' at the Fair and offer to start a Five."

"You never thought of 'standing forth' yourself, Gwin?" asked Diver.

"No," she said. "I was too shy. A leader is easily seen. Brin, my own pouch-child, was a leader from the first, though I say it myself."

"Tell us about the message skein," said Narneen.

"Well, I had been about in Cullin and I had seen certain young persons and been seen in my turn. A few days before the Fair a child came to me at my loom with a little message skein. It said 'Beautiful Gwin with the long hair, look for the green mat where I stand forth,' and it bore the name of Tarr Gabroyan. This Tarr was an especially tall and handsome young fellow that came from a broken five, where the pouch-mother and the ancient had died of fever. He had earned respect after this calamity by staying on in Cullin, not travelling to another town or taking service in Rintoul . . . but he was still not my mother's idea of a worthy suitor. As the time approached I could not help thinking of him.

"The Family Fair at Cullin was magnificent in those days. The whole fairground was fenced with brushwood and decorated with flower carpets; the season was early spring. Musicians played night and day and there were food stalls. Only those who came to make families were allowed into the main enclosure; there was space for the standing forth and the necessary dancing. When we went into the enclosure we wore straight linen robes woven in the pattern that is called five-petal, with no decoration except girdles of flowers.

"I went alone into the enclosure; it was a strange feeling I can tell you. I was turned loose, cut off from my birth family for the first time, with nothing but their advice in my ears and a little wooden charm from Malbo Otru, our dear old Luck, who was a mute. I wandered among all the others and did as the threads told me. I made the rounds of all the mats where a person stood forth and looked well. I came past Tarr's green mat; there he stood alone, but there was a crowd before him because he looked so fine. The crowd of choosers have the right to question any that stands forth and many of the young females were calling out to Tarr Gabroyan. I quickened my pace and went round again. One, two, of the richer persons called my name; I stood awhile before the mat of my female friend Leen, who had been joined by a promising young hunter.

" 'Gwin,' she called, 'dear Gwin Felmroyan, come be my sib and we will manage this hunter between us!'

"I passed on, smiling, and as I came towards Tarr's green mat for the second time I saw that one person had already joined him. I was filled with fear that I should be too late; I all but ran the last few steps and pushed through the crowd to see who had joined him. Surely, it was another female and very sweet-faced, a stranger that I had never seen before. Then Tarr saw me approaching and spoke to the pretty newcomer and the crowd parted and I stood at the very edge of the green mat.

" 'Beautiful Gwin,' said Tarr in that rich voice of his that I had heard in my dreams, 'we await your coming. Here is Roneen, come to be your sib.'

" 'I am Roneen,' she said. 'Come to us, dear Gwin. Let us make Tarr's Five!' So, seeing them both, I was persuaded; I believed that the North Wind meant me to join this Family and no other. I stepped onto the green mat and the watchers cheered and sang. We took hands, all three, and did the first proving dance without one false step, which proved that we would match well, and so we did."

"How came the rest of the Five?" asked Diver.

"The Ancient is most often close kin of a Five member," said Gwin, "so came to Tarr's Five that night his elder, Old Therel, a kind and useful person."

"And how do you find a Luck?" he asked.

"Bless you, a Luck finds a Family, not the other way about!" said Old Gwin. "There is a lot of haggling and unseemly competition for a good Luck. An unscrupulous Luck or its birth-family can accept great gifts of cloth and credits. But a true Luck concentrates and sees in its mind where it should go. So Little Griss, the Luck of Tarr's Five, came straight to us, that same night, carried in a basket by its normal-sized sib. A dwarf, he was called but truly he was more of a fairy person . . . perfectly made but very small. A Luck that could have fetched thousands of credits in the city. He was a sweet-natured creature; the thing he loved best was to knit and we never had a leg or an arm bare of his skill."

Old Gwin and Diver talked on, but by this time Nar-

neen was asleep and I was becoming drowsy; I curled up
on the sleeping bag. I peered at Old Gwin's face; I loved
her dearly but it pained me a little when she spoke of her
youth. I could not see a trace of "Beautiful Gwin with the
long hair" who had danced the proving dances long ago
at the Family Fair.

Diver took advantage of the general good spirits to put
forth an idea; it was not a time when the Luck can be
refused very much. I knew what he was asking, and I was
afraid, lurking in doorways and behind trees to hear the
others reply.

Finally Mamor said, lazily unpicking a spoiled pattern:
"It might be done."

Then the Harper, mending Gwin's lace pins: "If you
think it is safe . . ."

Last of all Brin, with the family at midday, braiding her
hair: "You are our Luck. Do it . . . but remember our need
of you!"

Next day before the rising of Esto, we all turned out to
haul the *Tomarvan* to the top of the great rock.

The machine rode easily over grass and rock; it was
well-balanced, live in our hands, like a bird eager to fly.
The shepherds, Varb's Five, had been warned; and we
could see them standing aside by the fold. Certainly they
had no need to fear. The glider was pointed far out into
the inland meadows; its own shape would take it there if
it refused to fly. Brin stood away from the ropes and
looked out and down, fretting again because we had no
wind chart. Diver and Mamor had taken readings from
the rock and watched the course of the flitterlings, but a
wind chart would have helped.

Once the *Tomarvan* was in position, Mamor and the
Harper descended onto the plain. They were going to
watch the landing, so they said, and keep an eye out for
Petsalee or any other watcher. We all knew they were
going to pick up the pieces. Diver, in his woollen mask
helmet and goggles, sat in the pilot's chair; the *Tomarvan*
creaked and swayed a little in the morning wind. Diver
was divided from us, and I was cold now, in spite of the
climb. Brin stood apart coiling our good ropes over her

bent arm; Narneen was crouched in my "tower room"
among the bushes. I remembered the time of day; a gold
rim of Esto showed above the horizon, and the Far Sun
was still high in the sky, silvering the damp fields. I wished
hard, I prayed, for some comforting sign from our protec-
tor. Be near us, I thought, our Luck is flying today! But
there was no sign; no voice answered in my mind; no
warming presence visited the summit of the rock. The
morning wind, stronger than before, shook the vines and
rocked at the tail vanes of the flying machine. Mamor
high-called from the north and Roy from the south; it was
time.

I got into position as Diver rose in his chair for a last
wind check. Brin stood to the other wing; we made hope-
ful signals to Diver, and when he lowered his arm, we cast
off the runner ropes and shoved with all our might. The
Tomarvan slid off the rock without a sound, and I nearly
went with it. I had to fall flat and cling to an outcrop of
rock. The *Tomarvan* was out in the air, nose a little upward, but the whole machine was falling. Then it rose and
held steady in a longish gliding motion. Diver had caught
a current of air that would take him safely down.

Suddenly the machine checked visibly, shuddered, and
began to climb to the north in a wide, jerky spiral. There
came back to us, on the rock, a thin sharp buzzing sound.
We saw that the spin-toys were in motion and with them
the *Tomarvan* was transformed . . . it was an engine. All
three of us—Brin, Narneen and myself—cried out in excitement. Diver climbed still and curved, finding wind
currents and urging the *Tomarvan* to follow them. From
the plain came a cheer—Mamor, Roy, even the shepherds
were waving their hands and dancing.

The *Tomarvan* flew in a wide arc and swooped and rose
again. It was not so much a bird as a bright insect, darting
and buzzing and at times being lifted and carried by the
wind currents over the inland plain. Diver turned it back,
drew in easily over the rock, stooped low over the fixed
house—where Gwin and Tomar would be standing on the
roof—and crossed the river. I had time to be afraid; I felt
sick and giddy, as if I were flying in the machine myself.

Diver had gone, he had flown off to the islands. Then I heard Narneen laughing as if she had read my thoughts. She had crawled up beside me, out of her niche, and now she laid a hand on my arm.

"Here he comes again . . ." said Narneen.

"Great North Wind!" whispered Brin. She stood tall and warm at our backs; her hair was unbound, she flung back her head, watching the sky. I saw her as Eenath the Spirit-Warrior, not a pouch-mother, ruling from the loom.

"Children," she said, "our Luck will *win* this Bird Clan!" The *Tomarvan* flew low over our heads, spin-toys whirring, and flew out and round, crossing and recrossing the Troon, wherever Diver wished it to fly.

Diver flew every day after this proving flight, and we became accustomed to caring for the *Tomarvan,* holding its wings and so forth. Soon we prepared to leave White-rock Fold and began sorting out our entry fee for the Bird Clan. I felt secure and happy: plenty of food and something to look forward to. But as I lay in the sleeping bag at night or in the early morning before the suns penetrated the Ulgan's house, I had moments of deep unbelief. Was this all happening? Was it some long dream and would I wake on Hingstull with the snow coming down? How was it possible to endure such changes? I looked at Tomar in his swing basket with a sort of fear; soon he would be grown, time would run away with him as it had with me, with all of us. How could I have believed, last spring, that Dorn Brinroyan could *grow used* to a fixed house and a flying machine?

One night, while the last of the little darkness still held, I was awakened by a cry. Narneen was sitting up in the sleeping bag crying out for a bad dream. I told her to lie down again, but she would not. She cried out, between sleeping and waking, until Brin came to her. I was burrowing down to sleep again, but the talking did not stop and someone brought up Diver's magic lights.

". . . no dream," sobbed Narneen, "for I can listen again!"

"You were questioned?" asked Brin.

"There were two, and they asked my name and my Five name."

I was wide awake now. We all sat round Narneen, my young sib, and she had a staring, strange look in the cool light. Old Gwin had begun to chant softly under her breath, a chant of praise for a blessing.

"What does it mean?" asked Diver at my elbow.

"I think it means that Narneen is a Witness. Some other Witness has found and questioned her."

Brin had her recite all that had happened from the beginning.

"I thought it was a dream," said Narneen. "I was called, and I answered to my name. Then the questioning went on, and it was inside my head."

"It is a blessing," said Old Gwin, "a power wanting in our family since my mother's birth Five, Abirin's Five. Go on, child . . ."

"There is a Witness," said Narneen, "a female. One other questions through the Witness, for she asks always on behalf of another and sometimes speaks aside. She called first of all, 'Narneen, Narneen'; then when I replied, she asked my age and my Five name."

"I don't like this! This is mere sleep-spying!" said the Harper.

"I think you are right," said Brin, "and it is pure chance that Narneen has strong powers and can wake and tell us what has happened."

Diver was baffled by all this, and we made shift to explain. The minds of all Moruians have this linking power, especially strong in childhood . . . the same power, I supposed, by which the Maker of Engines made contact with me upon the rock. Children and young persons can also be questioned in sleep, and it has been used for curious purposes, good and evil. In one song the Harper sings, a young weaver is called in her sleep by two hunters: "Will you leave your mother's mat-loom and look for us at the Family Fair?" But there are also tales of this sleep-spying being used for gain, to find out where a merchant's treasure is hidden.

Old Gwin asked: "What did you tell them, child?"

"My name, my age, my Five name . . . the names of our Five. And then they asked a strange thing. Who was the newest member of our Five. So I told them Tomar, new-shown."

"Wait!" said Diver. "Was that what they wanted?"

"No," said Narneen shrewdly, "it was you they wanted, Diver dear, for they asked again, 'Has any stranger come to your Five, little Narneen.' "

I shivered at this; too many thoughts were reaching out towards our Luck. Narneen turned to me and shook her head. "Don't be afraid, Dorn," she said, "for I know this questioner, I know this Witness. They speak the truth when they say they mean us no harm."

"What did you answer them?" asked Brin.

"Nothing more!" said Narneen. "I cried out and broke the link, for I was afraid."

"It was right, I suppose," said Old Gwin, "but remember, child, that a Witness should not lie, in reporting or in any question, mind-to-mind, else your sacred power is betrayed."

"Hush," sighed Mamor, "this is weighty stuff for so young a child. I don't like this whole business."

Then Narneen was given a herb drink to make her sleep; but the rest of us found it hard to settle. Next day we packed up again, cleaned the Ulgan's house and prepared our new work for market. Mamor made sure the Ulgan's barge was waterworthy, and Diver prepared the *Tomar-van* for its journey downriver. I put Tomar on my back in his wicker carrying cradle and went up to the top of the rock, to bid farewell to Whiterock Fold. It was a day of bright sunshine, but to south and north, where we had come and where we were going, the river Troon was lost in shimmering mist.

When we were back on the barge, I expected another journey like the one from Cullin to Whiterock, long days of sun and shadow on the water. But I quickly learned that every voyage on the river is different and part of the difference is in our mood and understanding as travellers. We came back to the barge in darkness—what was left of it—and loaded our bird, our treasure, by the light of Diver's torches and swaddled it in the pieces of our tent. One or two fishers passed by as we were working, but there was not much to be seen. The Far Sun was rising, full and silvery, as we cast off, and our spirits began to come up just a little. The Troon took us back kindly, and Gwin's prayers for a wind were answered.

We passed more boats . . . they should have been fishers but instead of gray or black they were striped in bright colors. In the Far Sun light we could see the crews winding trails of green and red vines high on the masts and along the sail ropes.

"What are they doing?" I cried to Brin, as we stood huddled against our wrapped flying machine.

"What are they doing?" It was Diver asking the same question.

Mamor, at the tiller, began to laugh. "I didn't think it would begin so soon!" And the crew of the nearest boat let out a strange hail, almost a high-call.

"Lee-va-ban Otolor!"

It was the fair-call, the cry for Otolor Great Fair. Suddenly we were in the midst of a wave of decorated boats . . . barges, fishers, birders, crossing boats, even paddling mats with one bold swimmer and a tail of vines . . . a fleet spread out across the full width of the Troon, stretching downriver as far as we could see.

"But there are miles to go before we come to the fairground!"

Still the cry echoed up and down the river. There zigzagged past a round-bottomed boat full of flowers and drunken shepherds, singing that spring was in the New Year and the New Year was in the spring. We came, with the fleet, to the first hamlet, and then another soon after it, both on the west bank. These places were decorated too and their crossings full of craft, loading up and setting off for the fair. I saw at the second landing stage a family of weavers, true mountain folk and nomads, our own image. I pointed them out to the Harper, who was tuning his instrument in the stern. We watched them and hailed and high-called. There they stood, trembling, about to step on a bird-boat—a sturdy Five, with leggings and a carrying sled of new work, perhaps not as fine as our own. Their hair was tied with bright skeins, and one mother wore a cream vented robe, heavy from her hidden child. Brin held up the wriggling excited Tomar in his little holiday wrapper, and the bush weavers saw us and took heart. Yet already I imagined that they looked upon us strangely . . . we were of them and not of them, in our barge, with its strange cargo and Diver, standing among us in his sun-goggles.

So it went on, the whole fleet scudding downriver under a fresh breeze, with as much noise as a fairground itself. About the rising of the Great Sun, the wind dropped, and there was a creaking of paddle wheels and much work with the paddles. The barge lumbered along, wedged in the crowd of smaller craft, and the talking and singing flowed naturally from deck to deck. We were excited and looked continually through the boats for Beeth Ulgan or for Gordo her apprentice, who was to meet us at the fair. Harper Roy sang and watched; I knew he had eyes out for trouble, even here. In particular he and I were on the lookout for that watcher . . . the escaped twirler, Petsalee, who might be the Pentroy's creature. It was difficult in the midst of all this laughter to think of the long shadow cast by Tiath Gargan. We bartered food and ate well. I looked at the water, inching past between the boats, and had a perverse longing for those days alone on the water with only the flatbills for company.

We knew there would be scarcely any darkness, but it was still difficult to sleep. I dozed, thinking of the white rock and the Maker of Engines. I tried to send out thoughts to this great personage: We are coming. We are on the river, bringing Diver, our Luck, to Otolor Spring Fair. Take care for us.

The *Tomarvan* took up most of our deck space, but there was room for one or two to nap out of the suns' light in a small tent. In the late afternoon it was my turn to go under the flap; Mamor pushed me in, and I found Tomar, asleep in his basket at last, and Narneen. We were coming to the largest village before Otolor, in a flat calm; there was not a breath of wind on the Troon, and we could hear the creaking of paddles below the shouts and songs of the merrymakers. I lay down and really slept for about an hour, then I woke suddenly with Narneen urgently stroking my cheek.

"What is it?"

"Ssh," she whispered, "let Tomar sleep." There was a thin, unchildish look about her. "I am called again by the same Witness."

"Who is it? Shall I get the others? Is there danger?"

"No, it is friendly. Dorn . . . I see them. It is two persons, Witness and Questioner. They do not know how clearly I hear and see."

"What do they ask?"

"My Five name, the same as before. What shall I answer?"

"The truth." I said. "Remember what Gwin said? But steer clear of our Luck. Narneen . . . I must fetch the others."

"No, no . . . you still don't understand. They are *close*. We are going to sail past them. They are standing on the east bank by a landing stage, right now."

"We could see them!"

"Yes!" said Narneen, her long eyes blazing. "Go to Diver, get the seeing glass, you know? Look to the landing stage for a tree, and there they stand. The Witness is short, female, wearing a gray tunic like a town worker. The Questioner is male, older, in a straight blue robe and a straw shade-hat with a veil. He wears this. . . ." Narneen drew breath and bit her lips but went on. "He hides his face because it is horribly ugly. It is burned, I think, on one side."

"Will you come with me?"

"I will lie here," she whispered, "and answer their questions, so that they stand still."

I tumbled out onto the deck into the bright sunlight and the singing, paddling riverful of travellers going to the fair. I found Diver beside the wrapped wing of the *Tomarvan* and gasped it out to him.

"Where are they?"

He had the glass and let me search the east bank. We were past the landing stage of Geelar, the large village, but some way beyond it another small jetty stood out beside a spreading red-wood tree on the river's edge. I shivered although the day was hot. There they stood, exactly as Narneen had described them. I saw the quiet, listening face of the Witness, the odd, straight cut of her short hair, the broad silver band clasped around one sleeve. The Questioner stood like a pillar of gray rock; his face was youngish, pale and fine; the veil of his hat, half drawn, hid any scars. Diver examined them and Brin, when she came up and heard the story. Old Gwin went at once to Narneen in the tent.

"The Questioner wears a scribe's pouch," said Brin. Her voice was hard and angry, full of mistrust.

"That's not all . . ." growled Mamor. "I can read the garments of those two like a new skein. They come from Tsagul, the Fire-Town."

We were so close now that we scarcely needed the glass to see their features. Instinctively we bent down and approached the tent flap. Narneen lay on her back, eyes wide and sightless, her body stiff. Tomar began whimpering, and I crawled inside and went to him. He chuckled and was happy again when I came to him, and I felt a new love for my younger sib, a comradeship. I was pretty sure he would never become a Witness. Old Gwin prayed continually beside Narneen but did not touch her. After a few long moments Narneen shut her eyes, went limp, then sat up—an ordinary weaver's child, full of mischief. "They are going," she said.

At the same time the Harper gave a whistle from the bows, which meant: "birds flown." I turned to a hole in the tent and caught a last glimpse, between two boats passing, of the gray-clad Questioner moving away, limping.

Brin reached into the tent and took Narneen by the hands.

"Now child," she said, "you must give account of what passed, like a true Witness."

"They asked as before," said Narneen, "starting with

my age and my Five name. And this time I answered all these things truly."

"Did they give reasons?"

"No, but many promises of friendship. The Questioner was very particular about meaning no harm."

"What else?"

"They asked me about Stone Brook. Had I ever lived at Stone Brook on Hingstull, in a cave. And I said indeed I had."

We were mystified at this and could find no reason for it.

"Then they asked the names of all my family, but I did not answer clearly. I sang and said I could not hear the question."

"You sang?" asked Diver.

"I sang inside my head," said Narneen. "Have you never done it? It blocks questioning. So next they began, gently, to ask all the things we did . . . and I admitted to weaving, of all kinds, and to hunting and to playing harp music. I hope that was not wrong . . ."

"Of course not," said Brin, "you have done very well."

"But there was more," said Narneen. "They asked if I could read and I told them truly I knew my woven script and part of the written. Then they went on . . . I agreed that my Five could read and weave message skeins. And they asked about making pictures, drawn pictures, blue ink on white willow paper."

Narneen's voice trembled for the first time and her upper lip crinkled, for weeping. "I said yes, one among us did such drawings. Then I sang and wouldn't answer, for I remembered . . ."

Diver gave a startled exclamation in his own tongue. He drew aside and spoke to Brin and Mamor, then turned to comfort Narneen, assuring her that she had done no harm. We all understood, more or less; I saw us in the cave at Stone Brook with the blizzard coming down, teaching Diver new words while he drew us pictures. By some means those pictures had reached this scribe from the Fire-Town.

"Ah, but they said one other thing that makes it certain," said Narneen sadly. "They spelled a word to me. They asked if I knew what is M-A-N." She spoke the sounds in our tongue . . . and we remembered still more. Diver had drawn his own race: a male, a female; then some common objects: a tent, a chair from a fixed house, a sort of wool-deer; and Brin had lettered in our own sounds below his script.

"I said no more," said Narneen, "at least I answered no more. But I *asked*. The Witness is called Onnar; I asked quickly, and she replied before she could think of other things. And the Questioner—"

"You got his name?" asked Brin.

"He is Vel Ragan," said Narneen. She lay back sleepily on the folded bags. "He is a scribe from the Fire-Town, Tsagul. He was surprised when I asked the Witness what burned his face."

"What did he reply?" chuckled Gwin. "Cheeky wretch to question a child in this way."

"I think he said it was a firestone . . . a clinger." We shuddered and fell silent at the thought of this terrible violence, brought close to us. Firestone clingers were a fabled device for evil clan-creatures and grandees' quarrels, not for honest mountain folk.

I burst out, finally, as I rocked Tomar inside the tent. "But there is still the mystery of how they reached Narneen!"

"I know the answer to that," said Diver heavily. So it was explained, and we remembered. Diver had drawn Narneen's picture, and Brin had marked it with her name.

"I have brought this upon the child," said Diver. We all spoke together, reassuring him. We could not bear it when he spoke in this way, or blamed himself.

"Diver," said Narneen, "I know one thing . . . they spoke truth. They will do us no harm."

The wind had risen, so we could use sail, but still the press of small boats bound for the fair was so heavy we could make no speed at all. When I put Tomar on my back and went on deck, the land had changed around us. We were sailing through tamed country, with fence ropes and bird farms and food gardens on either side of the river. I found Diver sitting astern beside the shaded spinner-basket, lifting the flap to give them sun, as Gwin had taught him to do. An ancient weaver, on the deck of a bird boat, cried out to him: "Two new hatched . . . for a whole keg of good sunner?"

"Forgive us!" said Diver. "These beauties are not for sale."

"Too bad," cackled the ancient, turning back to his braiding frame. "Ours died a'winter."

I sat on the deck, with Tomar between my knees playing with a string of dried seed gourds. My sib was strong and brown, with his first-fur already lifting. There was no doubt that we had the best baby and the best Luck and the best barge and even the best spinners in the world. Far in the distance, between the bird farm nets and the no-fishing skeins, I could see one, two balloons tethered, riding above the walls of the city of Otolor. The Bird Clan was near.

VI

The launcher wore a scarlet robe, kilted up with a cord under his belly, to show his fat, pasty legs and leather boots.

"Va-ban!" he shouted in a voice of thunder. The Bird Clan vassals heaved on the ropes; Diver, Mamor and the Harper steadied the framework. *Tomarvan* slid up the ramp to the level of the Bird Clan grounds. The vassals lifted it bodily onto the wheeled wicker cradle and trundled our precious bird into the enclosure. The Launcher surveyed it calmly, hands on his waist.

"Cullin!" he cried. "Where in blazes will they come from next! Every bush weaver is Antho, this time o' year. And why don't ye *fly* it in . . . eh? eh? Because the flaming thing won't fly, do you suppose?"

"It will fly," said Diver.

He loomed up at the Launcher's side, and the fellow flinched at his height. Diver looked as impressive as we could make him; it was a time for dressing-up, not for hiding away. He wore his own blue suit and, as a cloak, a magnificent silk hanging, one of Gwin's treasures, ordered and not paid for, long ago, by Elbin Tsatroy, a mad old grandee, one of the last of her clan. The fire clan emblem blazed forth, flame on ochre; suns and stars whirled over the silk. I wondered, each time I saw it, how Gwin and her first-family, Tarr's Five, could weave and embroider such a fiery piece of work. Diver's hair was a sandy red; his hood was pale blue, over a basket helm, worn by fliers, and he had his own goggles.

"Peace, sir!" said the Launcher. "I believe you. Now, the matter of your fee and escort."

We were perfectly prepared; old Gwin had even rehearsed us in the proper responses, but in fact the ceremony was not formal. At least two persons must escort a flier into the enclosure, and it is traditional that females are lucky . . . because they partake of the nature of the North Wind, our Great Mother. So Brin was First Escort, and my prayers were answered, I was the second. Mamor was needed to berth the Ulgan's barge and the Harper to earn credits with his playing. They had withdrawn to the barge while I stood shivering next to Brin at the top of the slope, beside the booth where a pair of scribes entered the records. The Launcher bowed, as if we were all grandees, and I was pleased that Brin, at any rate, was a splendid person, straight and tall. I stepped forward and presented the fee.

"On the bench, my friend," said the Launcher. "What have we here?"

He examined the bolts of cloth—fine, plain work of three weights and an embroidered robe for good measure —then counted the silver credits. It was correct for him to chaffer a little; he must either demand more or hand a little back. The scribes were feeling the robe and twitching their eyebrows.

"Fly or not, you can certainly weave," the Launcher muttered. He counted three credits back into my hand; I bowed and uttered the correct response. Brin signed our names and knotted them into the skeins. The elder scribe, a sharp-eyed ancient with a Wentroy pectoral, handed out our tokens: wood and metal on elegant braids of blue silk. Still tight-browed, we had only time to wave to the others on the barge; Narneen waved a green branch, Old Gwin held up Tomar. They all chorused, "Good Luck" to Diver; Mamor shouted something encouraging to me. The barrier was lifted again, and we strode into the Bird Clan.

We found ourselves on the lower edge of an enormous

tilted field, larger by far than the whole fairground at Cullin, and turfed with tough brown grass. Oval tents, for quartering the machines, blossomed all around, and beside them, to show what exalted company we kept, were the little field tents of the grandees, panelled in silk and decorated with banners. A vassal in the familiar blue green of the Bird Clan ran up and bowed.

"Garl Brinroyan? Ablo, your humble servant and mechanic. This way, gentles . . ." He led us to *Tomarvan*, outside its tent. Five or six of his fellow vassals, all younger and nimbler than Ablo himself, were standing or crouching or lying on the grass, examining the machine most minutely.

"Away!" shouted Ablo. "Flaming spies! Get to your own broken-winged flitterboxes!"

He seized Diver by the arm. "Send them away, excellence . . . they must not know its capacities!" Diver laughed, drawing off his own strange five-fingered gloves, and the vassals drew up short at the sound of his voice.

"Peace," he said. "The capacities of the *Tomarvan* are no secret."

"Excellence," begged Ablo, "noble escorts . . . the vassals carry tales and make bets." He lowered his voice and moved closer. "They often have a Witness or an apprentice diviner who can guess the place this Machine will fly and the round that it will reach."

"If you say so," said Brin, smiling. She reached down and dragged a small vassal from beneath the wing. "Begone friends!" she ordered.

The "spies" all scrambled up and drew back a little, then scattered suddenly, on an impulse from elsewhere. Another pilot was approaching; I stared, taking in a grandee. Spare, short, businesslike, magnificently dressed in dark red overalls and cloak, a flowing black wig, and with a basket helm of white, dangling from one long hand, marked with a crest. I bent sideways to read it. Two blue flax flowers. Luntroy, one of the oldest of the five clans.

"Jebbal!" said the newcomer in a bright, harsh voice. Diver bowed and gestured towards the *Tomarvan* as if to say: "Look well" or "Be my guest."

Jebbal circled warily, twirling the spin-toys with a fingertip; Diver was on hand, with the respectfully chattering Ablo to point out various refinements.

Brin touched my arm, and we moved quickly to raise our own field tent. I saw the townee vassals struggling with the grandees' beautiful butterfly houses, but our plain green, with a banner for Cullin, went up in record time. Brin looked around at the hangars and field tents and stalls; some fliers and their escorts were eating and drinking at legged tables of wood and carpet-cloth, set upon the grass. She whistled for a little greasy-headed vassal, the same she had dragged from under the wing, and sent me off with him, clutching two silver credits. Presently after a discreet scrimmage with some others of about our size outside two of the stalls, we had a table and a tray of refreshments. When Jebbal and Diver came up for air, Brin bowed and bade them sit down.

Jebbal looked us up and down. "Bush weavers, eh? Is this your Officer, Garl Brinroyan?"

"Not so, Highness," said Brin easily, "I have the honor to be the head of Garl's family. Brinroyan, of Gwin's blood and Tarr's Five and the distant mothering of Abirin, Felm, Felrin and Narbreen. We have lived and woven upon Hingstull for more than a great five of years, on land now owned by the Great Elder."

"Good luck to you!" Jebbal sat down and sampled the fruit wine. "Whose is that stripling?" she asked. "Come on, young Hazel, who is your pouch-mother?"

"I am Dorn Brinroyan," I stammered, "and Brin is my mother."

"Wind save us!" cried Jebbal, rude as ever. "I respect mothering above all things! You may not guess it, Friend Brin, but I pouched four sucklings before I took up flying. You must send Dorn to my tent to play with my younger clan-brats. Not all Luntroy—which is a mild clan, as you will find—but infused with Galtroy wildness."

"We know a Highness of Galtroy," I babbled.

"Indeed?" she grinned. "Well I guess that it is my cross-cousin Rilpo. He hunts in the mountains. Yes? I thought so."

She took up a handful of crystal fruits from the table and began to play Hold Stone, a game for two players. We had played three or four hands together—Jebbal was winning—when I looked up and saw Brin and Diver laughing aloud at the pair of us. Jebbal was like the taste of the crystal fruits: tart, sweet, surprising. She had only two loves in the world: flying and children; everything else, we found, bored her "utterly to death."

Jebbal, having checked out the *Tomarvan* and declared that it would probably fly but hadn't a chance against the favorites, led Diver and me to marvel at her machine. It was certainly very beautiful: a double improved pedal fan with an enormous wingspan and lighter than a feather. It was called *Peer-lo-vagoba,* which means, more or less, "Forever Soaring in the Blue."

While Diver was examining this wonder, I looked for the wild clan-brats; I was anxious—perhaps they would eat me alive. When I peered into the dark red silken tent, I sighed with relief and a touch of disappointment. The two sprigs were nothing like their fierce mother: the male, Valdin, was taller than me and older, the female, Thanar, a little younger. They were beautiful, I admitted, and richly dressed, but timid and engrossed in strange games. They had been at the Bird Clan every year for four years and were still afraid of the young townee vassals who bullied them when the escort was not looking. I sat in the stuffy tent and tried to learn their bead placing; there was no doubt they were grandees—they squabbled in sharp voices and their moods changed. Finally I took out a credit and suggested we buy honeycups at the stalls.

"Those flaming vassals will catch and beat us," whispered Valdin.

"Not while I'm around!" I said firmly.

"It's dishonorable to go about without an escort," said Thanar, "for us, I mean."

"Oh come on, I'll be your officer!"

So we slipped under the back flap and marched boldly to the nearest stall. A few of the young vassals did attempt to jostle us, but I made a feint and sent the largest one into a mud puddle.

"Hands off all cubs of Highness Jebbal!" I said. "For I am their Officer!" The townees murmured about Mountain Beasts. "Yes . . . and I will fall on you like a mountain wolf!" I said.

We went back to the tent and ate our honeycups. The "cubs" were thrilled with their adventure. They talked confidingly of the place they liked best, a villa on the salt marsh to the east owned by their Galtroy kin, where they had a little sailboat.

The difference between grandees and mountain folk was suddenly illustrated.

"In ten days then," said Thanar, "we will go to the villa at Salthaven to be with our father." I blushed, and Valdin looked at me sideways.

"It is no shame," he said. "Jebbal has a pair-marriage with Faldo Galtroy. He is our father."

"We follow the old threads. . . ." I muttered. There was a mirror of silvered glass on their tent wall, and I had not seen my own face for some time. I looked now, and the two Galtroys smiled.

"Oh come, Dorn," cried Thanar, sweetly. "What do you see? Does it help you to find a father?"

I looked in the mirror and saw what I had always seen, in mountain pools, perhaps, or the Ulgan's metal cooking pots or a glassed window in a fixed house. "Yes," I mumbled. "I see which is my father."

I had hazel eyes, a strong, squarish face; everyone who saw me in our family or out of it must have known at once; I looked exactly like Mamor.

Before I left, with Diver, I saw Jebbal with the two children, absorbed in their games, chivying them a little, like a mother and a child at the same time. I trailed on the way back to our tent—the bright days never seemed to end, and there was never time to sleep—trying to piece together all I had learned about grandees. They were something like a honeycup, a treat now and then; or perhaps they were like a visit to the fair, an excitement once a year. There was too much Jebbal did not know about her children: they feared and hated the Bird Clan and were all for sailing at Salthaven. But I still found the Bird Clan a marvellous place, except that our Five could not be together.

"Enough!" said Brin, standing over me. "Sleeping bag for this noble escort."

I staggered into our green tent. "Wake me . . . wake me if anything else happens!"

There were fifteen entries in the Bird Clan rounds that spring, the highest for twenty years. Most flew in and were signalled down. A few came to the river gate as we had done and were wheeled into the enclosure. A red and white Antho, with a dirigible rudder and two small balloons called wind-catchers flew in from the west as the Great Sun rose. It made a few daring and illegal passes over the vast complex of fairgrounds across the river and hovered over the citadel of Otolor on its island where the stream divided. Then it flew in steadily to land, but the wind-catchers worked too well. It was twisted up into a spiral of warm air, the balloons became interlocked, then one deflated over the pilot's chair. The machine blundered down, bounced, with a scattering of marshals and vassals, then splayed its runners and broke a wing. The pilot, a young Dohtroy, climbed out cursing.

It was not the first elimination. Three of the earlier arrivals had elected to do their first exercises on the first day, while I slept. Two were traditional gliders, the third, a strange patched-up craft called *Tildee,* entered by a merchant from Rintoul. One of the gliders snapped in half at the starting blocks, the other, a silver gray, piloted by another sprig of the peaceable Dohtroy clan, caught its air currents well and soared normally. The *Tildee* took off and flew doggedly with a thrusting motion, which Brin described to me.

Diver laughed and shook his head. "Tildee will be hard to beat!"

"That one?" I asked, "but it is ill-made, of patched fabric."

"This merchant . . . is his name Mattroyan? . . . has been dabbling in fire-metal-magic."

"True Excellence," put in Ablo, "you are a good judge

of machines. For I have seen this ugly *Tildee* on the ground; it rings when a hand hits the panels, and it gives off a hot stink. White air comes in puffs through wooden pipes behind the pilot's chair."

"What merchandise does Mattroyan sell?" asked Diver. He was fishing for information but could not ask more plainly in front of Ablo.

"Excellence, he is a tanning-factor who runs horrid hide-boats up and down the coast of the great ocean sea." Ablo grimaced as he told it. "He visits Itsik."

As soon as I had a chance, I explained about Itsik to Diver. It is a strange place, barely respectable, between Rintoul and the Fire-Town, on the coast. "Go to Itsik" or "Go back to Itsik" is a common insult meaning, "You have not washed . . . you stink." All the burning, the tanning of hides, the curing of fish, the rendering of fat and lamp oil necessary for the great city of Rintoul is done at Itsik. Lawbreakers are sometimes sent to Itsik for a term, or if their offence is less serious, to Gavan in the east, on the salt marshes.

As I told this, we were wandering around the edges of the ground, between the tents and hangars, a pilot and his young escort. We came to Mattroyan's hangar, where *Tildee* was housed out of sight, guarded by an escort of monstrous omor. Mattroyan himself came out presently: a burly brute who put me in mind of no one so much as Hunter Geer, although he wore very fine garments of silk and wool floss. The pilot was with him, a young, dark-skinned, blood-haired flier, with a strong likeness to Mattroyan.

"Must be the merchant's child," whispered Diver.

"Yes, but don't say so if you speak to him."

"I'll remember my manners," said Diver. "I must not say 'your child' to a male person. Only 'a child of your family.' " We stayed at a discreet distance, however, and did not approach the merchant.

"I wonder how this custom came about?" asked Diver. "Is it because a person's family tree is reckoned from mother to mother."

"Partly. And partly because the child belongs to the

family, not to any person. To say 'your child' to a pouch-mother does not mean that she owns the child. But if the child has, well, a father singled out . . . Do you understand?"

"Partly," said Diver.

A splendid craft lit down: a double tier of scalloped wings, the upper span set forward and both activated in a flapping motion. We went through the tents and saw the pilot being lifted out by the escort; the Wentroy crest, a bird's head, was on their tunics. They had hardly time to set their highness upright before the clappers were sounded all around the field and three more entrants began their exercises. Two were set in the blocks attached to the launching catapults and the third had chosen the tower.

The Launcher stood on his platform, far away across the field, but when he shouted through his gourd, the sound seemed to echo around the world.

"U-va-ban!" The vassals hauled the lever and stood from the drums on the first catapult and a yellow Antho sailed off, straight and light.

"Uto-va-ban!" A black glider with an enormous wing-span went up and twisted from the second catapult.

"Yo-va-ban!" All eyes were on the tower. It was taller than the tallest tree, and flimsy, with crazy ladders and a ramp for the flying machines. More points were allotted for a tower take off; it made me feel dizzy just to see the vassals crawling on the upper beams, and I was mountain-bred.

Diver and I stood near the tower's base, and we could see through the maze of bentwood poles and flax ropes to the very runners of the machine. It was squarish, rather ugly, like a child's kite, with the pilot spread in its rigging. There was a twang, and the thing was launched, soaring down from the tower in a long curving arc, lower and lower over the field. Just as we felt sure it must ground, the blunt nose turned upward and the "Kite" rose gracefully. The pilot caught one of the mapped currents over the field, "stole the wind" of the black glider and went into the qualifying turns. The black glider, called *Hadeel*, staggered in the air and shook, then the pilot, who was very

skilful, bore straight upward, in the only current near
enough, and reeled into the turns. The yellow Antho,
meanwhile, flew carefully in circles further down the field.
Its turns were in fact oval . . . not true circles; all gliders
had this difficulty on circular turns.

This was not a speed test; when the three machines had
done the turns and performed any simple maneuvers that
the pilot felt the marshalls must see, they lit out, one after
the other, to the First Mark, inland to the east. Another
tower was there, and to complete these first exercises the
machines must round it and come back to land. These
three easily completed their exercises, but later that day
two machines were not so lucky. A pedal fan that had
come upriver from Linlor on a barge tipped the First
Mark and blundered into a strange craft, one of Diver's
favorites, a dirigible balloon that everyone had christened
"The Pod." The wretched pedal fan twisted away and
came down in the sandy plain beyond the First Mark,
which is called Gwervanin or Bird Bone Place, because so
many fine machines have fallen there.

When this happens, according to the threads, the pilot
should climb out and walk away from the wreck "without
looking back." The machine must lie where it has fallen,
struck down by the winds' bane, unless another can send
it into the air again, proving that the winds have been
appeased. So Diver soon came to understand that we had
acted correctly in "refloating" the *Tomarvan*. This judge-
ment of the winds could be harsh; in old times it had been
a subject of debate at the Bird Clan and throughout Torin
as to whether an injured pilot could be dragged out of a
wrecked machine. There had been quarrels between the
clans on the one hand and the weavers and townspeople
on the other, for the common folk would not leave a pilot
to suffer. They rushed straight in, chanting to avert the
winds' bane, and rescued a fallen flier.

This day the pilot of the pedal fan did climb out unharmed and limped back, shame-faced, to the enclosure.
"The Pod," poor creature, struggled round the First Mark
and flew back leaking. It touched down with a loud, sad,
hissing sound, like a giant tree-bear, and the beautiful

striped casing crumpled slowly before our eyes. The two
pilots, a pair of young town grandees from Otolor, stood
and wept. The third machine to exercise at this time was
Peer-lo-vagoba, and Jebbal was in fine form. She made a
perfect tower takeoff, exquisite circular turns and a quick,
clear run to the First Mark. She was given a special ova-
tion as the only one of this group to survive the test, for
clearly she had "averted the winds' bane" or proved her
superior skill.

I was determined to stay awake for a full thirty hours
or more until the lists closed at the next rising of Esto. At
about the third hour past midday the marshals came and
told Diver to get ready for his first exercises. He had
inspected the launching catapults carefully, with Ablo, and
decided to use one, rather than the tower. The weather was perfect, with a great head of white cloud coming
in from the east to provide a wild current besides the ones
that lived over the field. There were only two machines
exercising at the time: *Tomarvan* and *Utofarl,* or Double
Hope, the splendid Wentroy flap-wing. The Wentroy pilot
and a numerous escort took the field proudly. Too proudly, I thought, knees knocking as I shaped up with Brin and
Diver for the formal salute. I had the luck skein in my
hand, ready to exchange, but we stood there, emptily
waiting, and the Wentroy contingent went straight to their
catapult without a glance in our direction. I heard Ablo,
the mechanic, muttering angrily behind me and turned to
Brin, questioning.

"We've been insulted?" whispered Diver.

"The Wentroy insults itself!" she replied. "Dorn? You
know the next part?"

My knees knocked so that I could hardly run, but I did
it; and the piece of ritual was unexpected: Bird Clan for-
mality had fallen away of late. I ran out into the field and
threw the luck skein, which the Wentroy had ignored,
high into the air. I expected it to come back down again
and lie discarded in the field, but there was a gasp from
those watching: Wentroy's rudeness had already swelled
the crowd. The long silken skein was caught in a current
and whirled upwards in a broad spiral. The winds had

accepted my offering, and the Wentroy's luck was tossing round and round above the ground like a seed. The Wentroy escort, young and old, could hardly restrain themselves; they must catch the skein, the most foolhardy pilot could not allow it to be carried off or dashed to the ground once the wind had taken it. I saw the old Wentroy scribe speak to the pilot, and at last the word was given. The escort swarmed over the field, jostling, eyes on the sky, hands uplifted. Brin nodded, and we three walked off to the *Tomarvan*. The crowd laughed and cheered and clapped palms against their buttocks; I realized they were applauding us.

Now we thought our first trial was really at hand; Diver was in the pilot's chair, the catapult was attached, Brin and I stood to one wing, Ablo to the other. Diver had already given a few runs to his spin-toys, which made the vassals duck their heads. But suddenly the clappers sounded; there was a confusion of marshals and a loud chopping buzz in the air above our heads. A large winged shadow dipped and zoomed across the field, and its buzzing was echoed by the crowd. The Launcher on his platform was speaking to a large escort of more than twenty persons in black and white quartering. Now he spoke on the hailing gourd.

"Diver!" Brin reached up, trying to pat his arm in the chair, "he is addressing you directly . . ."

"*Tomarvan* pilot . . . how say you? Will you give leave for a new entrant to make a display?"

A marshall had come up with another hailing gourd; he gave it to Diver, who looked down at Brin with raised eyebrows.

"It is a shame!" cried Ablo. "You need not give leave, Garl Brinroyan; you need not! He asks because you are in the blocks."

Brin said: "See who it is. Say, 'Noble Launcher, who asks this leave?' "

So Diver spoke into the gourd, and his voice echoed sharply across the field. "Noble Launcher, who asks this leave?"

"Truly it is Murno Peran Pentroy up there, who asks leave."

Diver hesitated, the crowd was still; he looked at me and saw how I gaped with excitement. "I give my leave. I give my leave freely to this noble contestant!" said Diver.

There was another spatter of applause as the Launcher boomed his thanks. Diver climbed down, and we went back behind the barrier.

A hand plucked at Brin's sleeve, and there was Jebbal Luntroy's officer, a tall ancient, who bade us follow around the enclosure to Jebbal's viewing stand, a little row of raised seats outside her tent. There was Jebbal, lounging and smiling, in her red gear.

"Take a seat, gentle friends," she said. "Let's see what flaming marvel Blacklock has to offer!"

So I sat down at Brin's feet on the grass and watched the black and white escort march onto the field. My friends Valdin and Thanar came and sat beside me, chattering excitedly, but I could hardly speak. I was in a dream state, about to see Blacklock for the first time, and my excitement was tempered with a strange dreaming sadness. I ranged in a moment from the here and now at the Bird Clan in Otolor far, far back to our tent on Hingstull. The warmth of the spring sun on my arms became the scratching cold of winter, and I saw Odd-Eye's face. "I have dreams for you, as fine as Blacklock's mantle."

The incoming machine swooped and circled; Diver stood up, flinging back his helmed head to observe it. It was sleek but short-winged with a large whirling vane, a giant spin-toy, mounted centrally; we could see wing-flaps and a dirigible tail. It caught the currents and used them, but it had a curious thrusting motion as well, and suddenly it hovered, like a water-fly. The escort had formed a circle in the middle of the field; now they ran in together like dancers and quickly drew back again. I heard myself squeak with excitement. They had unfurled a huge net. The machine hovered, increased height, and at last I thought I could see movement by the pilot's chair. Then separating, falling, a bundle of cloth, but moving, surely . . . a body, struggling, flapping arms in the air. I stood up with all the others and screamed like them, and a great bubble of silken cloth stretched and blossomed over the falling body. A tall Moruian in a shiny green flying suit floated down calmly under the green canopy, bounced deliberately in the net two or three times, then skillfully stood still and drew the folds of the silk together. Blacklock had come to the Bird Clan.

Everyone laughed and cheered; I had never heard such a slapping of buttocks. Even in this very first exploit that I had witnessed, there was some of that special magic that made Blacklock's audience laugh, even in sheer relief. Diver was laughing too; Brin leaned down and touched my shoulder. I saw that the flying machine was moving away to land at the end of the field, with a second pilot, of course, whom no one remarked greatly. The crowd was streaming onto the field to cheer Blacklock, so I took the clan children by the hand and ran with them. We managed to wriggle in fairly close, followed by Jebbal's officer. Between the shoulders of two vassals holding the net we saw him: tall as a tree, broad as an omor, his helm was off now, and he seemed to be beaming straight at us. Blacklock is the handsomest Moruian anyone can imagine; he has a rather broad, jolly face and his skin is tanned, like a bush weavers', with no trace of grandee pallor. His eyes are wide as a baby's and set well into his temples; they are a clear yellow brown. He has an enormous shock of light brown, almost blonde hair, and from his brow there flows back a broad black streak of dye . . . his black lock.

As we all gaped and cheered, the circle of the escort parted at the very place we were standing, and a little creature, a female in the black and white uniform of the escort, cleared a space and reached up to the net. Blacklock gave a final flourishing bow, shrugged out of the thongs that held on his green canopy, then took her hand and stepped out of the net. He allowed himself to be brushed down, then the little escort was making way for him through the crowd. She had a brisk, cheerful voice, and her face, as she led the hero, was creased with worry, like a mother fussing over a toddling baby, ten days shown. Yet it was a pretty face, young and pointed, rather like Thanar.

Blacklock was saying as he passed, ". . . didn't even split a seam. . . ." I felt a stab of envy for the little escort, Blacklock's familiar.

"That is Spinner," whispered Valdin Galtroy, reading my thoughts, "Blacklock's first officer . . . or maybe his mothering nurse."

Now Spinner was whispering urgently to Blacklock, who was still bowing to right and left.

"What?" boomed the hero, "hmm, yes, well . . . flaming courteous of the flier in the blocks . . ."

He waved his hand in a wide circle or two and shouted a command; the escort packed up and made tracks with admirable precision. I realized that it was Diver's turn to fly his exercises; I left the clan children and ran back through the crowd to do my escort duty. The clappers were sounding, and the Launcher repeated his orders to clear the field; I found Brin and clung to her arm. Diver was beside us, showing his teeth in a grin. His nerve was much better than mine; he was keen and eager to be in the *Tomarvan*. It came to me that Diver loved to fly; the time he spent above the ground was actually less nerve-wracking for him than the time he spent hobnobbing with Bird Clan pilots and officials.

So it was all done over again. The excitement had died down, and the fickle audience of the Bird Clan had drifted away, so that Diver and the Wentroy began their rounds almost unnoticed. Ablo was still fuming and fretting by the *Tomarvan,* and Diver leaped into the pilot's chair. The catapult was attached; Brin and I stood to one wing, Ablo to the other.

Diver looked down at us and said, "There goes the machine to beat!" We saw Blacklock's odd craft wheeled away through the barrier to a heaving mass of black and white cloth: its hangar being erected. I had time to read the name on Blacklock's machine, then the Launcher spoke, once, twice and the *Tomarvan* was sent aloft, followed by *Utofarl,* double hope of the Wentroy.

We marched smartly off the field; Brin and Ablo stood,

shading their eyes, and I ran, bent low inside the barrier, to the end of the field to see better. Diver had made a good launch, but not so good as the Wentroy, who caught a wild current, lucky wretch, and spiralled up as surely as the good luck skein, so rudely rejected. Then I laughed, for the *Tomarvan* eased into a series of perfect circular turns and a double circle, twisted, like the script letter which has the sound "ee."

There was a chuckle at my side, and I saw that I was standing next to a short, spare, brown person, probably from some escort, for he was middle-aged, with wrinkles netting his green eyes. No grandee, more of a townee, and I felt at ease with him. He was watching Diver's performance as keenly as I was. The Wentroy tried to steal Diver's wind and could not, for Diver had no need of a wind. The *Tomarvan* banked and turned; the Wentroy tried a few circles, with fair success, then caught the wind again . . . through skill this time . . . and flew off towards the First Mark, high and fast. Diver flew after him in the darting, buzzing *Tomarvan*.

"Fine! Fine! Oh excellently done! Is that your pilot?" said my companion.

"My pilot!" I agreed proudly. I tried not to think of Bird Bone Place, up ahead.

I was about to reply in kind when I saw the insignia on his tunic and the white basket helm dangling from his strong, brown hands. I was speaking to Blacklock's copilot, who had landed the machine. I was excited then and almost went off into a flurry of childish questions about Blacklock, but something held me back. Politeness, for my companion was interesting in himself; or perhaps I had a moment of divining power of my own. I asked instead, "Good sir, who designed the noble machine that you brought in to land?"

His green eyes twinkled as he replied. "A good design is never the work of one mind. Your pilot, for instance, adapted that glider, with a device I call a wind-blade. Not new upon the land of Torin . . ."

I felt my blood pound in my throat and answered boldly, "Nothing is new under the suns. I see your craft is called *Dah'gan* or Maker of Engines."

"It could be Maker of Looms!" He laughed. "What shall I call you, young escort?"

"Dorn Brinroyan. And my pilot is Garl Brinroyan, our Luck. What shall I call you, sir?" I had thought for a moment that he knew something about Diver, but now I was not sure.

"I have had several names," he said, "just as we all have several families, from our birth family onwards, as the Great Wind blows us through the world. Now I am called Fer Utovangan."

It was a plain name, signifying no more than Fer, the Second Pilot, or even the Other Wing-Maker. He pointed across the field to a certain glider and commented on its design, then went on talking pleasantly and knowledgeably about flying machines and every sort of device that helped them to fly. We heard a sound and I stiffened, then I could not hold back a cheer. The *Tomarvan* returned, fast and sure from the First Mark; Diver swooped low over the field and boldly circled the launching tower before coming in to land. There was a landing net in position, but Diver had never used one and had determined to use only his own power. The marshals were there to hold his wings, but I could not stay . . . I slipped under the barrier and my companion did the same. We ran to the left wing of the *Tomarvan,* which touched, bounced, but not high, then came in for a perfect landing. The wing rode right into our hands, and the spin-toys or wind-blades were quivering but still.

Diver climbed out as I shouted to him; he came down happily and stood beside us on the field. In his excitement he pulled off his goggles as well as his flying helmet, and I instinctively touched his arm. Hiding his eyes was a game we must always play. He turned his head aside, but Fer Utovangan said quietly, "No need to replace your visor on my account, Garl Brinroyan."

Diver glanced at me, questioning. "This is Blacklock's copilot," I said warily, "called Fer Utovangan."

"A good flight!" said Fer, clasping Diver's hands between his own. He stared at Diver; blue eyes met green. Fer flinched a little but was not afraid.

"The Maker of Engines did not expect to find the *Tomarvan* and its pilot at the Bird Clan!" he said.

"Do you mean your machine or that One who gives others wings to fly with?" I asked.

"Both!" he said smiling. "I would give much to see what makes the *Tomarvan* fly."

"In time I don't doubt you will see," said Diver, "and frankly, the *Dah'gan's* engine is more new and wonderful to me."

"A thing I call a long-spark-maker," said Fer. "I wonder what you would call it?"

Diver replied with a few suggestions, totally unpronounceable to me at the time but in fact they had to do with "electricity." Fer laughed in delight.

"I have heard all the speech on Torin and words in two ancient tongues, taken from rock writings, but now I find there *is* something new under the suns."

He bade us farewell and walked off the field; Esto hung low in the sky, he walked into sunset colors. A few notes twanged in my memory, but I could not unravel the thread. We walked back ourselves and saw Brin coming proudly to meet us. It was not until we reached the tent that I found the answer to the puzzle; it was such a rich, impossible secret that I hugged it to myself. I murmured that plain name over to myself as I watched an improved Antho wheeled out of its hangar: Fer Utovangan, Second Wing, Second Pilot . . . or *Former Bird Farmer*. The winds had not taken Antho the Bird Farmer very far after all.

Now it was the eve of the New Year. Esder was already rising in those sunset clouds, no more than forty pulse beats after Esto sank below the horizon, and Esder would shine on, long after Esto rose again. It is more difficult to fly by Esder light, but some pilots make it their art; the second round went on, by lot, without a break. Flags and mirrors were set up at the Second Mark, inland to the northeast, still on the eastern bank of the Troon, at a place not far from the landing where we had seen Narneen's questioners, the scribe from the Fire-Town and his Witness.

We went into this round with good spirits; but Ablo, who knew more than we did about the ways of the Bird Clan, was very nervous. The second round is the most hazardous of all because it is an elimination round. We sat in our tent, ate a good meal of farm fowl with greens and washed it down with honey water. The first decision was when to sleep: wakefulness had been the downfall of many a brave pilot and escort. Ablo sat blinking in the darkness of the tent, picking his teeth and fidgeting with our lot skein, which marked the *Tomarvan* to fly at the second hour after midnight, paired with *Hadeel,* the black glider. "Seven hours!" he exclaimed. "Seven hours, Garl Brinroyan! Sleep or wake, it's your decision . . . we have a light escort."

"I will sleep and so will the escort. Will you watch for us, good Ablo?"

"Yes, yes . . . but *can* you sleep, without wine or the preparations the grandees use? I have heard that Blacklock sleeps by the laying on of hands—sleep-stroking-magic."

"We can sleep," put in Brin, "have no fear. Wake us in good time."

So we slept before his eyes: Diver by the use of a small white piece of medicine from his pocket vest, and Brin and myself from natural weariness, plus a pinch of herbs in our honey water. I slept and dreamed a long ordinary dream that I was on a summer journey, walking, pitching the tent, weaving, with my dear family all together again. Then I woke up, lonely for a moment and displaced, but filled with the excitement of the Bird Clan, as I saw Diver fastening his buckles.

Brin and Ablo parted the tent flap and came in, silvered by the light of Esder.

"Six out!" cried Ablo. "Six fallen by the way . . . never seen such an elimination round. The winds are blowing for you, Garl Brinroyan."

"What has gone?" asked Diver.

"*Utofarl,*" panted Ablo, "double hope of the Wentroy,

indeed, tipped the Second Mark; the yellow Antho did the same—or was it a tree. At any rate, it nearly came down. The copper boiler that came by the river went back into the river again, but the crew were saved, thanks to our Great Mother."

I was suddenly afraid. "Jebbal?" I whispered, staring at Brin.

"Safe, child."

"Continue with the eliminations," said Diver coldly. Ablo saw that his enthusiasm must be tempered; he went on:

"The Kite lost wind . . . had it stolen by *Tildee,* the steam engine. The winds took that pilot, first casualty this year. The improved Antho with the green tail had a wing and wind battle with Highness Jebbal and lost out. The other elimination was the gray glider that flew its first round with *Tildee* . . . called *Margan,* the Peacemaker, flown by another unlucky sprig of Dohtroy, and named, doubtless, after her relative on the Council, Dohtroy out of the Fire-Town."

We went out into the bright Esder light on the field of the Bird Clan, with the business of the contest still going on, the constant coming and going of the escorts, the cries of the marshals. I felt we had dropped out of the world for several hours simply by going to sleep. And now all that remained in the contest were

PEER-LO-VAGOBA   *pilot Jebbal Faldroyan Luntroy*

TILDEE   *pilot Ullo Mattroyan*

DAH'GAN   *chief pilot Murno Peran Pentroy, called Blacklock*

HADEEL   *pilot Deel Giroyan, a town grandee of Otolor*

TOMARVAN   *pilot Garl Brinroyan, the Luck of Brin's Five*

Ablo was still very nervous as Diver made his last check of the *Tomarvan* before we wheeled it to the blocks. I thought this was because he had not slept, but in fact he had another thing on his mind. A member of Blacklock's escort approached to a respectful distance, and Ablo nearly exploded.

"I knew it! Flaming privilege and grandees tricks . . . Murno Pentroy is going to issue a challenge!"

Diver looked about, and we noticed then that there were a surprising number of vassals and escorts, including some from Jebbal, watching our reaction to the message skein that the young Pentroy omor held out to Brin.

"I have heard of this right to challenge. What can be asked of us?" said Brin, holding the skein.

"Blacklock has no partner," hissed Ablo, "and he scored well for that display. He could ask to fly the second round in company with *Tomarvan* and *Hadeel* . . . but I think he has other devilish plans!"

Brin read the skein and smiled. She drew Diver aside and made him hand read as much of it as he could while she explained. "A challenge: *Tomarvan* and *Hadeel* to waive the Second Round and fly altogether, with Blacklock and the two other survivors in an immediate deciding race. Its formal name is Great Circle for the Winds' Favor."

"I will do it!" murmured Diver. "What say the rest?" Ablo bobbed up at his elbow, still fuming.

"Garl Brinroyan . . . think what you risk! Against *Hadeel* you will survive and gain points. You have never flown the Great Circle . . . it is thirty weavers miles over a strange course!"

Diver laughed and looked into the sky, a dark translucent blue, where faintly in full Esder light keen eyes might find the stars. I remembered he was another creature, a Man, from the void, who had flown further than anyone under the two suns. It seemed a very little thing to ask him to do . . . but I was still afraid. He was our Luck still, our poor sib whom we had nurtured, our bonded kin; and he could be cast down and killed here, flying the Great Circle.

"Where are the charts, friend Ablo?" he asked.

"You are determined, Garl Brinroyan?" Diver nodded gravely, and Brin's fingers whisked over the skein filling in the answer.

"The challenge is accepted!" she announced. The watchers stirred and chattered; some gave shouts of encouragement.

It turned out that we were the last to accept the challenge; the other contestants were ready, even the *Tildee* had a second head of steam. Two Bird Clan gliders flew off, on the instant, to patrol the Circle and land marshals at the towers. There was a sound of music and chanting and a band of Bird Clan vassals, with scarlet tippets over their blue green, marched around the field in a ceremony for the winds' favor. The pilots and their escorts were bidden to center field for a departing rite and a good talking to from the Launcher. We set out boldly from five corners of the field; Blacklock, conspicuous in his green cloak at the head of an enormous wedge of black and white followers; Jebbal with hardly less, bearing the flax flowers of Luntroy on their white cloaks; Deel Giroyan with twenty, richly dressed, bearing the crest of Otolor; the young Mattroyan, attended by forty omor in striped bag-hose, each one carrying a green tree branch. From our place marched Diver, fine and tall, attended by just three, for Ablo marched with us, grumbling still.

We had gone only a few paces into the field when Blacklock halted, maybe from Spinner's prompting or his own goodness of heart, and dismissed all but three of his escort. He walked on attended only by Fer, his copilot, by Spinner, and the young herald who had just visited us. It was a stroke of great courtesy. Jebbal immediately did the same, then the Giroyan and the merchant's child. I guessed at their reluctance, poor things, because Town grandees have a deep love of display and feel that it increases their honor. So we marched on and came to center field where Blacklock made the mood easy and laughed as we passed around the cups of honey water.

I stared my fill at Blacklock and found that he was covertly sizing up Diver. Presently, after Deel Giroyan had made a greeting round of the circle, Blacklock gestured to his copilot and they strode up to us. We exchanged bows and salutations, but Blacklock was unable to stand on ceremony.

"Well met!" he said, "and from what I hear, Garl Brin-royan, you are a strange bird indeed, to fly so far."

"Not beyond the sound of your name, Highness!" said Diver. "It has been heard on Hingstull."

This was a smooth answer but it did not please or satisfy Blacklock. His handsome face was alive with curiosity; he nudged Fer Utovangan and burst out: "Speak up, old bird! I've been misled . . . here is some courtier! Ask a question."

Fer chuckled and scratched his chin. "You must know Blacklock cannot stand a mystery," he said with a wink, "so I will ask: who are you, Garl Brinroyan?"

"He is our Luck!" I said.

"He is our bonded Luck," echoed Brin.

"Where does this Luck hail from?" asked Blacklock.

"It has been suggested that I am an Islander . . ."

"Surely a devil flown from the void," put in Fer.

"One might say, Highness, that the winds themselves sent Garl Brinroyan to my Five," said Brin.

"Well, if we're talking about *possibilities*," cried Black-lock in exasperation, "one might say he is Eenath the Spirit Warrior!"

"One might say this is another Maker of Engines," said Fer.

"One might say," I piped up, "that Fer Utovangan is Antho the Bird Farmer!"

Fer and Blacklock stared at me with expressions of comical surprise; Blacklock roared with laughter. "Blazes, old bird, the mountain child has you netted!"

"Hush child!" whispered Fer. "Do you not know that the winds have taken that old-time designer?"

"I'm in exalted company," said Diver.

"Indeed we are," said Brin, "and I will suggest a bargain. When the Great Circle has been flown and *Tomarvan* has returned safely to the field, together with *Dah'gan*, whoever leads the other home may question freely and hear the truth."

"Agreed, Brin Brinroyan," said Blacklock.

"Agreed again!" said another voice. It was Jebbal making her rounds, accompanied by the young Mattroyan. "Well Murno . . . what there, Friend Brin, young Hazel.

I like that *Tomarvan,* whatever damned fire-metal-magic makes it fly. I never believed in your wind-blades much, Fer Utovangan, until I saw Garl Brinroyan fly in circles. This shy person is Ullo Mattroyan, who heaves *Tildee* through the air . . ."

The Merchant's child *was* shy, without a trace of arrogance; she was very strong, half omor already from her exertions with the *Tildee,* but awkward in company. She bowed and Jebbal led her on, brisk as ever, smoothing the way with her talk.

The Launcher pounced on us suddenly; he stumped into the midst of these pleasantries and began a ferocious harangue. "Safety!" he boomed, "and no wing cutting. We fly for sport and the honor of the Bird Clan. Winds forbid our dear flying machines should be used as weapons! Clean flying, skill and care and no fancywork."

He gave more of this pattern, but I heard little of it. I was becoming afraid for Diver, in spite of all this good humor in the center of the field. My legs would scarcely carry me to the new row of launching blocks, where the *Tomarvan* was already mounted. I stood stiffly erect and smiled at Diver and at Brin, but inside was a scared, bewildered creature, a mountain child indeed, ready to burrow into the sleeping bag when a wolf howled. The five machines launched at the third hour, each one steady, and flew off due east, to the First Mark, where the first red streaks of Esto burned above Gwervanin.

I sat down beside our launching blocks, shuddering, and Brin sat down beside me. Ablo came up with a bag of fresh honey cakes and flung them into my lap with that cross manner that masked his concern.

"Eat up, Dorn Brinroyan. Show these vassal youngsters we have stomach for the Great Circle!" I nibbled feebly, then with more interest because the cakes were very good. The machines were out of sight. The vassals were clearing the field, even tearing down tents and stalls that stood near the edge. A thick yellow net was being unravelled at the field's lower boundary, beside the river gate and the closed bridge that led to the citadel of Otolor, then leaped in another span to the fairgrounds across the river.

"It will be over in less than two hours. Then the gates will be opened and the crowds will come to the nets to cheer the winner," said Ablo.

Brin sprang up and helped me to my feet. "Go to the river gate, Dorn, and ask for a message from the Harper," she said.

"Will they come to the nets?" I longed to see them again: Mamor, the Harper, Narneen, Old Gwin and Tomar. I pictured them cheering the winner . . . our own Luck!

"Maybe they'll come," said Brin, "but it is a crush. Better if they waited in their camp on the fairground."

I turned to run off but Brin called me back. She held out Diver's viewing tube, his sailor's glass. "Perhaps you can find a vantage point." I took it gratefully and ran to the river gate.

Already there was a crowd of spectators packing the gate, waiting for the finish and a good place at the nets. It was strange to be on the inside looking out of the Bird Clan; I fingered the blue silk braid of my emblem and scanned the faces out there, expecting every moment to be hailed by one of the family. Then I approached the gate-keeper, and he went haughtily to his booth and returned with a message skein. I gave him a silver credit and stood, reading the skein in my fingers, feeling the Harper's words as I turned for one last look at the crowd. I saw a face I knew and my heart thumped, but I gave no sign and ran off again into the field.

I stood in the shelter of the tower and raised the glass; the tall, brown figure had edged back . . . I saw a narrow face, a flash of blue rags and feathers. Petsalee, host of spirits, and dressed as a twirler! Could he harm us here, in the Bird Clan itself? I folded the glass and carried the Harper's skein to Brin; she read off the location of the camp, on a good site by the cloth market, and the Harper's good wishes. I said nothing about what I had seen and sent my wishes and prayers after Diver in the *Tomarvan*, rounding the First Mark. I strolled off again and when I was out of sight of Brin and Ablo, I put Diver's glass in the pouch pocket of my tunic and climbed to the top of the great launching tower.

About twenty vassals and escorts had had the same idea, the nimbler ones, children like myself. We clung to the supports and felt the winds tug at the tower. I hunched down, straddling a sturdy crosspiece, and found the tower no more frightening than a tall tree on Hingstull. I extended the magic glass and searched for a long time until I found them: five dots, no bigger than birds, flying bunched together halfway to the Second Mark. The rays of Esto, rising for the New Year, flashed silver or blue or green off one flying machine then another as they dipped and soared. I adjusted the glass and began to distinguish the challengers. *Hadeel* overhead, then *Tildee* thrusting towards the Second Mark, and surely that was *Dah'gan*, Blacklock's big machine, close behind. *Tomarvan* flew beyond the *Dah'gan* and trailing a little, high in a spiral behind the field, *Peer-lo-vagoba* soared in the blue.

The sunlight caught the mirrors at the Second Mark, which was another wooden tower, tall as the one I was perched on. I moved the glass on to survey the Great Circle: there were four marker balloons, one drooping from a leak, then far off by the fixed houses of Otolor, the Third Mark. There was one of the Bird Clan gliders flying in uneasy ovals on the farthest edge of the fair ground, and there were the streamers drifting out from the Fourth Mark. I flicked on quickly over the markets and stalls and dancing platforms to the gaudy Fifth Mark, still on the far bank of the Troon, a good distance downstream from the river gate. When I looked back, the five machines had crossed the river and were flying low over the fixed houses, low enough to wake sleepers, if any slept in Otolor at the New Year.

Suddenly one caught a wild current—was it *Hadeel*, still holding a narrow lead?—and the group spread outward and upward like birds alarmed by a fowler's slingshot. *Tomarvan!* I saw Diver catch the current and improve his place, but below came *Tildee*, heavy and dark, chugging even further ahead. Then I could see no more; the angle of the light made me weep and blink and lower the glass. I wiped my eyes and kept taking a look, but the machines were too far away, slow-moving dots, crawling through the sky to the Third Mark. So I sat on the tower for a long time, watching those five dots, hardly able to think of them as flying machines, the objects of so much hope, thrust through the air by living persons. Every so often I would identify one or other of the contestants: Jebbal wheeling to take the lead, *Dah'gan* hovering in close with *Tomarvan;* but then the pattern would change. All the machines became silvery drops or wisps of cloud, or I would find I had tracked a passing bird by mistake.

I sat rocking and blinking on the tower, below the other chattering youngsters who pointed and whooped and thought they saw this leader and that. Sometimes I rested my eyes and almost slept, then woke in panic and found the machines no nearer . . . but was that *Dah'gan* following the *Tomarvan?* And suddenly I was wide awake, frantically adjusting the glass, for they were rounding the Fourth Mark and the view was clear. *Dah'gan! Dah'gan* well ahead, and *Tomarvan* above, then *Tildee* closing to the right; far above, the two gliders, *Hadeel* and *Peer-lo-vagoba,* battled for each other's wind. I could see the other Bird Clan glider and the marshalls in it. The three leading machines continued their desperate fight: *Tildee* challenged and *Dah'gan* banked and *Tomarvan* tried to cut between but failed, ran out of sky, and had to fly wide and low, back into third place. *Tildee* sliced in to take the lead, and I could feel the breath of the wind-blade as Blacklock brought the *Dah'gan* close enough to slice a wing. Now Diver . . . take the lead now! And the *Tomarvan* did take the lead, but *Tildee,* the stinking *Tildee,* undercut, hacking at Diver's wing—where were the flaming marshalls?—and *Dah'gan* flew round-about, doggedly, and came up ahead of the two others. Then *Peer-lo-vagoba* lit down from high above, catching the wind perfectly, to take the lead, and there was *Hadeel* following.

"Come down!" The tower was rocking crazily, and the Launcher stood at its base calling in his thunder voice, "Down you wretched fledglings! Down, before we dismantle the tower with you clinging to its branches!"

Two clan vassals and a marshal were already on the platform shoving the youngsters to the ladders and attaching ropes to the tower. I scrambled for my life, with the rest, and we had scarcely hit the ground when the tower was skilfully twitched in half by the ropes. In a moment our perch was nothing but a heap of sticks and binding, dragged off the field in a transport net. I saw that the gates had been opened and a jostling crowd were pressed against the yellow ropes of the barrier. I ran back to the blocks, or the place where they had been, and found Brin and Ablo waiting among the silent, ranked escorts of all the challengers. I could hardly believe that they had seen nothing.

"Soon . . ." I panted, "approaching the Fifth Mark!"

"None down?" panted Ablo, "good, good, winds' favor indeed! Where is the *Tomarvan?*"

"Battling with *Dah'gan* and *Tildee,* last I saw."

The voice of a marshall, with a speaking gourd, reported calmly from the pavilion. "Now at the Fifth Mark. All challengers approaching . . ."

There was a buzz of relief from the escorts.

"*Dah'gan, Tildee, Tomarvan* . . . followed high by *Peerlo-vagoba* and *Hadeel.*"

"But how can they tell? How can they see so far? They must have a seeing glass!"

"They have something better, child, and could have told us the entire contest if they dared. There is a voice-wire stretched round the whole of the Great Circle, with answering places at every mark," whispered Ablo.

"Fire-metal-magic," said Brin. "And how do you know so much, Dorn Brinroyan?"

I looked at the brown turf. "I was on the tower with Diver's glass."

Ablo grumbled at that, about mischief and taking risks, so I handed him the seeing glass. He puzzled over it a little, and I helped him. Then, as he exclaimed in wonder at the powers of the glass, the cry went up.

They flew in at some height on the long southern curve of the field, *Dah'gan, Tomarvan, Tildee,* in line, then with *Tomarvan* shifting up and back a little. The gliders were nowhere to be seen. Blacklock's escort raised a clamor, and the Mattroyan omor began to chant, waving their green branches. I shouted, but then fell silent, like the anxious escorts of *Hadeel* and *Peer-lo-vagoba*, but for a different reason. I knew what would happen. There was a landing target set down, a circular mat of white woven straw in the center of the field; the trick was to turn and land, facing the river. I knew, I knew that Blacklock must peel off his heavy machine to the east leaving a strip of sky; and surely, as we watched, the *Tomarvan* turned half upside down, stood on its wingtip in midair. I saw Brin raise both hands and shout, summoning the winds, as Diver came through. The *Tomarvan* slotted between *Dah'gan* and *Tildee*, like the shuttle on a loom, then turned as the crowd began to roar, cut under *Dah'gan*'s runners with a hand's breadth to spare, turned again, and came down gently as a leaf, on the white mat in center field. Ablo seized my hand—he was weeping—and we ran, with Brin, to hold the wings. And that was how the Bird Clan was won.

I have thought of this moment and dreamed of it all my life since that time. I remember how the *Dah'gan* lit down beside us, how Blacklock ran to embrace Diver and call him friend and sibling. How the *Tildee* came in, red-hot in patches, and the pale young Mattroyan was lifted out by Diver and Blacklock to share the moment. Then the platform was wheeled up, the same one that had brought *Tomarvan* into the enclosure, but decorated this time with flowers of spring and blue green banners and tall silk lilies, the sign of victory. The *Tomarvan* was lifted aboard, and Diver, our Luck, unable to keep the smile off his face, stood beside his machine while silkbeam copies were made by the marshals. Then we climbed up beside him to share his triumph ride, and Blacklock himself stood to the flower-twined ropes with the cheering, laughing band of marshals and vassals. We were drawn towards the barrier and the cry went up, again and again, "Garl Brinroyan," "*Tomarvan*," "Brin's Five and Cullin." Here my dream should end; here I should remember no further. I have awakened in the darkness or in Esder light, on land and on the ocean sea, crying out for the dream to stop, stop and show me no more.

We had reached the barrier when the cheering began to fade; I saw Blacklock check and look at the sky. The cheering dried up, ebbed away completely. Diver made an exclamation in his own tongue. *Hadeel* and *Peer-lo-vagoba* had appeared together high above the field, moving, both of them, with a strange shuddering motion. Then I saw that they were locked together. The slender wingtip of Jebbal had pierced the black glider behind the pilot's chair and would not come free. They swung down together caught in one current that lived over the field, then were carried up in another; at the greatest height *Hadeel* wrenched free and came soaring down safely, far to the east, almost on the First Mark. *Peer-lo-vagoba* looped over, still graceful, and began to turn, to turn faster, to spin like an autumn leaf, spinning down, down, faster and faster towards the hard ground. I screamed but no sound came; there was a heavy silence over the whole of the field. The glider was a spinning blur of blue, a twirler; I could not take my eyes from it, but at the last Brin turned my head away and buried my face in her cloak. All I felt was a jarring thump, no more than the closing of a wooden door in a fixed house.

The silence was shattered after a few pulse beats; it was a scene of dreadful confusion. I saw Diver leap down and run, followed by Blacklock; the Launcher was roaring somewhere; the crowd broke the barrier and swarmed onto the field. Brin and Ablo had to stand to the *Tomar-van* on its triumphal platform to protect it. I saw a tall ancient rush past, tearing the clothes from his back and scratching his face in token of mourning: it was Jebbal's chief officer. I had only one thought. I leaped from the platform and ran and fought and burrowed through the weeping, jostling crowd until I came to Jebbal's fine silken tent, where the children were waiting. There was a clear space all around it; the escort were not there, except for two body servants, one an ancient sitting on the ground, tearing the flax flowers of Luntroy from its cloak, the other a young officer rifling through a kitbag. The ancient shrieked at me as I went to the tent flap that the place was accursed. Would I draw down the winds' bane?

"I carry the winds' favor!" I shouted.

I stepped into the darkness of the tent and waited, searching the darkness until my eyes became accustomed to it. They sat there on the cushions, pale as ever: Valdin and Thanar. They were richly dressed in honor of the day; the bead game lay between them. I saw myself in their silvered mirror, wild-eyed, dirty, full of the fear and excitement that made up the Bird Clan. I felt sure they had not watched the race, that no one had told them how it ended, and at the same time I was sure they understood what had happened. For four years, until this time, they had waited in the dark tent; and they knew the worst, although no one had brought them word. I stumbled forward and sat by them; Valdin moved a bead on the board, and Thanar clapped her hands silently and took four of his beads. Valdin sighed and handed me a beaker of honey water. "She is a baby," he said, "she likes to win." I sipped and choked.

"Has anyone . . . ?" I gasped.

"Not yet," whispered Thanar, "you are the first, Dorn. You are our officer." She replaced the beads carefully, every one in its correct socket, then began to move about the tent, collecting their belongings.

"You must make a report," said Valdin. I stared at him, dry-mouthed.

"Is the Bird Clan won?" he prompted.

"Yes, by Garl Brinroyan."

"And Jebbal? . . ."

"The winds have taken her." I hated this empty formula but I was glad of it; I could not tell them any more.

Thanar brought Valdin his cloak and he put it on, as she had done with her own; scarlet lining turned out, in token of mourning. I talked with them about sailing. We sat there for what seemed a long time, and the eddies of sound from the field became fainter, as order was restored.

"What will you do?" I asked.

"Go to Salthaven," said Thanar. "Some clan folk will see to it."

There was a faint hail from outside the tent, and I went to the doorway. I saw that the escort had all returned, shame-faced and weeping; they sat in a circle, giving the tent a wide berth. In the midst of them stood the hawk-faced old scribe with the Wentroy pectoral, first officer for the pilot of *Utofarl*.

"Who is that? Who has braved the winds' bane in that tent?" he demanded.

"Dorn Brinroyan!"

He took a few steps towards the tent and said, "Aren't you afraid, child?"

"No, I am not," I said truthfully, "for I carry the winds' favor. We have a Great Luck, victor of this Bird Clan, and besides, I have a special duty to their highnesses Valdin and Thanar."

"Well, you have taken the edge off this accursed place." He stepped into the tent and bowed sorrowfully to the children, who stood together, holding their velvet satchels. "Highnesses, my liege of Wentroy has your barge ready."

I cannot remember what we said in farewell, but the ancient took them away, quickly, by the back flap of the tent and bade me stay longer. I looked out and saw the two scarlet cloaks heading a slow and melancholy procession towards the river. Jebbal's escort trooped silently among the tents and stalls to the Bird Clan stockade and crept out through a broken place onto the bank of the Troon, where the barge was waiting.

I drew back into the empty tent and sat on the ground. I was alone and in an accursed place, but I did not want to be with anyone at that moment. Even the winds' favor weighed heavily upon me; I could not think of our good fortune. I could not wish myself back on Hingstull; for the Dorn who had run about on the mountain was gone forever. I would meet that child, become that child again, only in dreams.

"So you have seen the Bird Clan," said a dry whisper inside my head.

"I have seen it."

"Then you know that the winds can dash every hope to the ground."

A beam of sunlight, the rich light of the two suns, blazing outside for the New Year, struck the silver mirror left on the tent wall. My eyes were dazzled; a figure dark and bright grew in shadow at my side. I caught a movement of the green-hemmed robe.

"Do you hate the Bird Clan then?" I asked aloud.

"It is a testing ground, no more," said the Maker of Engines.

"Our Luck flew well . . ." I said defensively.

"Too well!" the voice was harsh. "Now he is known, marked down for the strange creature that he is. He must come to me at once or my protection will have no power."

"Someone is coming!" I said.

"Those I have summoned."

There was a muffled shout of "Winds' Favor!" outside the tent, and Blacklock strode in followed by Diver.

Blacklock checked in his stride at once for he saw who was there, a familiar presence to him. His handsome face wore a rueful expression. "At your call," he said.

"Another victory for the Bird Clan!" said the Maker of Engines sadly.

Diver came on into the tent completely unaware of any other presence. "Are the children taken care of?" he asked.

"Yes," I said, "but Diver . . . hear me . . ."

"Dorn, poor fellow . . . my dear sib . . . come up off the ground!"

"Diver . . . someone else is here," I said.

"What?"

"Garl Brinroyan," said Blacklock. "Meet this other, whom I call 'teacher,' 'guide,' even 'my liege.' "

Diver looked carefully round the tent and said in wonder; "Some other person . . . here in this tent?"

Blacklock waved his hands in exasperation. "There! I've never seen a better demonstration of thought-blindness! By the fire, I believe what Antho, our wise old bird, says of you, Garl Brinroyan. You are not of this world!"

The Maker of Engines said in that dry inward voice,

"Thought-blind indeed! Yet, I wonder. Dorn, ask your Luck to stand still and take off those flying goggles."

I was about to pass on this message when to my surprise Diver did as he had been asked.

"Why did you do that?" asked Blacklock slyly.

"No reason," said Diver, "or perhaps . . . I felt . . ."

The Maker of Engines uttered a sighing laugh; that radiance I had felt on the rock grew very strong. I saw the Great Diviner in and out of my head, everywhere around me, as if reflected in a hundred mirrors, so clearly that my head ached. Tall, narrow-faced, with a great fall of dark brown hair held across the high brow by a band of green brilliants. The eyes were black and piercing; I shut my own eyes and seemed to fall into a deep pool of black light where there was only this dazzling figure.

"Enough, Nantgeeb! You will have us entranced!" cried Blacklock. I dragged my eyelids open and saw Blacklock reeling back, an arm before his face. Diver suddenly cried out in his own language.

He took a step forward, his face very pale, his blue eyes staring, for he was very much afraid. "There *is* something . . ." he whispered. He mastered his fear and stepped forward again into that light, which we could scarcely bear, peering warily like a hunter entering a cave.

"Commend me to the Maker of Engines, Dorn," he said.

"Commend me to your Luck, Dorn Brinroyan," said Nantgeeb.

The light had already faded, and the Maker of Engines was a more comfortable presence. "This Luck—what is his true name?—is certainly very brave. The report I have from the Ulgan of Cullin does justice to him."

"He flies as well . . . as well as I do," murmured Blacklock. "And I smell more fire-metal-magic about the *Tomarvan* than any other machine in the Bird Clan."

"Murno, my firebrand," said Nantgeeb bitterly, "I have given my time, my riches, even those I might call my kin to this Bird Clan, and I grow weary of its wretched excesses. Remember where you stand . . . if this place is accursed it is because I curse it. Once, long ago, I was an officer in the escort of Jebbal Faldroyan Luntroy."

"We are all sorrowing," said Blacklock, "and at least our team came through without accident. Will you speak with Antho and Spinner . . . and take comfort from their safety?"

"I will see them soon enough."

"What is your will then?" asked Blacklock sulkily.

"I will have this Garl Brinroyan and his *Tomarvan* as quickly as the winds can carry them, for the newcomer's safety. Dorn . . . give my words to your Luck."

I passed on the words as I was told, but the plans outlined were shocking to me. Blacklock and Diver must fly out together in their machines *Dah'gan* and *Tomarvan* to a place far away, east of Rintoul, where Nantgeeb would be waiting. Agents of Tiath Gargan were supposed to be in Otolor; Diver's existence, even his identity, might become well known now that he had won the Bird Clan.

I put this all to Diver exactly as it came to me, and he made the reply that I had already made in my mind. "Ask the Maker of Engines what is to become of Brin's Five?"

"They are very rich, with even a portion of the Bird Clan winnings. Let them take land or return to Hingstull; they have played their part."

"Not so!" exclaimed Diver. "For I am their Luck, and I will not leave them, especially in Otolor where danger threatens."

"My care is for your person and the knowledge you bring to Torin."

"You are the Maker of Engines, so I will give you mine to study. Let Fer Utovangan, or Antho, if that is his name, fly the *Tomarvan* and my scripts on its engines to your meeting place. I will go on with Brin's Five to Rintoul and ask for news of my air ship."

"I can see why this new bird is your sib, Blacklock," said the Maker of Engines, "for he is as tender in his feelings and as stubborn as you are."

So it was arranged; I gripped Diver's hand with relief, for I had seen our Luck snatched away from us. But Nantgeeb was eager to have the *Tomarvan*. Blacklock promised to find us all passage to Rintoul before he flew away also.

"Tell the Maker of Engines I look forward to a true meeting," said Diver.

"Tell Garl Brinroyan to take care," said the Maker of Engines.

I knew this was the end of our audience. A last whisper grated at my ear: "And do not ask in Rintoul for the air ship. Tiath Pentroy has lost his prize. I have it now."

Diver sprang up when I said this and questioned the empty air, but Nantgeeb's presence had been withdrawn.

Blacklock walked about flexing his shoulder muscles like a weary omor and cursing under his breath. "Garl Brinroyan, this is an old quarrel you have come upon. Nantgeeb hates the Bird Clan," he said.

"I like it less than I did," said Diver, "but with your help, Murno, my good friend, we will fly by all these nets."

Blacklock smiled again and even laid a hand on my head to make me more cheerful. "Escort, you have served your Luck well!"

We walked all together out of the silken tent into the sunlight of the New Year and made our way, through subdued cheers and salutations, to the green tent, garlanded now, where Brin and Ablo were waiting.

When I saw Brin again, my eyes stung with tears, like a child who does not cry after a fall until its mother brings promise of comfort. But I did not weep. We sat in the tent, and I reported faithfully all that had passed. The task of making these reports, as a Witness must do sometimes, is not easy, and I did not envy Narneen, who was going to have a lifetime of it.

Brin turned to Diver when all had been told. "We have a great Luck," she said, "not because he wins the Bird Clan, but because he is faithful to his bond."

VII

The closing ceremonies of the Bird Clan were shortened because of Jebbal's death on the field. Even so they took several hours, part of them spent in sorting and counting our winnings. These were lodged in five wheeled wicker caskets, each one big enough to contain two or three Moruians, inside the Launcher's pavilion. Ablo was given a generous share and left to head a guard chosen from Blacklock's escort; this pleased him almost as much as the cloth and credits he had won.

The gates had already been opened, and the members of the Bird Clan were streaming across to the fairgrounds to celebrate the New Year. A bridge of decorated barges stood at the river gate; the double bridge past the citadel was twined with flowers. Flying machines still passed overhead, taking their leave. Diver instructed Fer Utovangan in the control of the *Tomarvan,* and he flew a brief practice flight. It was arranged that Fer and Blacklock should fly out the next day or the day after that.

"I will care for this bird of yours," said Fer. "No harm will come to the *Tomarvan,* and I hope you will fly in it again." For he could see that Diver loved the flying machine and did not really wish to part with it.

At last we were ready to leave and find our family at that good pitch the Harper had told of in his skein, by the cloth market. It was customary for the winner to leave in

triumph, with Bird Clan vassals playing music all the way
to the Sun Carpet, the famous dancing place in the center
of the fairgrounds. We did not use this escort, and it was
understood that this was out of respect for Jebbal, but we
had other reasons as well.

We set out at the third hour after midday, three nonde-
script Moruians, two adults and a child, muffled in plain
gray silken cloaks. We joined the crowds thronging the
double bridge, and I felt at last a lifting of my spirits.
Home again. Home to the tent after so long, with Mamor,
the Harper, Old Gwin, Narneen, and Tomar waiting for
us. It was a day when nothing but friendship should pre-
vail. The faces I saw everywhere were smiling; there was
no ill-will, no ill-natured jostling. Children ran about
among the crowd waving fair favors of colored wool that
twirled on a stick. As we passed the citadel, Brin checked
suddenly, then we walked across the second arch into
Otolor.

"Something wrong?" asked Diver.

"I thought we had a follower . . . in twirler's dress."

"Petsalee!" I squeaked. "I saw him, I saw him . . ." It
seemed ages ago, before the race was won, before Jebbal
died.

We stood in the shadow of a cook-stall awning and
looked back for a long time but saw nothing suspicious.
Then we threaded our way down a long alley full of cook-
stalls, and the scent was so delicious that Diver and Brin
took pity on me and we stopped to buy roast wild fowl
stuffed with berries. Then, feeling open-handed, we
bought a carrying hamper of food to take to the tent and
spent so much that the cook-shop owner gave us towels
when we washed at the fountain. We wandered on well-
fed, and then I saw two twirlers, neither of them our
watcher, lounging in their blue rags under the window of
a fixed house, a common sleeping house for fair travellers.
They stared dully about and accepted offerings but certainly paid us no heed.

"I will feed these birds a little grain," said Brin. We
followed her and stood to one side as she approached the
pair.

"Greetings to the spirit-warriors," she said, dropping a credit into their gourd.

"Eenath's blessing!" was the soft response.

I stared at them, feeling the same mixture of fascination and disgust that I had felt for the twirlers in Cullin. They were both still young; their brown bodies were thin and stringy, scarred from head to foot with the marks of the sharp shells. I have heard townees complain that the twirlers are dirty, but I hardly noticed. I saw their expression, gentle, sad, dazed. Could Eenath bring this fate upon her followers?

"Dear friends," said Brin, "share this food and answer me a question."

"What pleases you, in Eenath's name." A gaunt hand came up for the food, but Brin held it out of reach.

"Where is the twirler Petsalee?"

The twirlers were silent; their faces grew firmer, their expressions almost sly.

"Petsalee . . ." prompted Brin. The twirler who had reached for the food held up two fingers and whistled softly. Brin reached a second game bird from the basket.

"The spirit-warriors dance at the Sun Carpet," said the twirler.

"At what hour?"

"When the spirits call . . ."

"About the fourth hour after the New Year Shout!" put in the second twirler who was very hungry. "The Leader Petsalee will call the dance."

Brin gave them a bird each, and we left them eating. Diver was curious about Petsalee; how could he be Leader still and recruit a new band of twirlers? Did this mean we had misjudged the creature—he had not bought a life but only escaped Tiath Gargan's massacre?

"Twirlers have their own laws and their own secrets," said Brin, "Petsalee must hold great power for them."

We were still passing through a part of the fair given over to eating and drinking; then we came to a place for all kinds of sports and games. Brushwood fences separated the stone-placers from the teams of skip-rope and the ringers, who twitch down wooden pegs from a high stand

with a reed ring attached to a strong thread. A whole pen
of ancients were taking part in a knitting contest, with the
colored work growing before our eyes until it flowed over
their knees, so fast their needles flew. Diver announced
that he could knit; he had had it from his mother and all
his female ancestors. We laughed in disbelief, until Brin
fetched a ball of thread and needles from the knitting
marshal and cast on a few stitches, as she used to do for
me, when I made my winter stockings. Diver took over
pretty unhandily, but he knitted, both first and second
stitch; anything requiring more skill or more than two
needles he said was beyond him.

"Knitters are born," said Brin. "Dorn here is still battling with his third twist and double plaits. The best knit-
ter I ever saw was Little Griss, the Luck of Tarr's Five,
my birth family. He swore he could knit a tent, given the
right thread."

Diver explained, as we walked on into the pottery market, that knitting had been a dying art on his world, but
had grown up again in something called the Craft Revival.

So we passed on, through the pottery market, the place
for music and singing—where we looked for the Harper—
and the fortune-tellers' lane, where we kept an eye open
for Gordo Beethan. We skirted the edge of the Sun Carpet
and took a side trip into the fixed houses of Otolor, beside
the old curtain walls of the town, now tumbled down and
planted with flowers for a memorial. We came at last to
the cloth market, and I was impatient, for the stalls of
cloth reminded me of our winnings and the great news we
were bearing home. Behind the cloth market is a wide
field, especially planted with red-wood trees for the bush
weavers to use for the support of their tents. We stood on
the edge of this field and stared, and I saw it. Our tent
. . . our own good tent, with the three new panels replacing
those we had left in the glebe on Hingstull. It stood a long
way off on the distant boundary of the field; there were not
many people about, and none that we knew; everyone was
at the fair. Yet somehow I thought of the Family all sitting
in the tent waiting for us. I began to run.

"Hold . . . in the Winds' name, hold!" I looked back and

saw a lithe figure in gray dart out from behind a tree, a stranger, frantically hailing our approach. Then I thought I knew it . . . the Witness who had called Narneen! Before I could think of her partner, I was caught and held in a firm grip.

"Still! Be still for your life, Brinroyan child!" said a strong accented voice. I looked up into the scarred face of the scribe from the Fire-Town. I must have showed fear, for he slackened his grip at once and turned his face away in an odd cringing motion, as if protecting me from the sight.

"Don't be afraid," he said. "I am Vel Ragan, ever your friend."

Diver and Brin converged on us fiercely, with Diver already fumbling under his cloak.

"Let the child go!" ordered Brin.

"Hold, I pray," gasped the Witness Onnar. "We bring a warning." Vel Ragan released my arm and held out his hands empty in the gesture of peace.

"We have waited for your approach since the rising of Esto," he said. "Pray hear us, for your safety."

"You are Vel Ragan," said Brin, "and this your Witness, Onnar. You come from the Fire-Town, and you sleep-spy upon my child Narneen."

"This is true," said the scribe, "but I think Narneen, that excellent Witness, has also told you that we mean friendship and we do not lie."

"Trust us both," begged Onnar. She kept looking about anxiously. "Come to this tree," she said, "where we can sit down like a Family at their food."

"What are you afraid of?" asked Diver.

"The creatures of the clan Pentroy," said Vel Ragan. His voice had a rich timbre, almost like Diver's; his gray eyes flashed fire; I could guess what hand had guided the firestone that burned his body.

"Are they safe . . . our Family . . . ?" I blurted out.

"Come and sit down."

We sat down together under the tree, and Vel Ragan looked keenly at Diver. "Let me see your face," he said.

Diver threw back his hood and removed his goggles. Vel

Ragan stared and gave a long sighing breath. "It is true then. Strangers have come to Torin from the void."

"One stranger," said Diver, "and no longer so strange thanks to the love and care of Brin's Five. My poor companions still work in the islands. No doubt they think I am dead."

"How many? An army?"

"Three," answered Diver, "a team of scholars."

Vel Ragan drew out from his sleeve a worn sheaf of willow paper: Diver's drawings, copied first at Cullin, then in other parts of Torin.

"Yes," said Brin. "Diver made these drawings and I wrote on them, at Stone Brook. But now, tell us your warning."

"Hear us out," said Onnar, "and do nothing rash." So we heard them out, although the tale they had to tell was a terrible one, outweighing any sorrow or danger we had passed through till now.

"We came to the fair after questioning Narneen on the river," said Vel Ragan. "It was only then we were certain that this child was the one named in the Stone Brook drawings. We believed that your Luck was the one we sought, and we had heard tales of the landing all down the river. We had planned to go to Cullin or even Stone Brook itself, but in fact we landed our glider at Wellin with a damaged runner and took up the search from there twelve days ago. There was plenty to hear. The Strangler had left a trail much wider than Brin's Five. So we came on to the fair and gleaned a few snippets of gossip out of the Bird Clan, and at last the news today of your good fortune. But before that time, about the first hour of Esder shine, or what would be night, Onnar was called by Narneen. The child, as you know, is a powerful Witness, destined for a great career in this strange art if she desires it. Narneen had a dreadful tale to tell. The members of your Five have been surprised, sleeping, by seven armed vassals of Tiath Gargan. The Harper was absent from the tent when this happened, but we could not warn him in time and he was taken when he returned. No—be still and listen! No one has been harmed or even questioned, although Mamor and the Harper are bound and gagged. Narneen lies, feigning sleep; Gwin nurses the baby. The vassals are simply waiting for the return of Garl Brinroyan; they are disguised, but make no secret of their allegiance to the Great Elder. There are four among the seven who say that they have a score to settle . . . your Luck has already dealt roughly with them on Hingstull and in Cullin town."

I could not speak after this for the fear and helpless anger that I felt. But Diver had flushed. His blue eyes blazed, and he was as keenly alert as when he was flying the *Tomarvan.*

"The score will be settled, believe me!" he said. He peered around at the field and the tent, far off, and the few passers-by.

"Are there any Pentroy vassals keeping watch *outside* the tent?"

"No," said Vel Ragan, "not that we have seen."

"There are only seven," said Brin slowly. "It is a thread I never expected to unravel. These creatures have united in Gulgarvor, a seven-fold cord, a covenant to perform a certain task."

"My capture," said Diver. He felt under his cloak and asked Onnar, "How are they armed?"

"They have knives, and the two who stand at the door of the tent have a bludgeon and a limed net."

"Nothing else?"

"They mean to take you alive," observed Vel Ragan.

"Diver," I croaked. "Blacklock will help you!"

"Against his own clan's vassals?" inquired Vel Ragan. "That I would like to see."

"It is a different branch of Pentroy," said Brin. "Diver, shall we send for his help?"

"We need help, that's certain," said Diver, "and Blacklock would do it . . . but time is short. I will not have those creatures in the tent any longer. It is a long way back to the Bird Clan . . ."

I thought of the fairgrounds we had crossed, two or three weaver's miles at least; I felt myself running the distance.

"Not so far!" said Brin. She pointed to the southern

corner of the tented field, where there stood a wooden tower, decorated with drooping flags. A mirror flashed from its summit and I realized what it was: the Fourth Mark of the Bird Clan circle.

"The voice wire!" I cried. We all explained at once.

"Thank heaven for fire-metal-magic!" said Diver. "Will it still be working?"

"If our luck holds," said Brin.

"Can we use it?" I asked. "We have never seen a voice wire."

Vel Ragan laughed. "I have seen too many," he said, "but none so welcome as this one!"

We left Onnar watching under the tree and made our way quickly back through the outskirts of the cloth market and across a patch of nettle bushes to the tower. There was a small tent of Bird Clan blue green at the tower's base and it was sealed with waxed threads bearing a warning message. Diver snapped this seal impatiently, and we crowded into the empty tent. Ragan stayed back however, peering up at the tower.

"Still firmly in place," he said over our shoulders, "but how are the cups?"

Brin adjusted two window flaps, and we saw it. Two innocent looking clay cups, for all the world like ordinary drinking cups, but covered at the base with a fine mesh of wire and linked by a thick cord to a leather bag on a pole.

"Where is the outlet?" demanded the scribe. He came past us and took up the cups in a familiar way.

"In the pavilion? Well, we'll see what the Bird Clan staff do when it is all over . . ." He pulled on the linking cord and rattled the two cups together so that they made a hollow clopping sound.

"I was wondering how you would do that," murmured Diver.

Vel Ragan went on clopping at intervals, and I found suddenly that I did not believe in the voice wire. It was impossible that what we did here could be sent to the Bird Clan pavilion. Then from one of the cups there came a loud rattle. Vel Ragan immediately pressed the cup over

one ear—which I thought was a very brave thing to do—
and proceeded to speak resonantly into the other.

"Are you there? Bird Clan pavilion . . . answer!" There
was a breathing sound, another voice, and he held the cup
from his ear. The voice spoke from the cup, magically, and
it was a real voice, a voice in accent and tone quite unmis-
takeable.

"Who calls? What cheeky wretch is bothering us in the
course of our duty? Who is that, I'd like to know?"

Brin and Diver and I all shouted together.

"Ablo!"

Diver stepped up and took the apparatus from Vel Ragan. "Ablo, this is Garl Brinroyan calling from the Fourth
Mark."

"Excellence, I hear you wonderfully clearly," said
Ablo, "but you had no need to check. The escort is doing
a fine job of protecting our winnings!"

"Good Ablo, you have served us well," said Diver, "and
now you must render the greatest service of all. You must
save my Family from peril!"

We heard Ablo gasp. "Excellence, anything, anything
. . ."

"Then leave the senior member of the Pentroy escort in
charge and take the next in rank with you to the tent of
Murno Pentroy. Tell the Highness himself or Fer Utovangan that my Family is imprisoned in their tent near the
cloth market by a Gulgarvor who seek my own capture.
Tell them that the one who has ordered this deed is the
same who lost a silver ship. And as proof of my good faith
say all this in the name of the Maker of Engines."

Diver said more, giving the location of the tent and
schooled Ablo in the message, which he seized quickly.

"Go then," said Diver, "our prayers go with you. We
will not wait Blacklock's coming but make shift to free
those who are trapped by ourselves, if we can."

Then Diver returned the cups to Vel Ragan, who broke
the link and left us forlorn and still helpless in the stuffy
tent. Diver was filled with energy, like a twisted thread or
a metal spring. He led us, very fast, to a place behind the

patch of nettles. We were much closer to our tent and in a desolate corner of the fairground where no one came.

"What weapon have you?" asked the scribe. Diver brought out his stun-gun; Vel Ragan whistled in admiration and produced a wooden box from his sleeve.

"This fires a dart . . ." he said. A metal tube with a wooden grip lay in the box.

"The tent has a blind side," said Diver. "I think the brutes are watching the door and the eastern wall."

"Correct. Narneen, the ancient, and the baby lie on that blind side," said Vel Ragan.

"Then Mamor and the Harper are tied to the tree," guessed Diver.

"You see it well."

"What is your plan?" asked Brin.

"The stun-gun?" I whispered.

"Dangerous in a confined space," said Diver. "They must be lured out."

"You will not budge them," said Vel Ragan. "They will not stir until they can take you, trussed, to their cruel liege. Their own lives depend upon it. Surprise is their main weapon."

"Then they have lost the game already," said Brin, "for they cannot surprise us. Diver . . . I have a plan if the scribe Vel will cooperate."

She told the plan, which seemed good, and then I went with her, back to Onnar under the tree. "Narneen asks if you are coming," said Onnar, "and I have told her not yet. But I cannot lie to this Witness . . . I can barely shut her out."

"Do it, I pray," said Brin. "The less she knows the better."

She outlined the plan to Onnar, then we moved on. We went to the northern edge of the field, dropped into one of the ditches circling the ground and made our way crawling through nettles and dead leaves to come up on the tent's blind side. It took less time than we expected. The tent loomed ahead, and we crawled again, from one clump of bushes to another. Brin took her amulet on its chain and caught the suns' light, flashing towards the field and the place where Diver waited with Vel Ragan. She handed me Diver's knife and drew out her own, pressing a hand to her mouth for silence.

There was an empty time of waiting; then we saw two figures approaching the tent, passing among the trees and the other tents as they came. Diver, still in his gray silk cloak, stumbled along oddly, pushed and urged by Vel Ragan. They came on until they stood before our tent's closed flap door. Then Vel Ragan shouted in a harsh ringing voice, "Gulgarvor . . . I have your prize!"

He wrenched back Diver's cloak, to show his blue suit, and shoved him to the ground, on his knees. Diver's hands appeared to be bound. "Here is the devil for you!" cried Vel Ragan. "Here is your release!"

The scene already attracted attention from the few weavers and idlers who were not at the fair. They stood peering around trees, poking heads from flap doors. Vel Ragan was a frightening figure; his scarred face was revealed, and he held a long knife in one hand.

"Bargain for your devil, Gulgarvor! Pay ransom or the devil will die!" He flashed the knife high in the air and made as if to stab Diver, who cried out piteously in his own language.

For the first time there was movement from our tent and the sound of voices.

"Hold . . ." A single figure stepped out; one of the intruders, heavily built, blinking in the sunlight. I thought I recognized the face of a vassal from the convoy, one who had gone back for the Galtroy litter.

"Not so fast, friend," said the creature, thumbs in its red belt. "Perhaps you have something there we need." Another stranger came out of the tent, by the back flap, and sidled towards Vel Ragan in a circle.

"No closer, or the devil dies and takes his secrets with him."

"Who are you to tangle with devils, friend?" asked Red-Belt, taking a step closer.

"A poor adventurer," said Vel Ragan smoothly.

Diver, groveling, cried out again, as if in fear of his life and suddenly the members of the Gulgarvor all burst from the tent together and rushed upon Vel Ragan. I saw Diver and Vel begin to run, drawing them away, then I was inside the tent with Brin, on the blind side.

They were all there, just as we had been told; Narneen sat up screaming and Mamor and the Harper were straining at their bonds. I hacked at their ropes while Brin closed and weighted the back flap and stood to the door, speaking to comfort Old Gwin and Tomar as best she could. Mamor wrenched out his gag and did the same for the Harper, as I freed their feet.

"What was that, for the fire's sake?" roared Mamor.

"A game to draw them off . . ." I said.

"Help Diver!" said Brin. "Mamor . . . Roy . . . can you fight?" I rushed to the door, but Mamor held me back.

"Stay here. Is that the scribe helping us?" He plunged out into the daylight, followed by the Harper, and at last I was able to get a look at the struggle.

Diver had his stun-gun out and had already felled one vassal as he drew away with Vel Ragan to the open ground at the end of the camping place. But the bond of Gulgarvor made them heedless of any danger, and Vel Ragan, unsteady on his lame leg, stumbled and fell in their path. They were swarming onto him; Diver rushed back, stunning two more, and dragged the scribe to his feet again. Diver, speaking plainly in Moruian, warned them to keep back, but they did not heed him. Then Mamor and the Harper joined the fray, each seizing a vassal from behind and wrestling. Diver had used his stun-gun with measured force; already those that he felled had bounced up again, and as he altered the setting two of the largest brutes leaped upon him. Vel Ragan, behind a tree now, fired his weapon, and I saw Red-Belt, the leader, clutch a wounded arm, pierced by a dart. Diver had one of his assailants down with a chopping blow, but the other was pressing him dangerously. A crowd was gathering now, to watch this strange, long battle.

Narneen crawled to my side and said, "There is a flying machine . . ."

Blacklock flew in low, with the big wind-blade churning the air and tossing the treetops. The crowd scattered and crouched, but the members of the Gulgarvor still fought on as if possessed. I saw the machine land on open ground then a present danger made me cry out for Brin. Red-Belt and another vassal, who had an arrow skin-sewn in blue on its upper arm, were racing upon us, determined to regain the shelter of the tent or seek hostages. Brin sprang to the door again, pushing me aside; she carried a loom board as a weapon and I heard Red-Belt grunt as she used it.

She held it out of the tent, prodding and parrying the assaults of Red-Belt and Arrow.

"Devils!" panted Red-Belt. "Nest of devils!"

"Keep back!" cried Brin. "I charge you in the winds' name!"

"Repent!" growled Arrow. "Make clean, mountain weaver! Give up your bond with the Foreigner!"

"Keep back from my Family, my children and my home tent that you have defiled!" said Brin, in a voice that made me shudder. "Or I swear by Eenath I will strike you down!"

Then she struck at them again, more fiercely still, and I felt Old Gwin come closer, placing the whimpering Tomar in my arms. She drew back the flap until she stood at Brin's side and in a sharp chanting voice she cried out, "Keep back, for the fire of Eenath has consumed your souls! We know you all, and you are all accursed! You will go down into fire and have Gulgarvor enough, for your very bones will be consumed to ashes . . ."

The pair of them, Red-Belt and Arrow, halted for a moment at the ancient's curse; then they came on, and Old Gwin dipped into a leather sack on her wrist and flung a handful of dust in their faces.

"Narneen," she shrieked, "call the names of the Gulgarvor for all the world to know!"

"VARADON!" cried Narneen, kneeling by me in the darkness, and I echoed her cry and so did Brin. The Leader gave a cry of pain and surprise, for Old Gwin was throwing the dust of the fireweed.

"MEETAL!" cried Narneen. The vassal marked with the arrow reeled back, and its eyes were stung with the dust.

"ARTHO!" cried Narneen. The two, backing away from the tent, half-blind, fell over another vassal coming to their aid. Brin, holding the loom board and Gwin with her sack of pepper, edged after them. I stood up, holding Tomar, and took Narneen's hand and we stepped out into the sunlight.

"TRANJE!" cried Narneen.

"Tranje!" echoed Brin and Gwin and myself at the tops of our voices. A vassal, wrestling with the Harper stood back amazed.

"TROY!" cried Narneen.

"Troy!" The shout rose up even louder, for now the Harper and Mamor had joined in the naming of the Gulgarvor. The wretched Troy broke loose from fighting with Diver. Mamor's opponent, still not named, rushed at Narneen, and Gwin threw another handful of dust.

"ALLOO!" cried Narneen.

"Alloo!" The cry went up on all sides.

At last the Gulgarvor faltered, and all rushed for open ground. They slammed full-tilt into Blacklock and Fer and two sturdy members of the black and white escort who had somehow crowded into the flying machine *Dah'-gan.* They were flung down and herded into a ring, wild-eyed, panting sweat-streaked creatures, some unarmed, some clutching weapons . . . they looked like devils indeed.

"BANO!" Narneen cried out the last name, and it was repeated. Then we saw that one member of the Gulgarvor lay still on the ground, apart from its companions.

Blacklock clapped Diver on the back and said in a matter-of-fact tone, "At your call, Garl Brinroyan. But with the power of Brin's Five, I see you have flown past this net."

"Let us make all secure!" said Fer. He gestured to the members of the escort, who carried ropes.

"What will you do?" asked Diver suddenly.

"Bind up these creatures," said Blacklock. "What, did you think I meant to string them up? My nickname is not Gargan, like my uncle's, I promise you."

With the help of Mamor and the Harper, the six living members of the Gulgarvor were bound all together and sat on the grass in the sunlight of the New Year, with their fallen comrade. Fer walked about and bade the members of the crowd go about their business and refrain from watching a private quarrel.

I sat on the grass too, at a safe distance, with Tomar, Narneen and Old Gwin, still shivering and muttering from the ordeal. Vel Ragan came slowly out from behind his tree and waved; the Witness Onnar came running to his side. They approached our group hesitantly, then Onnar held out her hands and Narneen ran to her. It was a moment, in all the terrible violence and confusion, that I was often to see in my thoughts. I felt as if some piece of weaving was complete; the last shuttle had gone through a certain panel and the pattern was ready to be seen. Brin came to join us and took Tomar in her arms.

"Let it be known that Vel Ragan and Onnar have saved this Family!" she said. She clasped hands with each of them in turn.

"It was the power of Narneen that made it possible," said Vel Ragan. He was a strange, shy person, made harsh, I guessed, by what life had brought him, including his disfigurement. His mind was the keenest of any Moruian I have ever known, for all the ways of city living and politics and the relations between one person and another. In this he surpassed even Nantgeeb, who was before everything a scholar and a ruling spirit, who could see only one way at a time.

Now, on the fairground at Otolor, Old Gwin took the edge off the day by squinting crossly up at Vel Ragan. "I forgive you the sleep-spying, young scribe," she said, "and wish you a Happy New Year."

We returned to our tent and purified it, and I had the joy of seeing Blacklock, the hero himself, together with Fer, that legendary flier, under our roof branches, sitting among us. But the New Year was not a happy one and all the soothing talk ringing in my head made the hurt and confusion I felt worse instead of better. I stumbled out of the tent and saw the members of the Gulgarvor sitting under a tree, dazed as twirlers, and I felt a stab of hopeless pity for the creatures. Brin and Blacklock had been at pains to tell Diver of the threat that they presented; they would never cease to threaten him with capture until death took every one of them.

Their naming, the death of their comrade, the offers that had been made to them secretly by Blacklock, a member of clan Pentroy, for pardon and release . . . nothing could sever them from the bond of Gulgarvor. They could not return to Tiath Avran Pentroy with the task incomplete; they were outcasts. . . . Varadon, Meetal, Artho, Tranje, Troy, Alloo and Bano. Even the dead member, Bano, was not released from the seven-fold cord, and indeed the spirit of this member weighed upon all of us. Bano, an omor like Meetal, Artho, and Alloo, had died at Diver's hands, not from stun-gun or dart or cudgel but from the single chopping blow with which Diver had felled her to the ground. The killing lay on him like a shadow; he had a special aversion to killing a female, even a strong, fierce omor, seeking his capture.

As I sat on the grass by myself, looking as dazed as the prisoners, Blacklock, Fer and Brin came out of the tent with Diver. They were talking about boats and plans, but it seemed like so much of the grown-up chatter I had heard so often that it went literally over my head.

"Dorn . . ." it was Brin standing over me.

"Dorn Brinroyan," said Fer. "The escort will stay here so we have vacant places. Would you like to fly with me back to the field?"

To fly . . . in Blacklock's machine! Part of me was ready to jump up, but instead I found myself coming up from the ground wearily and unsteadily.

"Thank you," I stammered, "but I would rather stay on the ground this time."

He smiled, green eyes twinkling, and exchanged one of those grown-up glances with Brin. "It has been too much for him," she said.

I was ashamed and sad and felt tears stinging my eyes as I stood looking at the grass. There was too much I could not bear thinking about, from Jebbal to the Gulgarvor. I turned my back on the whole of the New Year and went into the tent. I lay down on top of a sleeping bag beside

Narneen, and the last thing I heard was my sib, the Witness, cracking nuts with her teeth.

I slept heavily but not long enough, and I seemed to hear the New Year Shout in the depths of my sleep. I woke with Diver gripping my arm . . . the Great Sun had gone down, and the people had shouted to see the Far Sun rise up beside it at least two hours before. Now the fair was in a sleepy stage of rejoicing.

"Come, put on your gray cloak again, and we will walk through the fair to the river," said Diver. I looked about and hardly recognized my own tent for it had been stripped and packed while I slept. There were strange faces there; three weavers had been hired to help with the packing under the sharp eyes of Gwin and the Harper.

"Blacklock has hired us a boat," explained Diver.

I went to the water bag, luckily still unemptied and drew out water for my face. "Wait!" I said. "What will become of the Ulgan's barge? Has Gordo Beethan come to the fair as it was promised?"

Diver shook his head. "He has not been seen. Mamor arranged for a family to take the barge back to Cullin."

"I hope no evil has come to him."

They were calling outside the tent now, "Dorn!" and "Diver!" so we went out. Blacklock and Fer and the escort had gone; the Gulgarvor were no longer beneath the tree. Only Brin's Five stood there in Esder light beside a wheeled handcart, which showed that this Family had come up in the world. Once the tent was down and folded, the hired helpers set off on the paved ring-road, and we turned to walk through the fair.

We went into the cloth market and halted before a lace stall while Old Gwin examined the lace and collected credits from the stall keeper for some of her own lace that had been sold. I saw the Family, tired after their ordeal, with Tomar sleeping on Brin's back, for he would not ride with the others now that she had returned. There stood Harper Roy, tuning the good harp over his shoulder and Diver muffled up, with his head bent to hide his eyes, and Narneen leaning sleepily into the folds of his cloak.

I stood at the back with Mamor, and I saw us, side by side, making part of the family.

"What has become of the Gulgarvor?" I asked.

"Blacklock's escort and the Town Watch took charge of them."

"Will they be . . . put down?"

"It might be kinder!" said Mamor grimly.

"No!" I shuddered; the idea of a kind death was horrible to me.

"None would do it," said Mamor, "except their own liege. They will be parted . . . some sent north and some to the Fire-Town. Murno Pentroy's people will see to it."

Brin led us through the cloth market and the stands for rope-twisting and another place for eating and drinking that we had never visited before.

"Where are we going?" I called. The others laughed.

"To the Sun Carpet, where else?" said the Harper.

"Your friend Blacklock has a turn coming up!" said Mamor.

The press of people at the fair was greater than ever and still their faces were happy, the mood was one of friendship. But the light of Esder, strong yet silvery, made them strange, a parade of ghosts and shadows, revelling in some other world. I caught a gleam of Diver's eyes under his hood as the crowd jostled him.

I drew up to him and took his hand. "How does it really seem to you, among all these Moruians?"

He sighed and shook his head. "Very strange . . ." He threw back his hood and deliberately held up his head. For an instant, as he looked about, I saw what he saw: thin bodies, angular; faces that were long, peaked, shadowed, stripped to the bone or tilted and more firmly fleshed in youth. And the eyes . . . wrapping around the head in the way we admired, wide apart, in deep sockets, sometimes skewed to the sides in the look we called Gastil or South-North; eyes wide open, gleaming, or glazed with tipsy-mash and lack of sleep, eyes with thick natural lashes or lashes oiled into spikes, or painted white for the New Year. A flickering, glistening night-forest of eyes.

I tried to imagine a crowd of Diver's people, and I could

hardly do it: skins of every color from black to a whitish pallor; blue, forward-looking eyes . . . and what other colors might they have? Red eyes? Purple? Orange? Short folk and tall and the females oddly shaped; forests of curly hair like a crooked fleece or the wigs of grandees; all the shapes and sizes of Man milling about under a light even stranger than that of Esder, the impossible light of some reflecting dead little world called the Moon. It made me laugh, and I tried to tell Diver what I had imagined.

"Well, you are not far wrong," he said, smiling; "but if I have the colors right, there are no red eyes or purple or orange. Besides, Blacklock's eyes are nearly orange to my way of thinking." So he went on to tell me the colors of the eyes of men, and to point out those that came closest to earth colors among our family and the passers-by.

We came to the edge of the Sun Carpet, and there was a viewing stand filled with people from the Bird Clan, with a place in the middle for Diver. He put up his hood and greeted the Mattroyan and his child and Deel Giroyan, with an arm bandaged from a hard landing in Gwervanin. We looked around for Ablo, but he was not to be seen; so we sat comfortably and examined the great dancing floor. The Sun Carpet is one of the wonders of Otolor; it is not a true woven carpet but a huge tufted rug, made in sections like a flat loaf divided, on wicker frames that can be easily replaced. The colors are red, turquoise, yellow and tan in a waving pattern, with motifs of double circles for the two suns.

Harps and flutes were sounded, and the troupe of skippers who had been performing whisked away. There was a flutter of the familiar black and white; we cheered for Blacklock, and there he was . . . in bright orange, of all colors! Diver leaned down to me and whispered, "To match his eyes," and I laughed until I choked, and Mamor patted me sternly between the shoulders. First of all Blacklock did the triple leap—which meant springing over a series of high frames; then he rode the circle—a wheel with foot pedals in the center. In all these feats he was accompanied by members of the escort so that the whole performance was finished and perfect, like a dance

or lace pattern. At the end of each feat, he beckoned to the
crowd to try the same thing, and certain town grandees or
clan folk, including two from clan Dohtroy who had flown
unluckily in the Bird Clan, came forward and performed
well. But none were so fine as Blacklock himself, who had
a sweetness, a precision, a gift for pausing and seeming
about to topple and coming upright again, so that his
audience laughed and gasped.

For the finale, the escort brought on a whole raft of
fleece cushions until the Sun Carpet was nearly covered.
Blacklock stood alone, and the escort clambered on his
shoulders; two stood still, then more clambered up until
he supported a rack of six, seven persons, and a little one,
Spinner herself, went up and was balanced on the top.
Then Blacklock began to groan and rock like a tree in the
wind, and the others with him; and with a final whoop,
while we laughed ourselves into tears, the whole structure
came toppling down upon the cushions. But more was to
come, for Blacklock stood before our viewing stand and
gestured; we knew who it was he wanted. Diver climbed
down, grinning, and stood in the midst of the Sun Carpet,
side by side with Blacklock, their arms linked to make the
base for a double rack. Up went the escort, placing themselves differently this time, six, seven, eight, nine, eleven
and Spinner was the twelfth. Diver, taking his cue from
Blacklock, began to groan, and Blacklock echoed and the
whole crazy rack swayed; the crowd hallooed with delight
and down they all came. Everyone, even Old Gwin, was
doubled up with mirth.

"Well, it is childish stuff," she said. "I don't know why
I laugh . . . except for that cheeky sprig of Pentroy. And
if Hunter Geer has shaken Blacklock by the hand, well,
I have had him in my tent and well-acquainted with the
Luck of my own Family."

Then Blacklock left the Sun Carpet, and there was a
dive for the fleece cushions, which he left as pickings for
the crowd; soon there was not one to be seen.

Brin gave us the sign, and we left the stand to go to our
boat. I saw, as we left, that the Sun Carpet was being
removed to reveal the bare brown earth under its beautiful

frames, but I did not realize what this meant until we were some way off, on the western edge of the circle. Diver had come back, panting, from his feat.

"Wait!" said Harper Roy, drawing us to a halt. His sharp ears had caught the jingle of shell bracelets. We turned back at once and huddled together in shadow beside an empty stall; Mamor lifted Narneen to the counter shelf to see better.

There was the same furtive jingle of shells as the twirlers came to the dancing place, then fire shot up in the center of the circle. Petsalee! There he stood once more, gnarled and long and brown, dipping his hands in and out of the cool flames. There was an enormous host of twirlers—three bands at least—but the Leader was Petsalee, and he began to chant at once in his queer, penetrating voice.

"I am returned from the dead!"

And each time the twirlers echoed his name, "Petsalee!"

"I am returned from the grip of the Enemy!"

"I am returned from the river depths!"

"I am returned from the black barge of death!"

"I am returned from the Strangler!"

"I was spared, and my spirit-warriors were taken!"

"I was spared to do the work of evil!"

"I was spared to betray Eenath!"

"I was spared to watch by the river!"

The beat had quickened, and the heels of the twirlers were thudding upon the earth; in the shadow we quivered like a taut thread, knowing too well the meaning of this chant.

"Avert!" shrieked Petsalee, raising his staff. "Avert the evil might of the Strangler!"

"I am purged by the twirlers' fire!"

"I am freed by the power of Eenath!"

"I declare the truth to the land of Torin . . ."

Brin turned us all away, and we went through the crowd pursued by the rhythmical shrieks of the twirlers, who spun in ecstasy and fell and rose again. The message they were chanting rang in our ears as we made for the South Wharf.

"A spirit-warrior fell down!"

"A noble spirit has come upon Torin!"

"A hero has come, a hero who flies like a bird!"

"A hero is here among us . . ."

There was a large keel-boat waiting, and it bore our Cullin banner from the Bird Clan at its masthead. The captain and two crew members, all out of Otolor, bowed humbly, and we saw the reason: the Bird Clan winnings were safely stowed aboard. The captain handed us a message skein from Fer Utovangan, bidding us a safe journey in Blacklock's name and assigning us a lodging, the house of a wig-maker in Rintoul. We trooped aboard and began to make ourselves comfortable with our own furnishings, for the handcart had also arrived. It made me begin to understand what it might be like to be rich: work was done for you. Food had been laden and even flowers in a water frame.

We were about to cast off when a voice shouted, "Hold! Hold please, I pray you in the winds' name!"

The sailors stood still. What now? I asked and prayed for nothing more to happen. A plump figure in a townee robe was struggling along the wharf with a small wicker travelling basket.

"What do you want?" called Brin.

"Excellence . . . Noble escort . . ." At last I saw who it was.

"Garl Brinroyan . . . take me with you. I have striven at the Bird Clan every spring for ten years and never served a winner till now. I am discreet and handy and would rather serve a . . . a spirit-warrior than go back to my cross-cousin's woodwork shop . . ."

Diver looked at Brin, who smiled, and he said, "Come aboard, good Ablo."

So Ablo scrambled aboard, and the boat was cast off. We set sail into the New Year with a light northeast wind, and overhead a silvery bank of cloud, like fish scales, drifted across the sky hiding the light of Esder.

VIII

Every journey on the river is different, as I had learned, and our circumstances had changed. We were rich, we had friends, we even had servants. Slowly, slowly it came to Brin's Five that we did not ever need to weave again; we could, as the Maker of Engines had suggested, take land or become townees in some place on the Troon. For three days the adults enjoyed the sun of the New Year, then they could not refrain from putting up the largest of our looms as before, and Gwin got out her lace frames. But the spark of a new life had settled behind the eyes of the Harper, for one. How would it be, he asked now and then, if the Family had a bird farm, with a tent or a fixed house or both, whatever they pleased? How would it be if Mamor had a bird-boat to carry the birds from the farm, and the wild birds he might trap in the eastern hunting grounds, near Rintoul? Old Gwin was scornful.

"How would it be if wool-deer grew wings?" she said.

She was still mourning the loss of our spinners. They had gone with the Gulgarvor; a rack had fallen across their basket when Mamor was subdued in the tent; some had died, some had run off. Only Momo, the largest, had had the sense to crawl up the tree, and Old Gwin had coaxed her down again and had her alone in a cage beside her on the deck. Ablo assured Gwin that good spinners were to be found in Linlor, but she would not believe him.

The mat-loom did not sound at all on this journey; not from my usual laziness but because I was sick. Perhaps it had a little to do with the motion of the keel boat, which was greater than that of the barge, or perhaps it was some town fever from Otolor. At any rate I dragged myself miserably from the deck to the hold, so as not to miss anything, but by the fourth or fifth day I was flat on the box-bed in the hold, burning and shivering. I gazed through a small window over the Troon, and the members of the Family took turns sitting by me. I had time to think, too much time, and I believed that my sickness was a sickness of the mind as well as the body; it was born of excitement and violence. I first dreamed here of Jebbal's flying machine twisting to earth and of the dark faces of the Gulgarvor.

Up above me, on deck, life went on. Tomar fell overboard and was rescued by Mamor, but not before the little wretch had begun to swim. Every day Mamor set Tomar and Narneen swimming round the boat for practice, to save himself another wetting. Diver practiced his speech and his woven script and taught Harper Roy the "Song of the Young Harper Fallen in Battle," which, in Moruian, became a great favorite in the Harper's song sack, known far and wide.

I can lay out, on paper, three versions of this same song: the true words, the sense of it or paraphrase that Diver told the Harper, and the words written into Moruian. I do not know that the Harper's listeners will ever have the real sense of this strange, sweet, violent song. A lone harper, a young male, setting out for war deliberately, is something that belongs far in our warlike past, in the time of the Torlogans and the clan wars. And the loneliness of it ... "one faithful sword" and so on. But the beauty sings through very well; who could chose between "wild harp" and "turu geer" or "rorogaban torin-na" and "land of song"? One line, of course, caused great difficulty; it was impossible for the Harper to sing anything resembling, "His father's sword he has girded on" and when Diver suggested, "His mother's sword," the Harper jibbed at that too. So the Young Harper went into battle "with weapons borrowed from his Family," solving the problems of decency and fire-metal-magic.

Brin and Narneen sat by me one morning, and we spoke of Vel Ragan and Onnar, who were following us to Rintoul in their own sailboat. We were becalmed at the time and thought it must be the same with them. Narneen had a tale, half-understood, from Onnar, of Vel Ragan's friend and former liege, who had been a great leader in the Fire-Town, then had been disgraced and dismissed from his work with the Town Five. Tsorl was his name, and he had gone not long before to Rintoul to study some strange new metal, which Vel Ragan guessed must be Diver's ship. But Vel Ragan had no trust for the Elders and the Great Elder in particular, and what he had seen on the river and in Otolor made him fear for the safety of his friend Tsorl. I said this leader's name to myself, after this, for he was called Tsorl-U-Tsorl or Tsorl Alone; he would have no family name at all and not even a nickname, which is valued among ordinary folk. It seemed to me a proud and brave title. Could I be Dorn-U-Dorn, ever?

We had left behind the Pentroy lands, and from Otolor we had been sailing through the country of clan Wentroy. We came, with some work on the capstans, to Linlor wharf, and by now my sickness was lifting. I came up on deck and saw that Linlor was a sweet, well-swept town, smaller than Otolor but graceful and white, a foretaste perhaps of the townee districts in Rintoul. It lay in the midst of tamed lands and orchards on the west bank of the Troon, which was broad at this point.

There was a tall fixed house not far from the town in fine gardens; it was the home of the Wentroy Elder, Guno Gunroyan, whose reputation for bad temper and cussedness was as great as her reputation for justice and fairdealing. She was called "Guno Deg," which is difficult to translate, for it means Old Cross-Patch, but it is a term of grudging affection, almost a loving nickname.

Ablo took Old Gwin into the town, the pair of them tottering a little on dry land, and found out a place to buy new spinners. We put on new clothes, made from our winnings, for the Harper and Brin had been busy with sewing; they had taken Diver's measure, and he looked very fine. In fact our craft and our family brought inquiries from the Town Five. Brin had the Captain give it out that we were rich weavers from Otolor come to take up an inheritance in the delta. Every day hawkers and food-sellers and flower-sellers came down to the wharf offering us their wares, but old habits die hard and we shopped sparingly.

A wind sprang up after two days, and we made haste to leave; but just at the moment we were about to cast off, Narneen, who had been sitting silent by the mast, ran to Brin.

"Wait," she said. "Please wait for Onnar and Vel Ragan. I know they are coming!"

"Child, we need the wind!" said Mamor.

"They have news! They have been trying to catch us for days! Wait . . . we must wait!"

"You have been right before," said Brin seriously. So she bade the captain moor the boat again, and we waited. It was no more than two hours when a sailboat hove in sight, far to the north, and came beating down upon the wind; Narneen clapped hands with relief.

Through Diver's glass we saw them, sailing expertly, with Vel Ragan at the tiller and Onnar handling the sail. I saw that sailing, in one's own small boat, might be a great thing; I thought of Valdin and Thanar and hoped they still sailed in their boat on Salthaven. Vel Ragan came scudding up to the wharf and made haste to come aboard. There was something in his set face and fast limping gait that pierced me with fear, the old fear of Tiath Gargan. He spoke quickly with Brin and Diver, then drew into a close discussion with all the adults. Narneen and I crept close and heard at last.

The news was very bad. The members of the Gulgarvor had been held in the citadel at Otolor, heavily bound and under close guard. But one had a scrap of shell in its boot sole and managed to work on a single rope until it parted and freed another. Then, by lot apparently, or some other secret choice, three went free—the omor Meetal, Artho and Alloo—strangled all the rest of the Gulgarvor and strangled two guards and made off. No one knew where they were, but we all knew their purpose: to capture our Luck.

Blacklock and Fer had already flown out of Otolor when this occurred, and the Town Watch, fearing Blacklock's anger, might have hushed up the whole matter. But luckily some members of the Bird Clan escort were still doing guard duty and they made haste to tell Vel Ragan, so that he might warn Brin's Five.

Diver's face had its old harsh look, which I had hoped not to see again. "Are we well ahead of them?" he asked.

"So I trust," said Vel Ragan. "We set out at once, the day after the escape and passed no boat on the Troon that might have carried them. All were local fishers, small and untroubled. Onnar probed their thoughts if she could."

"What about a glider or a flying machine?" asked Brin.

"Hardly possible," said the scribe. "Even if they could come by a glider, it would not take them all."

"What do you advise?" asked Diver.

"Let us make what speed we can to Rintoul," said Ragan. "They call it the city of peace. Weapons may not be worn and vassals in particular may not appear in arms. Also, there is one there who should know of your presence."

"Do you mean Nantgeeb?" asked Brin, for Vel Ragan was already familiar with our story.

"That is impossible, if you will pardon me, Brin Brinroyan," put in Ablo. "I have heard that the Maker of Engines and even Blacklock himself are as good as exiled from Rintoul."

"I did not mean Nantgeeb," said Vel Ragan. "I will present you to Orn Margan Dohtroy, the Dohtroy Elder on the Council of Five. Margan, the Peacemaker, holds land in Tsagul and the west."

"Why should this Elder meet our Luck?" asked the Harper.

"I think I know," said Mamor. "Do you, Diver?"

"Something to do with the Fire-Town?" asked Diver.

"By no means," said Vel Ragan, laughing, "but for your

own protection, Garl Brinroyan. To show that you exist and that a clan member has set eyes on you!"

"You are a useful friend indeed," said Brin, "and we need you in the great city."

Vel Ragan sighed and said: "Any news of the air ship?"

"A little," said Diver. "We have it from a hawker that it lay over here at Linlor wharf for several days and met up with a small boat from Rintoul. But we cannot tell what this means. Could this be Nantgeeb?"

"I think not!" Vel Ragan said excitedly. He cursed under his breath and began to speak, with some hesitation and shyness, of his former liege Tsorl-U-Tsorl, Deputy of the Fire-Town.

"I believe Tsorl came in that small boat to Linlor to view the air ship. This is bad news . . . it means he saw the ship before its capture."

"Why are you anxious for the safety of your friend?" asked Brin.

"It is a strange story," said Vel Ragan, "and one that I cannot bear to tell. But Tsorl set out for Rintoul to serve the Great Elder by his superior knowledge of metals. He has not been seen by his friends since then."

"You have asked in Rintoul?" said Diver.

"One friend, a Highness of Dohtroy, Tilje Paroyan, was no more than a few days after him, yet he could not be found. She was in Tiath Avran's own house."

"Whew . . . I would rather keep out of that place!" exclaimed the Harper.

"It is a dull place, so I hear," said the scribe. "Tiath is not even his family head . . . Old Av still dodders about, and there are various high-bred old females . . . a tangle of the old threads."

"What is their Luck?" I chipped in to the conversation.

"I can tell you that," said Old Gwin. "It is the dwarf Urnat, that was born of a poor Five on Gurth Mountain, west of Hingstull."

"Clan gossip!" said Mamor. "Vel Ragan, what do you fear for your friend the Deputy?"

"I do not know," said Vel Ragan, "but the Strangler's

hand is in it. Tsorl hoped always for more freedom for the Fire-Town, but this is a dream."

Then the talk went another way, but I sat by Vel Ragan and Onnar and said to them, "Tsorl-U-Tsorl. . . . that is a very proud name."

"The Deputy is a proud man," said Onnar.

Vel Ragan laid a hand on the hand of his Witness. "I last heard his voice from Onnar," he said, "when she brought a certain message. I pray we find him again."

Then we all took advantage of the wind and sailed straight on, through the Wentroy lands, with Vel and Onnar out-running our keel boat. We lay over sometimes, and our friends came aboard and Vel Ragan instructed Diver in all sorts of practical matters: the government in Rintoul, the Council of One Hundred, the City Council, the inner Council of the Five Elders, and their laws and formalities. He told old tales of the Fire-Town and the last clan war and the more distant history of Torin.

We kept up our discreet inquiries about the barge carrying the air ship, with the help of the captain and the crew who knew the river. They knew something of our business, and Diver's identity was an open secret, as it had become at the Bird Clan. Ablo had been taken into our counsel, and he was the one who finally made the discovery. We lay over at a small hamlet on the eastern bank, close to the rich delta lands, and he went to buy flowers. He came panting back with a great load of yellow twin-suns and a strange story. A barge had moored at this place, Pelle, and the crew were taken in the night with sleeping sickness.

At the same time, there were comings and goings of strangers up the tiny stream, the Pel, that flows into the Troon at this point. A net and hoist were seen, said to be of metal, and a tall personage supervising the operation; the farmers in the village had been paid to see nothing. The crew on the barge and certain passengers woke cursing after a sleep of a whole day and made haste towards Rintoul. This told us enough: Nantgeeb had stolen the air ship at this point, by the use of mind powers or simple sleeping herbs. If Tsorl-U-Tsorl were on the barge examining the ship, then he slept with the rest. Perhaps the anger of the Great Elder had been vented on those who lost his prize.

Diver called to us one day, about two hours before the setting of Esder, and we found him standing in the bow with the captain. The land around us was particularly fine, with huge river meadows of reeds, where the water-fowl are bred. Not far away the Troon divided and divided again, for we had come to the delta. Diver pointed ahead and stared, like one in a dream; we all stared, and the dream took hold of us. A tracery of fine lines grew and wavered in the sky at the horizon, fading before our sight, then becoming solid; floating, then reaching firmly to the earth. It might have been a huge grove of white trees or the high columns and ridges of a mountain range; then the light changed and it was a net, a network of pure gold— the towers, the bastions, the spires, the skywalks, the sky-houses of the great city of Rintoul.

Rintoul has been raised up and cast down, even in my own time, but the dream remains; the habit of perfection and grace inspires those who build there, those who live in the city, so that it regenerates and grows more beautiful from age to age. It has had blood spilled in the broad white streets, but they have been washed clean by letting in the sea; towers have toppled and been replaced by more resilient towers. There is no seamy underside to Rintoul, it is all well-made, smoothly plastered, cleverly woven, with winding basket ways to the higher levels, and the curtain walls of former times gently folding into the skyhouses of glass and stone where the grandees live.

Rintoul is surrounded by beauty; as we sailed on through the delta lands, I gazed at the fields and trees and waterways and wondered how it would be to live there. The land was tamed and farmed but full of good places to fish or swim; Old Gwin was taken by the flower fields; Brin and Roy looked closely at the bird farms. Mamor was restless, standing in the bow with Diver's glass as we sailed on the eastern channel, which is called Curweth. The city rode up on our right hand, covering the world high and low, but Mamor looked to the east and on the next evening he gave a shout and called me to his side.

"There now!" he said, handing me the glass. I stared east and saw a line of light; it heaved and shifted, as if the sky had fallen to the earth, clouds and all.

"But what *is* it?" I asked, unable to look away. The line had turned to a flat plain, unbelievably vast, stretching further than the plain of Torin itself and shot with queer pale colors.

"Ah," said Mamor, "that is the North Wind's own sib, that quenches every fire. That is the Great Ocean Sea . . ."

That day Vel Ragan and Onnar took the sailboat ahead of us through another channel into the city. We sailed on and came in Esder light to the gardens and granaries and round, low store houses on the outskirts of Rintoul. The city lies between the sea and the land on the very edge of the estuary; we sailed through the eastern gate, Curweth-Ma, where the captain tied up the keel boat. Then we crossed through the wharves to the city canal and sailed in one of the painted pay-boats through miles of quiet streets. I sat with Tomar and Narneen, and we counted ten fountains, some still, some playing, in the dawn before Esto, until we came to a landing stage near our street. We walked a short distance and were received at the wig-maker's house, which seemed as grand as the citadel at Otolor. The lower level was a shop, full of wigs on stands, like so many grandees' heads; we were shown by a servant up a winding basket corridor to the third level and settled into a large room, with a view of the ocean on one side and the city on the other.

These two windows, glazed in many panes of white and colored glass, with stiffened rope between the panes, are something I remember whenever I think of those first days in Rintoul. We sat before them a great deal, watching and pointing; Old Gwin, who did not go out much, sat beside the city window for hours at a time, watching and laughing and shaking her head in a kind of bewilderment.

"Rintoul . . ." she would say in disbelief. "We've come to the city!"

The streets were never thronged with people, there was never such a crush as there had been on the fairground at Otolor, but we felt the presence of more, many more people, all around us. I could not wait to go out and explore, but at the same time I was nervous.

The Harper took me on a first expedition, and we became lost; we looked through a marvellous street of shops containing leatherwork and bought some presents. Then we read signs for the Fish Garden and set out for it but missed our turning and came to a most beautiful street full of paper garlands and pink windows. There were carrying chairs with their curtains drawn, coming and going, and the inhabitants of the street leaned from first floor windows with their arms bare. The Harper whistled and grinned.

"Truly," he said, "this is no place for one so young." I did not understand and we wandered on, taking in the exquisite little shops for eating and drinking and gaming. A pretty painted creature leaned from a window and threw a credit to the Harper.

"Play us a folk song, dear Weaver!" it said.

"You must excuse us, Friend!" he replied and threw the credit back again. The painted one caught it nimbly and stuck out its tongue at us.

"But what do they do here?" I asked.

"Let me put it this way," said Harper Roy. "For these folk it is Springtime all the year round!" So he bustled me along to the end of the street, and there we found a member of the Town Watch, an omor in a white robe, with the insignia City Friend.

The Harper greeted her and asked for directions. The omor was kind and cheerful; she told us the way to the Fish Garden.

"From the North?" she asked.

"Truly," I said, "from Cullin."

"I have kin still in Nedlor," said the omor. "When you have seen the Fish Garden go down the long steps to the Friends' Round. It is an open place where you can hear the news and meet other visitors. You can buy a map of the city."

"And it's more respectable than this place . . ." said the Harper. He pointed to the street sign waving about above our heads: it said Honey Dream Crescent, which sounded to me more like the name of a sweetmeat.

"City ways!" shrugged the omor. "Not many folk come here by accident."

The omor walked with us then, as far as the Fish Garden, and left us standing on a bridge looking at the clouds of green finger-fish and the big striped Sea Bear. Another City Friend turned up in the Fish Garden with a throng of tourists; there were townees, who might have come from Otolor or Linlor, a few bush weavers from further north, and a group I did not recognize at all.

"Who are they?" I asked Harper Roy.

"What? The ones in flax kilts? Oh they are real outlanders . . . from the far west, I should say, beyond the Fire-Town at the edge of the world."

We hung about at the edge of the group as they went up to the top of the promenade at the end of the garden and the guide began to point out the sights of the city. We saw the Old Breakwater—now on dry land—and the beautiful Corr Pavilion, where the Hundred meet, both buildings from the time of the Torlogan. We saw the clustered skyhouses of the grandees, rising from the third or fourth level; in this part of the city they seemed especially tall, cliffs of stone.

Figures could be seen moving about on the skywalks, like birds on the highest branches of a tree. On every skyhouse, clustered among the beams like strange fruit, were golden globes, painted with the gold paint the grandees use for their outdoor wickerwork. "Those are sleep-cells," explained the guide. "Little basket rooms where the grandees are rocked to sleep. The clansfolk in this city have a strange malady . . . they find sleeping difficult."

This made us all laugh; yet there were times I remembered when it *was* difficult to sleep.

We could look down on the Friends' Round, a pleasant place with trees and benches and cook-shops and a large mosaic pavement reaching out into the lagoon.

"What's that, Friend?" called a townee, pointing.

"That island?" asked the guide. "Why that is the glass island . . . 'halfway to Itsik,' if you know what I mean."

We could see the tall heaps of sand glistening in the suns' light and high-domed buildings with smoke coming from their spouts. As we broke off from the group and ran down the steps to the Friends' Round, the Harper said, "This city runs on fire-metal-magic. What more could they have in the Fire-Town?"

"Moving staircases," I said. "My feet are tired."

"Diver has been telling you Earth yarns!"

This was our first and one of our longest expeditions into the city. We all went together to the Friends' Round one morning and Vel Ragan met us there, with Onnar. It was a pleasant place indeed and one where we felt safe and comfortable. Old Gwin settled under a tree with Tomar, and the Harper had many requests for his folk songs. Brin took me to the message trees, which are wooden racks where skeins of news and other messages are posted; they stand at every street corner, and there are certain scribes who replenish them. Diver and Mamor stood at the balustrade looking out over the lagoon to the sea, marking the ships that sailed in and out to the wharves. Ablo took Narneen to buy a sunshade, and she came running back to Brin with another new thing . . . a carved wooden figure, dressed just like a grandee, in a long silk robe and a furry tippet.

"It is a doll," said Brin. "Ablo is wasting his credits on you, child." But Narneen hugged the thing and called it her dear little clan creature, her poppet, her pouch-child.

"What is it for?" I asked.

"It is a toy . . . a thing to play with, like the bow Mamor made you," said Brin. "The city children play with dolls, and I expect we might have found a stall of them at Otolor."

I looked at shops full of toys after that and wondered what kind of a toy I might like, but I saw none. Yet the city was full of things I did crave . . . writing sets, leather boots, pouches, wheeled carts; there was even a place on the city canal where small sailboats were made and sold.

Vel Ragan took the Five one day to wait upon Orn

Dohtroy—called Margan, the Peacemaker—in his sky house. They were gone all day, and we stayed indoors with Ablo at our lodgings. When they returned, they were disappointed but full of talk about the grandeur of the place. They had waited in the antechamber on the eighth level with many petitioners for the Peacemaker and had gazed into the sun room. This enormous golden room led onto a water garden, the Harper said, where there were tamed flatbills. But Orn Margan had been absent, so his servants gave out, or at least he saw no petitioners that day. Vel Ragan sent in his name, but not the nature of his business, and the skein came back with a polite addition asking him to call again in three days.

The scribe was worried and irritable because the Five had not been seen.

"Do not fret," said Diver. "I am sure it is chance that the Peacemaker did not see us."

"He is cautious," said the scribe. "Peacemaker is not altogether a grand title. Orn Margan is ready to compromise. I wonder if he thinks I am seeking Tsorl-U-Tsorl."

"You have no word?"

"None. And I must ask most discreetly. But this is another matter. I must get you seen, Garl Brinroyan, for your safety."

"Should we not go to the east and find the Maker of Engines and Murno Pentroy?" asked Brin.

"Perhaps," said Vel Ragan. "First, bear with me once more and we will try Guno Deg."

The little darkness had returned, though it was always very short in Rintoul; spring shades into summer in the south without a sharp distinction. We all rose up in Esder light, dressed in our best and set out for Guno Gunroyan's skyhouse in Rintoul. Old Gwin protested, but she was made to travel in a carrying chair with Narneen and Tomar. The scribe led the rest of us for miles, up and down, then only upwards, and we crossed our first skywalk. A wind blew from the sea, and the skywalk rippled; even Diver could not look down. The porters with the chair waited at the other side laughing, as we tottered across. We plunged into the shining levels of the house and came to the antechamber before the sun room. We were not the only petitioners, even at this early hour; we tried to send in a skein, but the servant in charge, the House Warden, would not accept it. Food was sent out on trays, and as we were eating it there was a sudden commotion and the curtains of the sun chamber were abruptly drawn. The room was of such magnificence that my eyes dazzled; three domes of colored glass flowered overhead, and there were three carpets, old and fine, each as large as a small field. There was a wicker throne on a dais, but it was empty. A little, stout, strutting figure in a brown robe was bustling through the spaces of the sun chamber, followed by a couple of vassals. A continuous stream of complaint and comment rang out. Guno Deg gestured with a staff and struck the floor with it. Eventually she came right on out into the antechamber.

"Good-day! Good-day, gentles all!" she cried. "What new work are you bringing me?"

Then she began by the door, speaking to each petitioner in turn and solving some of the problems on the spot . . . a matter of land claim, the need for a fishing licence. One or two groups of country visitors simply brought gifts of cloth or food, and she accepted these graciously and embraced an ancient who had brought her a young black wool-deer as a present. She approached our large party and looked us up and down.

"Great wind!" she barked, "an invasion from the distant north. No, good Mother, remain seated, I pray. Why are these children not asleep? Who is the Speaker here? A scribe, forsooth, and from Tsagul . . . what have you to do with this tribe?"

"We bring a wonder, Highness," said Vel Ragan. "Something that has not been seen under the two suns." He presented the skein with our names and his name.

"Indeed!" snapped Guno Deg. "Well, I don't believe you. I have no time for talking animals, healing stones or drawings of fantastic beings."

"Perhaps you mean the Stone Brook drawings, Highness?" put in the scribe.

"I do!" she said. "Is this your wonder?"

"Here is the artist himself," said Vel Ragan.

Diver stepped forward and bared his head and bowed to Guno Deg. She stared up at him in silence. "Garl Brinroyan?" she asked at last.

"So I am called on Torin, Highness."

"Did you not fly in the Bird Clan at Otolor?"

"I did, Highness!"

Guno Deg bit her underlip and rapped testily with her staff. "Humph!" she said. "Scribe, you do not lie. This *is* a wonder, and one I had hardly believed to this hour. Come in, all of you . . . yes and especially you, whatever you may be, Garl Brinroyan."

We were escorted into the sun chamber, and the curtains were drawn again on other unlucky petitioners. Inside we were all settled and made welcome by still more vassals and house servants, but I crept as close as I dared to hear Guno Deg speaking with Brin and Diver and Vel Ragan. At first Diver told a little of his coming and how we left Hingstull; then the Elder urged him to leave nothing out and tell all that had passed. We knew what she meant: the pursuit by Tiath Avran Pentroy. So Diver and Brin and the scribe told the whole tale, not leaving out the Gulgarvor and the harrying of the twirlers and the death-pact of the bird carriers.

The Wentroy Elder heard them out in silence, then she said, "You are wise to show yourself, Escott Garl Brinroyan. But I notice that in spite of your claims to come in peace you have fought several times with Moruians."

"In my own defense, Highness," said Diver, "and the defense of Brin's Five."

"What will you do now?" she demanded. "And do not tell me that you mean to seek out young Murno Pentroy, your flying sib. He is all but an exile, like his teacher Nantgeeb, and if you fly with him I cannot help you."

"I had thought, Highness, of seeing Brin's Five settled in the delta on a bird farm," said Diver.

"We can purchase one," Brin pointed out, "and the children can be at home there."

"Good enough!" said Guno Deg, "but what else?"

"Mamor . . . the hunter yonder . . . is also a sailor," said Diver. "We might sail to the islands—"

"Dangerous!" Guno rapped with her staff. "Do you sail upon the oceans of *your* home?"

"Indeed, Highness . . . and under them as well. But our ships move with engines."

"If the truth is told, so do some of ours," said Guno Deg. "Did you not fly with Mattroyan, the Merchant of Itsik? He has ships that leave the harbor under sail, then stoke up a boiler when they are in the open sea."

A vassal came and brought the Elder a reminder of some appointment; she turned aside irritably. "Work does not wait, even for a wonder such as this. Garl Brinroyan, wait on me again, with Brin and the scribe here, and I will do what I can about your safety. In the meantime, inquire for your bird farm and stay out of trouble!" She pressed into Brin's hand a Wentroy token of a bird's head colored and glazed on gold; then she cried out to us all. "Take your time . . . eat up. Call a chair for your ancient and use that token."

She bustled away. We ate our fill and wandered about the sun chamber talking with the vassals of Wentroy.

I sat with Tomar and watched the flatbills—two common Narfee—playing in the water garden; and thought of the distant north. Tomar was walking and climbing well now; his first-fur had all lifted, his front teeth were through, and he said "Bin-bin-bin" for his pouch-mother, "Een" for Narneen and sometimes "Dar" for myself. It seemed strange to me that he might grow up and never recall Hingstull, where he was born and hidden. I made a vow that he should return one day and hear the story of our old life there and of how the Luck came.

So we amused ourselves one day longer and were planning a trip to the delta to seek out bird farming land. I walked out with Ablo and Diver at the setting of Esto to buy fruit from a stall; we turned up a short basket way, empty save for a porter with a net lounging against the wall. As we passed, I noticed that it was an omor. I had no warning until Diver gave a shout, and they leaped upon us from three directions. The omor with the net had Diver down before he could help us; I hardly felt the blows that brought me down, but I saw Ablo shouting and fighting. Then a blow from a cudgel made blood stream from his forehead and he lay still. I heard the voices of the Gulgarvor, panting and rough; I remember the cart being wheeled up, then as I struggled, a foot struck my chin. My head bounced on the cobblestones, and I dived suddenly into a black pit; my last thought was, Ablo is dead.

So the Luck of Brin's Five was taken easily in the midst of Rintoul by the three omor, Meetal, Artho and Alloo, still bound in Gulgarvor. For good measure they took me along too, as a member of Brin's Five. But our luck had not quite run out, for Ablo was not dead. He was left bleeding in the street after the Gulgarvor wheeled off Diver and myself in their cart. He dragged himself back to the wig house and the alarm was given.

IX

I came to my senses slowly and painfully. For a long time I saw nothing but a blur of yellowish white; I felt a rocking motion and dreamed I was on the barge again or the keel boat bringing us to Rintoul. I heard voices and bell chimes and a long way off someone laughing and sobbing. Then I was fully awake; none of my bones were broken; I was wearing my own clothes and I could still feel my Bird-Clan token around my neck. Yet the waking made no difference, I was in a place so strange it was as if I could see for the first time. I lay on a bare shelf stuck to the wall of a small room shaped like a teardrop. The wall, which had no corners, was a smooth yellowish expanse of plaster, drawn up to the top, like the folds of a cloth bag. In front of me was a big bubbled piece of glass that distorted whatever lay beyond it. Colors and shapes moved on the other side of the bubble glass, and I saw that there was a small round door in it.

My head ached but I oriented myself as best I could and put a foot down from my shelf to the curving floor. The whole room rocked gently. I lay back again, thinking I was dizzy, but then I saw a water bag hanging across from the shelf, and it rocked by itself. I wriggled a little on my shelf and sure enough the whole room responded. The place hung suspended in some way, like a basket. I was struck with the awful notion that it *was* a basket, or a honeybee's cell: I had been enchanted and made small and stuck in some insect's larder! I stifled a cry and lay still.

There were voices and footsteps and shapes swelled as they passed the bubble glass then faded away. I became calmer and more naturally sleepy as I experimented with the movement of the room, and, like a beam of light penetrating the darkness, it came to me where I was. This was a sleep-cell. It was not a prison or a place of punishment but one of the golden globes of painted wicker that nestled under the beams on the highest levels of Rintoul. Through the round door was a solid corridor, a courtyard or even a sun chamber and a water garden. Another thing was sure—for me the place *was* a prison. I doubted very much if the door would let me out. Before I had time to pursue this thought, the sobbing laughter I had heard in my dreams sounded again, very close.

It was a horrible despairing sound in a voice quite light and young; another person, another prisoner, lay in another sleep-cell close to my own, so close that I could hear the broken words and pleading.

"Let me out . . . let me see you. I am the only one, they have need of me, my teacher has need of me. It has been so long. There are fifty fixed stars in the constellation of the Loom, I could name them all, but I have forgotten—they have been stolen from me. . . ."

There followed a dreadful sobbing. "Blue . . . the eyes were blue . . . it made no secret . . . I have told, and I will tell again if only you will not leave me in this awful place . . ."

I sat up, trembling, on my shelf.

"There is a cave above Stone Brook . . . please let me out, let me see your faces, let me die. Send me back to the north. The blessing has all left me. Oh my dear Teacher, the power has waned, and I have lost the blue barge and the mountain Five with the devil will be utterly destroyed. Three comets . . . this is a three comet year . . ."

I braced myself against the wall, although it rocked crazily, and shouted with all my might: "GORDO BEE-THAN!"

There was an absolute silence, and I shouted again. *"Gordo Beethan!"*

The voice came again, so low I could hardly hear it. "Who calls me?"

"Dorn Brinroyan. I am in the next sleep-cell."

"You are dead. You are a ghost come to mock me, for I have been kept so long, and I have betrayed you all."

"I am alive, Gordo, and so are we all. The blue barge is safe."

"Dorn, Dorn Brinroyan . . . is it you?"

"Truly Gordo. Have courage."

"Dorn, what is this place, this dreadful swinging basket room?"

"It is what they call a sleep-cell. The grandees use it when they cannot sleep."

"But where? In what place?"

"In Rintoul, of course."

"RINTOUL!" There was a pause, and I heard muttering and thought he had lost his wits again.

"Gordo?"

"I was taken before the New Year, returning from the east to Otolor, having delivered the Ulgan's message."

"Have you been . . . mistreated?"

"At first, a little. Then I was left here. It has been so long, Dorn. There is food put through the door, but I cannot eat much. I have lost my powers, perhaps forever. I sleep and dream and remember all that I told the questioners."

"Please Gordo, you are not to blame."

"The old one is *kind,* Dorn. All it does is ask and send me back again. I hate the blanket, I am wrapped in a blanket when they take me out of here, so that I cannot see. But no more beatings . . ."

A distant set of bells chimed, sweet and silvery.

"Gordo?"

"Quiet, they are coming!"

I lay quietly on my shelf, although my heart was pounding so hard I felt it must make the cell rock. I prayed to the North Wind; I prayed to Eenath; I called upon Odd-Eye to give me strength. I reasoned that they could not hurt me or make me mad as they had poor Gordo. I was protected by all that I knew, and I was given power by my duty. I must find Diver or at least where he was being held. I must find this out and return to my Family.

Then a shadow of yellow and gray appeared before the distorting glass of my door, almost destroying my courage. The round door opened and an ancient peered inside, smiling.

"Have you slept well, child?" My visitor was a grandee, I saw at once, and probably a male. I sat up a little.

"Come along, come along," said the old one. "We'll take a walk." There was no sign of the blanket Gordo hated so much; I slithered across the curved floor and half fell out of the door into the corridor.

It was frightening enough without the blanket . . . indeed it may have been another "kindness" not to let Gordo see where he was perched. The walls of the corridor were glass and wide-meshed wickerwork; we seemed to be on a narrow strip of paving, high, high up, with the blue and white and golden gulfs of the city reaching down on every side. The ancient wore an elegant robe of yellow silk, with gray facing, and carried a wooden staff, set with milky pink jewels. Yet there was something old and dusty and food-stained about these clothes; the long hands gripping the staff were furry and tremulous; only filmed eyes glittering in its temples told of a mind still alert.

"Come along, little string!" I followed the wavering figure along the bright corridor; we passed two omor, in neat gray, effacing themselves in alcoves opposite the sleep-cells. I counted five sleep-cells; they looked every bit as strange outside as they did in, oval gold baskets with the glass doors like bulging eyes. They were strung irregularly on the beams of the skyhouse so that each could move freely; between them one could see daylight, the empty air, yet the winding of the corridor allowed each one a firm entrance. Could Diver possibly lie in one of the other three?

As we passed, I asked in an innocent voice, as loud as I dared, "Highness, where are we going?"

The ancient replied without turning. "Into the sun chamber, child."

I was seized with a terrible frustration and began to have an inkling of Gordo's plight. This was the time, surely, when I should run away, bang on the sleep-cells to see if Diver were there, climb bravely up or down, elude the omor and the ancient . . . but it was useless and I knew it. There was nowhere to run to; the omor would have me instantly or I would fall to my death. I could only follow as I was bidden.

The sun chamber was as spacious as the one I had seen already but made more homely, less grand, by the use of furled cane blinds and circular tan mats and dwarf redwood trees. It had been turned into something more like three rooms: in the first space we passed were three females, all in filmy vented robes, although they were middle-aged and past the time for carrying children. They were carding and spinning; I had never seen grandees at this work before, but they seemed to know it well enough.

"Time for honey water!" one cried in a shrill voice as we passed.

"He is busy!" said another.

"Playing games . . . playing games . . . playing games. . . ." said the third, in a mad bird voice. Then all three laughed aloud, and the ancient waggled his staff at them.

I examined the sun room carefully, still hoping for a way of escape but it offered even less hope than the corridor. There were two or three servants, tending to the flowers and making refreshments on a tall, wheeled piece of furniture, with racks and drawers and little colored paper sunshades to cover the trays of food and fruit. Another omor, this time in pale gray, and another still, in striped gray and green, lounged in the second room of the sun chamber. The blinds were open and on a beautiful carpet a dwarf was practicing a dance before the omor. A young musician, half-hidden among vines, played for the rehearsal on a pouch-pipe, repeating the phrases as the dwarf practiced turns and somersaults. I felt a sudden chill spreading through my bones as we came to the next room, the most soothing place of all.

The chairs were of wicker, and there was a brazier of wood and metal, unlit for the summer and filled with dried red leaves. A big legged basket was overflowing with skeins and scrolls; in one corner stood a scribe's tall desk, with paper on the platten and skeins half-woven on the hooks. The ancient pointed briskly and cheerfully to a heap of cushions and sank down himself in one of the wicker chairs. In the other sat a middle-aged male in a figured black and tan robe and handsome, curled, gold slippers. His hair was lit by the sun through the blind: a reddish brown, heavily streaked with gray. The face in repose was full of scholarly concentration, the long eyes light and thoughtful under the jutting brow.

"Here is our young guest," said the Ancient, "and none the worse for a sleep."

"Then we have something to say to one another," said Tiath Avran Pentroy.

I was already seated on the cushions for I could not remain standing, from fear perhaps or surprise, or both. Yet where else could I have been? And how would the Great Elder look, at his ease among that family, which had been called "a tangle of the old threads." But I could only stare at this strong-faced, richly dressed Moruian grandee and see, in my mind, the black barge on a winter's night. I could hear, instead of the chink of glass dishes, the poison cups rolling about in the cabin of the old brown bird-boat. The twirlers drowned, or kicked out their lives on Wellin's trees; the Gulgarvor fought and died, like engines of destruction; a world of cold and death and darkness lived at the behest of this Highness in the scholar's robe and the curled slippers. And now he had his will—the devil from Hingstull was in his grasp.

The Great Elder gazed at me with a trace of curiosity. "Don't stare, mountain child," he said, "or the wind will blow away your eyelids."

"It is afraid," said Old Av Avran. "Perhaps it has lived too long on your land, dear sib."

"No," I whispered. "No . . . it is just that I have seen your Highness once before."

"Where?"

"At Wellin, by night. After you had . . ." I was about to say "held assize" but I choked on the soft words. "After you had hung the twirlers."

The ancient head of the family chuckled to himself. Not a ripple passed over the Great Elder's face. "You were at Wellin?"

"We sailed past in a boat."

"And the devil was with you?"

"All our Family was there."

"Including this foreigner . . . the one called Garl."

"Garl Brinroyan is our Luck."

"Why? Is he deformed then? Or mad?"

"His hand was burned when he first came to us. And he has blue eyes, as you have seen, Highness."

"I have not seen it," said Tiath softly. "I think it would frighten me."

I hung my head and let my fear and hopelessness wash over me in a great wave.

"One thing," said Old Av, knitting his bony fingers together. "Does your devil speak another language?"

"Surely. But he has learned Moruian."

"How many in its nest in the islands?" snapped Tiath. "Three."

"What is their purpose?"

"To find out what can live, what can breathe on Torin."

"The constellation of the Loom," murmured the Great Elder. "So far?"

"I do not know," I mumbled. "Please, Highness . . . speak with Garl Brinroyan. He comes in peace."

"Speak with the devil? I do not have it," said Tiath.

"No devil and no air ship . . ." chuckled Old Av. "What do you think of that, little string?" I hung my head again, and the ancient laughed. "I don't think it believes that . . ." he said. "Speak up child, what do you say? Has my sib got the devil or the air ship?"

"He has myself," I said.

"How does this follow?" asked Old Av.

"I was taken, on the streets of Rintoul, at the same hour as our Luck, by the members of the same Gulgarvor, who admitted to serving the Great Elder."

"Very reasonable," said Tiath Gargan. "You are a clever child, and bold. Nevertheless I say I do not have your foreigner, and I begin to think I do not have you, either."

"Lost! lost! lost!" said Old Av, cheerfully. "There are children lost every day, in the city."

"Quiet!" snapped the Great Elder. "This business is almost complete."

"Do you have Gordo Beethan?" I asked.

"I am not sure," he replied absently, reading his scroll again. "Do you think I have him?"

I made no reply but asked again. "Do you have Tsorl-U-Tsorl?"

The Great Elder crumpled the scroll in his hand and turned his gaze right on me. He looked pale now, implacable, just as I had seen him at first.

"Remove it, Av," he said. "Give it to Urnat for a short time."

Old Av flicked his fingers twice, and the gray and green omor came through the flower racks from the next room of the sun chamber. She dragged me to my feet and half carried me back between the flowers, then laid me on the figured carpet in the sunshine. The dwarf Urnat had finished dancing and was drinking from a tall glass cup. I could not tell whether the dwarf was male or female or whether it had any sex; it was, as dwarfs go, very handsome, with a noble head. The name Urnat was woven in red on its small green tunic; I remembered that it had been born of a poor mountain Five on Gurth Mountain, not far from Hingstull. It said no word but took up a long cane that stood against a settle and began to thrash me, mainly on my legs, while the omor held me. I buried my face in the carpet and did not cry out although the pain became very bad. The sun chamber seemed to swim and fade when I came up for a breath. Then I felt a hard hand in my hair, and it was Urnat lifting my head.

"Enough!" it said, in a child's voice. "Remove it!" The omor hoisted me into her brawny arms and carried me out past the female sibs, taking their honey cakes and fruit.

"Playing games . . ." piped the mad one.

The omor carried me back to the corridor and slotted

me into a sleep-cell, a different one. I was now, I thought, on the other side of Gordo Beethan. I called out feebly, but the cell rocked and no voice replied and finally I slept.

So I remained, in the power of the Great Elder, so helpless, so far removed from any hope or comfort for my Family, for Diver or for myself that my situation made me light-headed, almost carefree. I had stepped right off the edge of the world this time and lived in some other place, without day or night, where the only change was the coming and going of the omor with my food tray. I examined my cell and found that it was indeed an apartment for a grandee. A sliding panel in the plaster wall revealed a washing place and a waste closet; there was scented washing oil and a stack of soft amith leaves for drying or wiping. Gordo Beethan had been removed from his cell, and now I was alone in the row of five sleep cells. I heard the others being put to their proper use by the members of Old Av's family . . . the females came and sang and twittered in their cells until they slept and complained loud enough for me to hear of the fact that one cell was occupied.

The omor who attended me was always the same one, usually dressed in gray and green, who had carried me from the sun chamber. She seldom spoke, and I did not know her name, but she was not an unfriendly jailer. One day, with a solemn face, she asked, "Can you read?"

I told her that I could. She moved her thumb about on the cover of my plate of fish meal and inside, fastened in the lid, was a bright orange message skein. I was giddy with excitement and mistrust, but the skein was not what I expected . . . a message to me, Dorn, from outside. It was some kind of public message, of the kind purveyed at the Friends' Round. The skein read:

A Reward of Cloth or Credits
Will be paid to any person who can tell truth and
relieve sorrow
By showing the way or any part of the way
To these two Bonded Kin, who are lost.
Garl Brinroyan, The Luck of Brin's Five,

*A tall one of strong appearance who comes from a
distant place and whose eyes are blue.
Dorn Brinroyan, eldest child of Brin's Five,
A child thirteen years from its showing,
a male, whose eyes are hazel.
In the name of Our Great Mother, the North
   Wind.
Approach the scribe who stands every day in the
Friends' Round.*

I could hardly eat for reading the skein again and again
and wondering what the omor meant by showing it to me.
I guessed that Vel Ragan was the scribe, and I felt that this
was the sort of brave gesture my family might make. But
was it a trap?

Then, when the omor returned, I decided when I looked
at her broad face and its unaccustomed furtive look, that
it was no trap. The creature had no guile. She was a vassal,
serving in a favored place, the very skyhouse of the Great
Elder, and she had been tempted by the reward.

"Well?" she whispered. "Answer me one thing—how
can a mountain Five have cloth and credits for all com-
ers?"

"We have it!"

"By magic? From your devil?"

"From the Bird Clan," I replied. "For our Luck flies
better than any bird, and we have won that great contest."

She swiveled her eyes about, her head and shoulders
almost blocking the round doorway. "Write something on
the skein so they will know I speak truth."

"No," I said. "I have something better."

"Be quick. Guard changes in a few moments."

I drew out the Bird-Clan token from around my neck,
bit off clumsily about half a finger length of the blue silk
braid, and tied in the dangling threads one symbol of my
name. I gave it to the omor and returned the orange
message skein. Then she went off, and I refastened the
braid of silk with trembling fingers; I was disturbed and
frightened, for she had given me hope again. The rocking
of the cell would scarcely make me sleep; I listened and

waited for hours and then dreamed of orange message skeins strung all about the streets and gardens and sky-walks of Rintoul. I remained in this anxious state for two more days, then suddenly in Esder light, the omor and another vassal took me from the sleep-cell and led me away between them.

We descended to the next half-level, by steps; the omor left us, and when I looked back, gave a rueful grin and a wave. I never knew her name and her help came too late for the plans of the Great Elder. But I found out that she did in fact take her information to the Friends' Round and was paid for it; I hoped she was able to buy freedom. Now the other vassal turned aside, opposite five different sleep-cells, and led me into a large place for washing and dress-ing, probably used by the servants and vassals. Two ser-vants stood by a pool of water looking helplessly at a figure crumpled on the ground, weeping and shivering.

"We can hardly make it clean . . ." said one. I saw with horror that this creature with the matted hair and be-grimed tunic was Gordo Beethan.

"This one is in better shape," said my vassal. He pointed to a basin and a pile of fresh clothes, like the ones the servants wore, of fair quality.

I ran to Gordo and knelt by him. "Let me . . ." I said. "I can help him. He is my friend." The servants shrugged and stood watching while I spoke into Gordo's ear, sooth-ing, coaxing.

"Oh, Dorn Brinroyan," he said in a hollow whisper, "I thought they had killed you."

"Have courage!" I said. "We will come alive out of this net, I know it. Let me wash your face."

So he bent over the pool, and I sponged his face with the warmed, scented water that even the servants used in this place. Then the servants came with scissors and cut off his filthy tunic, and he stepped slowly into the pool. He was painfully thin but not marked with cuts or bruises, and the warm water revived him. We brushed at his hair, and the servants dried and dressed him while I washed and put on fresh clothes. I was careful to keep my own good leather boots and my Bird-Clan token—which I kept hidden—but I found new clothes of more or less the right size.

There were no mirrors, and I was glad of it. I did not want to see myself in Pentroy clothes; and it was better that Gordo did not see himself either. The Diviner's apprentice was thin and strange; his captivity had done it all; perhaps his brain had a more delicate pattern, being the brain of a Witness. We were led through the washing room and out at its farthest corner. I was about to ask the vassal where we were going, but the words did not come out; we were on a skywalk in a stiff breeze. Gordo balked; the vassal laughed and prodded us with his short cane. I looked far out over the ocean sea, pearl white in the light of Esder, and stepped out as bravely as I could, tugging Gordo by the wrist.

"Keep looking at the ocean!" I shouted. "Step out for Cullin and Hingstull." Gordo held up his head, and we crossed the skywalk. The air revived him; his eyes were not so shadowed. We were rounded up by the vassal on the other side of the walk, and he led us down a winding basket-way. I asked this time, "Where are we going?"

"To the Sea Flower Room."

"What is there?"

"Oh, it is a small place where the Council meets sometimes."

We entered the curtain walls of an old building with only two levels above ground and came to a beautiful, low-ceilinged, round room painted with sea flowers in an ancient style. All round the room was a wicker screen, about the height of a tall person, and set off-center there was a large oval table of wood, with comfortable chairs ranged at the edge. The vassal led us behind the screen and around the room until we were near the table; we sat on a wooden bench, and the vassal went away into the shadows.

"No tricks!" he said. "Listen well . . . hear how the old threads are woven."

We sat drowsily on the bench, and I found myself thinking of food and of my Family, two things never far from my thoughts in captivity. Gordo leaned back and shut his eyes. Before we knew it there were persons sitting at the table; a rustling of garments, hawking and coughing; voices echoed curiously in the chamber. The chairs scraped, and there were greetings; I leaned forward and heard a voice reading a report. It was long and dull, but gradually the sense of it penetrated and I was listening to every word.

The plan was to dredge the Troon north of Otolor; there was a report on the bad state of the river, its snags and sandbanks, which I could have sworn to from my own experience. The sand would be lifted from the river and used to improve river fields and cropland surrounding the villages, including Wellin. The problem was labor and credits to do the work. A contribution was to be asked from every clan, from the town grandees of Otolor and the landholders in the smaller places. This seemed to me an excellent plan, but other voices were protesting or at least raising difficulties.

"Yes, yes, yes," said one voice, "but the Old Bear will have its fur ruffled."

"I can give you workers, but I'm burned if I send credits to the north," said another voice.

"You have been burned before, Margan . . ."

Then I understood at last what was taking place and could not tell whether to laugh or cry. This was the Council of the Five Elders—or some of them at least. The old threads were being woven indeed, right there at the table. Most puzzling thing of all, the reader of the report, to whom the other voices seemed to defer, was the Great Elder himself. When I knew it, the old fear and loathing surged back, but I knew the report was still good, the plan excellent. Tiath Pentroy had been planning wisely for the north and surveying the river at the same time he harried innocent folk and spread his bane.

I could identify the others gradually—Orn Margan with his grumbling voice and the other on that side, only a dim shape through the screen, must be Blind Marl, Marl Udorn, Marl Noonroyan Luntroy, the Luck of Noon's Five. Then there came Old Leeth—though indeed they were all old—Leeth Leethroyan Galtroy, who approved everything the Great Elder spoke, for her clan was closely allied with his own.

"Tiath Pentroy," said Old Leeth now, "you must not keep us waiting, my dear. Bring it out, I pray." There were sounds of interest and approval; the Elders were asking Tiath to show, to display, to set their minds at rest.

"Dear friends," said Tiath in his strong velvety voice, "if I have spoken on this other matter, which is dear to me, it is partly to show that I do not go on a progress through the north in search of wonders. But here is a wonder and before anything is shown I will tell you plainly, as I am a plain speaker, that I need your help. I need a Ruling of Secret Hand and I need it within the hour, if the old threads are to remain unbroken."

Orn Margan coughed and replied uneasily, "There are rumors enough in Rintoul. What will you do if we give you this ruling?"

"I will keep Torin from danger!" said Tiath.

"Are we talking about the same thing?" asked Blind Marl querulously. "Is this Tiath's devil?"

"Blind Marl," said Tiath, "make use of your vaunted insight now and take this matter seriously."

"I would be blind indeed," snapped Marl, "to give a Ruling of Secret Hand to a Strangler!"

"Easy now . . ." rumbled Orn Margan. "Tiath Pentroy . . . what do we have here? I will not easily believe that another race has reached Torin from the void."

"We must believe it!" said Tiath. "But the danger will be averted if I get my ruling."

"One devil . . ." said Leeth Galtroy. "It could be put down in a moment. Is it an intelligent being? Does it have a shape fit to look upon?"

"More or less," said Tiath, "and its personal threat is negligible. I am talking of the security of the world and of the clans. Orn Margan, would you not be the last to precipitate another clan war? This creature has already travelled the length of Torin and been in certain contact with exiles and magicians."

"You mean Nantgeeb," said Blind Marl; "but this is your enemy, Tiath, not mine."

"Arr, I can hardly believe all this," growled the Peacemaker. "How did it come? How could it pass among us? Is it so dangerous and yet so harmless? Bring out your devil!"

"No!" squeaked Leeth. "Are we protected? They say its eyes are blue. Let the Great Elder have his ruling."

"Give me my ruling now . . . lest its enchantment work on you when you see it!" said Tiath, almost playfully.

"Oh if we must . . ." Orn Margan replied, humoring the Great Elder.

I was at the screen now, straining to see if Diver would be brought in.

"Dorn," said Gordo in a firm whisper. "Your Luck is close by!" His head was erect and his eyes blazed in the shadow. It meant that his powers were returning. "Back," he said. "They are coming to bring us forth."

I had returned to the bench when two vassals came from our left and bade us follow to a door in the screen. Then we came out into the lovely swimming light of the Sea Flower Room, which filtered down from glass panels in the walls which concealed oil lamps. There sat the Five—or four of them at any rate—looking exactly like their voices.

"These are two country children," said Old Leeth. "Are they the witnesses you mean? Child, what is your name?"

"Dorn Brinroyan, Highness," I replied. "Of Brin's Five and Gwin's blood and the distant mothering of Abirin and Felm. I come from Hingstull Mountain." The three elders laughed indulgently at this, as grown-ups do to hear a lesson well-learned; it made me furious and I determined that they would laugh no more.

"How came you here, child?" asked Blind Marl, reaching a hand in my direction.

I came a few steps forward and took his hand, gripped it, as is customary when speaking to blind persons. "Truly, Highness, I was set upon in the streets of Rintoul and taken, together with Garl Brinroyan, our Luck, by a Gulgarvor, set upon us by the Great Elder, Tiath Gargan."

This time no one laughed, only the Great Elder smiled a little.

"You speak without respect!" cried Leeth. "Wretched child. Have you used this devil as your 'Luck' because it is so ugly?"

"I speak truth, Highness. Escott Garl Brinroyan is our Luck. We do not find him ugly. He comes from a distant place, but I swear by our Mother, the North Wind, he comes in peace."

Orn Margan turned to Gordo Beethan. "What is this other youngster. Speak up, skinny one!"

"I am Gordo Beethan, apprentice diviner out of Cullin." The reply rang out strongly.

"Have you seen this devil?"

"I have seen it once, Highness, and it is a tall, well-made, thinking creature, in everything like a Moruian."

"Has it any magical powers?" put in Old Leeth.

"None, Highness. But you should ask it yourself—it is within earshot, behind the screen at your back, where the yellow sea flower is painted."

Old Leeth spun around in her chair, and the other elders reacted almost as strongly, protesting to Tiath Pentroy. He rapped the table with a piece of rock shaped like an egg. "Do not be afraid," he said, "but give me my ruling. Let us deal with the creature at *our* good pleasure."

He gave a signal and another door opened in the screen. Two vassals brought in Diver; he was naked except for a breech-clout and barefoot, his wrists tied with strongest cord. There was a gasp from the watchers; he had not been able to shave for five or six days, and a thick black growth of hair covered the lower part of his face. His pale skin and body hair made him look outlandish. Two vassals stood at my back but they were unprepared; I dived forward, under the table, shot between the chairs and long clothes of the elders and ran to Diver's side.

"Have they hurt you?" I gasped. "Oh, Diver . . ."

"Courage!" he said, and the flash of his blue eyes comforted me.

The vassals struck at me with their canes. "Leave the child alone!" said Diver.

"Great Wind!" exclaimed Blind Marl, "it speaks like a person!"

"Approach then," said the Great Elder genially, "child and devil both. How are you faring, Scott Gale?"

"I am cold, Highness, without my clothes."

"Have you taken to heart what we have discussed?"

"I have given it deep thought."

"You see?" said Tiath to the others. "It is an intelligent being."

"And trusting," said Blind Marl, "very trusting. I will question it. Gale, if that is your name, where do you come from?"

"The system of another star, Highness. I came by accident to Hingstull Mountain and was cared for by a mountain family."

"Do you have dealings with the magician Nantgeeb?"

"I believe I have spoken with this person, but I have never seen Nantgeeb face-to-face."

"Ah, what a voice," said the blind Elder. "It is truly not of this world. Can you sing, stranger?"

"A little, Highness."

"Foolery . . ." said Orn Margan. "Yet it is a flaming odd-looking devil to speak so well."

"Let me hear it sing," begged Blind Marl.

Tiath Pentroy nodded, and a vassal touched Diver on the shoulder. He looked down at me and murmured the song's name, and we sang together.

> *"Een Turugan arabor va-ban,*
> *Gwerdolee ma na dobaggarnee,*
> *Mor-roy anstar utothor ma-wen,*
> *Turu geer da, tu-u-uru geer da!"*

And when we had sung this, Diver sang the same part again in his own tongue.

> *"The Minstrel Boy to the war has gone,*
> *In the ranks of death you'll find him,*
> *His father's sword he has girded on,*
> *And his wild harp slung behind him."*

Then, for the sweetness of this song, and for the sweet,

safe time when Diver told it to the Harper, upon the
Troon, I hung my head and felt the tears coursing down
my cheeks.

The Elders were silent for a few pulse beats, and Blind
Marl, at least, seemed disposed to applaud the singing.

"My ruling . . ." said the Great Elder softly. He made
another sign, and a vassal set a cloak around Diver's
shoulders. Suddenly, at the other side of the Sea Flower
Room, a whole section of the screen was wrenched aside
and a short bustling figure in dark green burst angrily into
the chamber.

"Not too late!" cried a harsh voice. Guno Deg strode
or rather bounced to the table and thumped upon it with
a closed fist.

"Here is no justice done! You are cozened and made
into creatures of the clan Pentroy!"

"Hold your tongue, Old Spite!" said Tiath. "I call for
my ruling."

"If you ask for Secret Hand, you will not have it, Gargan!" cried Guno. "The thing has gone too far, beyond
even the reach of your ropes and your murderers and your
secret prisons. I heard a song sung as I came into this
chamber, by this visitor Garl Brinroyan. I have heard the
same song sung in the streets of this city. I have found this
skein strung from every tree and rack in Rintoul." She
flung on to the table another orange message skein, and
the Elders passed it quickly from hand to hand.

"Too far indeed!" said Tiath. His voice was hard as
stone, and his face had that brooding look I had seen and
known at the very first.

"The poison and madness this foreign creature brings
is at the very springs of our life. It seems like one of us,
but it is not . . . as we can plainly see when it is stripped
of Moruian clothes. We must deal with it by Secret Hand
. . ."

"That you may not do!" cried Guno Deg. She flung
down upon the table a short white staff. "I have canvassed
the Council of One Hundred, and our demand is that you
bring the person called Garl Brinroyan before them in two

hours, else the threads are broken and the Five Elders dishonored."

Tiath Pentroy's wrath was terrible to see. He turned on Guno Gunroyan Wentroy a look that should have withered her to ashes. "So be it," he said. "But when the Council votes for Secret Hand, then even you must be satisfied. None can say that I do not follow the old threads." He signed to his vassals. "Remove the witnesses and the devil!"

"With your leave," said Guno Deg, no whit softened, "I will add Wentroy vassals to their guard. I do not wish to hear in two hours that Garl flew untimely off a skywalk." She waved impatiently, and there were Wentroy vassals in the Sea Flower Room.

"Privilege!" cried Leeth Galtroy.

"Take the prisoners to the second gallery then," said the Great Elder. "If it please clan Wentroy . . ."

Guno bowed her assent, and the Great Elder did not wait to see the order carried out but leaped up and swept from the chamber.

Guno raised her staff to Diver and myself, but neither she nor any of the other grandees attempted to speak to us. Gordo came to stand with us, and according to some prior command, one of the Pentroy guards untied Diver and let him replace his clothes. He asked for leave to shave his face, but they affected not to understand. We stood in the Sea Flower Room in a knot of clan vassals, and I felt so weary that I could have settled on the tiled floor, among the engraved sea shells and small fish. Then we were marched off again, with Pentroy behind and Wentroy before, through another basket-way and across a street on the lowest level and into the walls of that most famous of all buildings in Rintoul: "the crystal sanctuary," "the rare shell," "the wind's own weft," the Corr Pavilion, summerhouse of the last Torlogan.

We were not alive to its beauties at that moment; we sat in the empty pinkish spaces of the second gallery, and I whispered with Diver.

"Where were you imprisoned?"

"Why, below that place—the Sea Flower Room," he

said in surprise. "There are floors below it . . . a labyrinth of old rooms, many used as prison cells, I think. Were you and Gordo somewhere else?"

"A little higher," I said. "Diver, do you know where the Five are?"

He shook his head. "I know the Pentroy went to the wig-house and found them gone. Tiath said they had returned to the north . . . He promised. . . ." Diver had a rueful look, as if he knew what Tiath Gargan's promises were worth.

"What?"

"The Five would not be molested any more."

"What did you promise in return?" asked Gordo Beethan sorrowfully.

"Information . . . the working of the engines. This ruling of Secret Hand means exile in some secret place here in the south."

"He will have it yet . . ." I said. "Oh Diver . . ." I thought of our poor broken Five wandering back again towards the north, without their Luck and their eldest child.

"Never fear," said Diver. "I made sure you would be returned to them."

"I cannot believe Brin's Five would give up so easily!" I went on to tell Diver of the orange message skein, and we laughed shakily together.

He told us a story of an imprisoned king in very ancient times in his own land, who was found by a harper who played a certain air outside various citadels until the king heard and replied. We rallied, thinking of Harper Roy strumming away at "Een Turugan," the "Song of the Young Harper," from the skywalks and pinnacles of Rintoul. Gordo Beethan had the exquisite idea of all the ropes and cables of Rintoul as one great harp, responding to certain tunes, until the whole city played music.

"Alas," sighed the Diviner's apprentice, "I wonder what will become of *me*. I was given promises too, but I am too unimportant for them to be kept. Yet I know even the Pentroy would think twice about harming the Ulgan of Cullin."

"Never fear," said Diver. "You will go north with Dorn, if that is how things must be. Guno Wentroy will not have the pair of you in captivity: trust her."

But I thought of Diver, left to his fate, disappearing into the secret hand of Tiath Avran Pentroy.

The vassals on guard duty were bored and restless; they gave us fruit to eat and water to drink. I could see that Diver was trying to keep up our spirits and I tried too, not thinking too deeply of all that had passed and all that might come, but enjoying this last time together. There was a cold sadness behind my eyes; I winced at the thought of having no Luck again, but it was Diver himself we would miss. Was this ancient thread, the need for a lucky person, a cruel thing after all, a matter of putting some other being to use to ward off a family's misfortune?

I walked to the fretted stone wall of the second gallery and peered out at the wonders of the Pavilion. I saw the huge, pale whorls of stone, overlaid with silken panels, stretching up and down; a floor had been removed since the time of the Torlogan, and the interior was more than ever like a shell. Curved tiers of plain white benches curled in a helix from the mosaic pavement, which showed two sea-sunners twisting their scaly bodies in battle, with fire coming from their mouths in a flourish of flame and purple tiles.

Already the place was filling up for the meeting; there were more grandees than I had ever hoped to see, for the Pavilion held many more than a hundred, and all clansfolk could attend and watch. Their voices echoed into our chamber; their clothes were dazzling to my eyes even yet, but I gazed on them sadly. They were remote, bright painted figures; their clothes were so many bolts of silk and fine cloth and the skins of dead animals; their jewels were heaps of little stones. Even cloth itself, which was the greatest wealth, the work one must do, the weft of life, had lost its value in my sight. There stirred in my mind for the first time the thought that there might be other threads for me to follow.

I laid my cheek against the cool stone and wished all the grandees away and my Family together again, not as we had been, for that was impossible, but safe at least, with Diver in our midst. Then I walked back and sat by him, with Gordo; they were talking of flying machines. I had a sudden flash that this had happened before, this sort of conversation, and I remembered just as the guards ordered us to our feet. Sailing—I had talked of sailing with the children in Jebbal's tent.

Diver was kept back by the guards, but Gordo and I were sent out onto a small railed platform in the side of one of the tiers. We were close to benches full of grandees, but none paid us particular attention. The whole spectacle of the crowded Pavilion lay before us, and however coldly I had looked on this sight a moment before, I could not remain unmoved now, in the midst of it. There were the Hundred, invested in their white cloaks; there were the galleries of spectators, rippling with color and the flash of gems. Below to our left was a shelf of sculptured chairs, each one grand as a throne, for the Five Elders. Wentroy, Luntroy, Dohtroy, Galtroy; they came in slowly, robed in the colors of their clans. Then the Hundred rose to the sound of hoarse conch shells and fell silent as the Great Elder took his place, robed in black.

The meeting was formal, controlled by ten Council officers stationed throughout the Pavilion and the High Herald, who strode about on the mosaic pavement and motioned to the trumpeters who stood in alcoves by the arched entry. The Pavilion was so made that the least word could be heard from any speaker; a single note from the conch brought silence and the formal opening of the Council by the Herald. Then Tiath Pentroy rose to speak.

"I have not summoned this council, but I am glad it is called," he said. "You are here to see wonders and you will see them." His voice was smooth, almost conciliatory, but there was a cold edge to it. I saw Guno Wentroy sitting stiffly erect and Blind Marl with his long listening face, half-turned towards the Great Elder.

"What you have heard is true. There are strangers on Torin and one is, by great good fortune, safely held here for you all to see."

A wave of sound and movement went through the

Pavilion; the spectators rustled and sighed and were quelled by the voice of Tiath Pentroy.

"This creature has been commonly called a devil, but it is no devil. We would be in less danger if it were a devil . . . for devils, according to the old threads, can be kept at bay by prayers and chants. This creature is called Man, and it comes from a distant world writhing in the grip of a fire-metal-magic that is profound and deadly. You will see that this creature is no monster—in many respects it resembles a Moruian. I have two young Moruians here, from the wild north, and the Man has lived among them. Dorn Brinroyan, answer to your name."

The vassal was about to prod me, but I stood to the rail, trying to forget the hundreds of eyes upon me, and answered, "I am Dorn Brinroyan."

The vassal did prod me this time, and I added, "Highness . . ."

There was a little swirl of laughter. "It is a mountain child," said Tiath Pentroy, reproving the audience for their laughter.

"Did the Man Scott Gale descend to the Warm Lake at Hingstull Mountain in an air ship?"

"Yes, Highness."

"Did it live in your tent and eat Moruian food?"

"Yes, Highness."

"That is all. Stand forth now, Gordo Beethan."

I drew back from the rail trembling while Gordo stood forth. The last chance to speak for Diver had gone and all I felt was an empty relief. I scarcely heard the Great Elder lead Gordo through his meeting with Diver.

"It was a tall person dressed like a Moruian but its eyes were bright blue." Gordo was parroting his lines as I had done.

Guno Deg rose up now and exchanged nods with the High Herald. "One question for Dorn Brinroyan."

I stood forth again, conscious of every rustle and titter.

"When you had rescued this being, Escott Garl, was he made part of your family?"

"Yes, Highness—he was made our Luck."

The reaction was neither more nor less, a little hum of

anticipation that quickly swelled to a babble of voices. The moment Guno resumed her seat, Tiath signed to his vassals and Diver was brought in. He had been stripped of his clothes again, and he stood alone save for one vassal on a larger railed enclosure beside the Five Elders. Tiath Pentroy stilled the clamor in the hall with a blast from the conches.

"Here is the creature from the void!" he cried, "and I will ask presently for a ruling for its control and the protection of Torin."

There was a tense stirring among the grandees and one not far from where we stood cried out, "Shame, Pentroy! Let it have clothes!"

This brought other shouts, and Tiath swooped in again, with a note for silence, and addressed Diver.

"Man . . . what is your name?"

"My name is Scott Gale. I come in peace to the land of Torin."

"Does it speak Moruian then?" came a shout.

There was a jeering answer from the same part of the chamber. "No . . . Tiath Gargan is a Voice Thrower!"

There was a cry of "Question," and a young Wentroy Councillor rose up. "Are you called Garl Brinroyan?"

"Yes I am."

"Did you fly a machine called *Tomarvan* to victory at the Bird Clan in Otolor?"

"I did, Highness."

"Call me rather your friend," said the Wentroy, stiffly but gallantly; "for I flew *Utofarl* and I am sad now that once I was discourteous to you and to your escort."

Then the cry went up again, "Question" and an ancient Councillor demanded, "Have you a nest of Man in the fire islands?"

"There are three of my people working there. They are scholars. I came by accident to Hingstull Mountain in a small air ship."

"Where is your ship now?" interposed Tiath.

"I do not know," said Diver. "Last I saw, it was taken down the mountain by Pentroy vassals, Highness."

"Do you not know that the ship, with all it contains of

fire-metal-magic, is in the hands of the exiled Diviner Nantgeeb?"

"I believe it may be so."

The name of the Maker of Engines rustled about the Pavilion.

"Do you use engines of fire-metal-magic for many purposes," continued Tiath, "for flying, for making silk-beams, for a weapon to strike down living persons?"

"I have small engines to do these things, but fire-metal-magic is not my thought."

"You think there is no harm in these engines?"

"Not in the engines themselves," said Diver cautiously.

Then a great questioning broke out from all corners of the chamber with inquiries, some of them serious, some jeering and foolish, about Diver's powers, his origins, even the shape of his body, and the conch blew for silence.

"I will call for a ruling of Secret Hand," announced Tiath Gargan, "so we may hold the Man in custody and answer all these things. Let the formal trumpet call for the motion to follow, according to our procedure, and keep the silence of the Council unbroken and the dignity of these proceedings intact, I pray."

The Hundred and the spectators settled down into a seemly hush, and I sat with Gordo, leaning arms against the rail, sleepy and defeated. I saw the vassal giving Diver his clothes again; the show was almost done, and Tiath Gargan, the puppet-handler, would have his will.

The High Herald was out of sight under the archway, and the conches blew a phrase of six, seven notes, high and low. I saw the Great Elder throw up his head; he broke the silence himself, angrily.

"Herald, what foolery is this?"

"Privilege!" exclaimed Guno Deg.

The silence in the Pavilion had become tense and deep; the Herald came to the center of the pavement and spoke. "The order is laid down!"

"What cause can precede this ruling?" demanded Tiath, "Guno Deg, is this your treachery?" And a chorus of voices said softly, "Privilege!"

"The cause has an absolute priority," said the Herald.

"It is a double claim of Life and Bond against the Great Elder and the Council of Five." Then the Herald gave the sign, and again the conch shells brayed out with that call of seven notes.

Through the arch onto the glittering pavement there came four persons; they had some marks of substance, but in that place they stood out plainly for what they were: weavers of Torin, the members of a mountain Five. The leader stood tall, supporting the ancient upon her arm; one male carried a harp slung across his back, and the other wore a hunting knife.

"Speak your names and face the accused with your claim!" bade the Herald.

"Brin Brinroyan!"

"Gwin Uto-Tarroyan."

"Roy Turugan."

"Mamor."

The voices rang out plainly, and the silence in the Corr Pavilion rolled back again, without another whisper.

"I am Brin Brinroyan and this is our charge of Life and Bond against those named and assembled here. The eldest child of our family, Dorn Brinroyan, is held here and must be returned to us . . ."

"The child has been held as a witness, together with the apprentice from Cullin," said Tiath impatiently. "There they stand unharmed, and they may both be returned. You live upon Pentroy lands, Brinroyan Family, and may return there when you will."

"Highness," said Brin, in a loud voice, "the charge is not complete. The child Dorn we take back, in right and bond, and we will gladly see the apprentice to his home. But we seek one other. Escott Garl Brinroyan, who stands there, is our Bonded Luck, and by every thread of law, we must have him back again!"

Then the silence was shattered, the Hundred talking eagerly until the conch was sounded. Tiath would have spoken first, but the Herald made the formal reply. "There is the charge stated, but have you a Speaker, known to the Council, if any dispute the charge?"

"We have!"

Vel Ragan came in, wearing his scribe's robe and a narrow hood, so that his scarred face was almost hidden.

"I dispute this cause!" shouted Tiath. "And I do not know this speaker!"

"Vel Ragan is my name, Highness, and I am known."

"He is known to me," said Orn Margan slowly.

"And to me," snapped Guno Deg.

Murmurs of assent rose from the clansfolk of Dohtroy and a few others.

"Yet I say I dispute this cause," said Tiath, "and I will not be told the threads by a scribe from the Fire-Town who has cozened these simple folk!"

"We stand here of our own will, every one of us!" said Brin.

"I doubt that," said Tiath. "You are suborned! Stand forth the hunter—you with the scar on your cheek. That is the brand given to runaways, I think. How dare you stand before us?"

"Anyone will dare to stand forth in a just cause, Highness," said Mamor. "We need our child back and our Luck. And the scar on my face came from a mountain wolf."

A voice called, "Try again, Gargan. He doesn't scare easily!"

"What says the Harper?" asked Blind Marl.

"Truly, Highness," said Roy, "I stand here to claim Dorn, our child, and Garl, our Luck. As the song says . . ." He reached over his shoulder in the way he had and struck four notes on the harp. Blind Marl chuckled approvingly; the four notes were from an old song, and they said, "True bond is best . . ."

"Let that ancient stand forth if it can," snapped Tiath. "Old Mother, what brings you from the mountain to stand before my face and before this Great Council?"

Old Gwin let go of Brin's arm and stepped forward, peering up to left and right at the assembly. There were a few soft cries of "Shame" and "Let it alone."

"I see the child of our family here," she said in a strong quavering voice, "and I see poor Diver, as we call him, our Luck, who came in answer to our prayers, and that is reason enough . . ." She looked up at Tiath Pentroy, then turned aside and made the averting sign.

Vel Ragan said, "There is only one question to be asked, and I put it to Garl Brinroyan: Are you here of your own free will?"

Diver stepped forward to the rail and answered strongly, "No, I am not."

"Then the Luck must be returned, according to bond."

"By no means . . ." said Tiath. "What is this bond? Have we seen it? Scott Gale, have you understood this bond? Think of all that I have said to you and answer carefully."

"I have understood the bond," said Diver.

"I have the skein here," said Brin, "and the name Diver is on it, for Garl Brinroyan, our Luck. I guided his hand, but he knew the ceremony."

Leeth Galtroy broke in angrily, "Witness! Here is the Great Elder questioned in the Pavilion itself and who knows by what humble creatures! It is a strong thread in this proceeding that there must be a clan witness or at least a person of more worth than these I see. The devil Garl has been no more than half a season on Torin—who has known him to be the Luck of this Five?"

"There is one," said Vel Ragan, "a clan witness who saw Garl Brinroyan at the first."

"I have seen him!" said a voice. It was the Wentroy pilot again.

"I have seen him," said Guno Deg.

"Thank you, Highnesses," said Vel Ragan, "but there are yet two others. I will not say the names but I leave it upon their honor."

There was a further call for silence. I had not taken my eyes from my Family, but now I allowed myself to look at Diver and smile. We began looking at the rows of grandees, but it was hard to single out faces.

Gordo Beethan whispered in my ear, "Who are they?"

Then there was a movement among the Hundred.

"I dare say I am one of the persons you mean, scribe."

"Yes, Highness?"

"My partner and I were done some service by the Harper here and the child and the one called Diver," said Rilpo

Rilproyan Galtroy. "But I will say I had not the least idea it was such a valuable creature."

There were exclamations of shock and excitement; I heard a grandee say to a neighbor, "That will cost Rilpo dear with the Pentroy." Tiath had a dangerous look.

"Friend Galtroy," he said, "are you sure of this?"

"Quite sure, alas," said Rilpo. "This is the Luck of Brin's Five. In fact dear Tewl and I made an offer for this visitor, by Cullin, to be *our* Luck."

"That would have saved a bale of trouble!" shouted some wit from the spectators. And the whole Pavilion dissolved into nervous laughter, rocking and fluttering, until the call for silence came again.

The Great Elder rose up again, his face still clouded. "The Elders are charged with holding this Man, and we do hold him and we must. This is no ordinary cause. Scott Gale is not a Moruian; he comes from a distant place; he cannot form a true bond with a family of weavers. All this has been mere foolery. He is of a different race and blood; he cannot partake of our customs. I have been strong in his pursuit because I will not have Torin divided and polluted with his new magic. He cannot be returned to this Five because there was never a true bond. A Moruian cannot enter into a bond with a foreigner."

The words seemed too strong for our cause. I thought, in that moment, that we had lost, when it seemed we must win after all. I heard words of approval and of dispute among the grandees. Then Gordo gripped my hand, and I saw that his eyes were bright. He leaned over the rail and beckoned eagerly to Vel Ragan, who limped across and raised his face to us.

"Dorn . . ." He smiled at me. "And is this Gordo Beethan?"